"SEE ME."

He started at her jaw. His fingers felt rough and clumsy, but her fingers kept him from opening his eyes. Reaching her ears, he smiled as he traced their curves, felt soft lobes. In his entire life, he couldn't remember touching a woman's ears with the same desire and need—to see with his other senses.

Her fingers stroked his closed eyelids. He learned the slope of her nose, the satiny feel of her face, then his thumbs caressed her mouth. "Sweet," he said. "Mattie, I think I have to touch you."

"You are," she said, her voice breathless.

"Not with my fingers. With my mouth." Then he opened his eyes, reached up to cup the back of her head with his hand, and drew her close.

SUSAN EDWARDS

WHITE DECEPTION

LEISURE BOOKS   NEW YORK CITY

A LEISURE BOOK ®

November 2004

Published by

Dorchester Publishing Co., Inc.
200 Madison Avenue
New York, NY 10016

ISBN 0-8439-5333-0

The name "Leisure Books" and the stylized "L" with design are trademarks of Dorchester Publishing Co., Inc.

Printed in the United States of America.

Visit us on the web at www.dorchesterpub.com.

To those who dared to dream.
Believe!

WHITE
DECEPTION

White Series Genealogy Chart

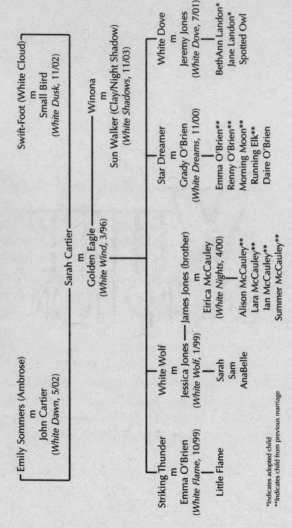

Emily Sommers (Ambrose)
m
John Cartier
(*White Dawn*, 5/02)

Swift-Foot (White Cloud)
m
Small Bird
(*White Dusk*, 11/02)

Sarah Cartier
m
Golden Eagle
(*White Wind*, 3/96)

Winona
m
Sun Walker (Clay/Night Shadow)
(*White Shadows*, 11/03)

White Dove
m
Jeremy Jones
(*White Dove*, 7/01)

BethAnn Landon*
Jane Landon*
Spotted Owl

Star Dreamer
m
Grady O'Brien
(*White Dreams*, 11/00)

Emma O'Brien**
Renny O'Brien**
Morning Moon**
Running Elk**
Daire O'Brien

White Wolf
m
Jessica Jones
(*White Wolf*, 1/99)

Sarah
Sam
AnaBelle

James Jones (brother)
m
Eirica McCauley
(*White Nights*, 4/00)

Alison McCauley**
Lara McCauley**
Ian McCauley**
Summer McCauley**

Striking Thunder
m
Emma O'Brien
(*White Flame*, 10/99)

Little Flame

*Indicates adopted child
**Indicates child from previous marriage

Prologue

Gray shrouded the land. Silvery clouds streaked with pewter hid the pale glow of the rising sun, while below moist air rose from the river. The dense yet cottony fog rose like so many ghosts soaring free from graves to glide up and over the banks. Thinning, merging, flowing, the mists wove as one around stands of grayish cottonwoods like satin ribbons before spilling across a sea of bright green grass.

Tendrils trailed outward as a gentle breath of wind swept across the land, molding the wispy fog into myriad images—some delicate and beautiful; others heavy and grotesque, mirroring the horrors of the world.

From high above, the brown blur of an owl dropped gracefully from the cloudy sky and swept across the river, parting the nearly translucent wisps with each downward thrust of its wide wings. The

1

bird allowed the breath of *Tate*, the wind spirit, to guide him between the trunks of two towering cottonwoods, and to carry him toward a solitary cabin enveloped by the cold fog.

"She dreams," Tate whispered.

"It is time," Owl replied.

"Time for what?" The wind followed the small bird in its flight around the single-story dwelling.

"Truth."

The darkness within the home called to Owl. He spiraled down, lifted his wings high and landed on the rough-hewn porch railing at the rear of the house. Folding back his wings, he sidestepped until he could see through the window to the bed where a woman tossed and turned.

"She dreams," Tate said again. He ruffled the feathers of his friend.

Owl flapped his wings. Tate was irritated with him, but this was as it needed to be. "She must. The truth must be revealed." Guardian of Dreamtime, Owl knew that important things often hid deep inside the mind, revealing themselves only in the solace of sleep. But the restless movements of the woman's tossing and turning finally got to him.

"Enough! Awake!" he cried. The tip of one wing brushed against the cold pane of glass.

The woman, caught in the dark world of dreams, cried out. Tipping his head back, Owl sent up a shrill shriek into the morning air. It was time for the dark-haired beauty to wake.

Chapter One

Fire!

Red. Orange. Yellow. Bright flames rose high overhead.

Mathilda's head pounded; a trickle of blood slid down her face. She had to get out. But which way? She blinked her stinging eyes. Smoke blinded her. Choking, gasping for air, she tried to stand. Flames and smoke spun wildly in all directions. Nausea welled deep inside her.

"Mathilda!"

Through the gleeful crackle of flames she heard her name. Opening her mouth, she tried to scream a reply: "I'm here. Help me!" A rough rasping moan was all she managed. Around her, the deafening fury of the flames rose a notch, blocking out all sound, consuming precious air.

Move. Get out, *she told herself.*

Frightened and hurt, she crawled on her hands and knees. The instinct to survive demanded she obey. A flare

3

of red-orange to her left revealed a stack of hay catching fire. It exploded, and a wall of intense heat struck her. Embers rained down around her head; popping with life.

Go.

Faster.

Get out. Hurry.

Her lungs burned. Desperate for air, she moved blindly. Smoke. Heat. Pain. Tears streamed from her eyes. Tongues of flame blazed all around, seared her flesh. She crashed into something. A saddle rack!

She sobbed with relief. She'd made it to the back of the barn. Here, the air wasn't so thick with smoke, and a faint glimmer of light beckoned from beneath the closed barn doors. Hope sent her heart racing. Reaching the door, she dropped her head to the space between floor and door.

Sweet air.

Fresh air.

She gulped it into her burning lungs. Standing quickly, she fought the dizziness that turned her world gray around the edges. Fighting to keep from passing out, she found the heavy wood bar that secured the barn's double doors. She gave an upward shove.

Safety. It was so close.

An ominous creak sounded overhead.

Hurry!

Around her, timbers fell in a storm of sparks and flame. A roar traveled through the barn.

No! Too late.

Sobbing, she heaved with all her might. The bar lifted, then fell from her trembling fingers, striking her shins.

Just as she shoved the double doors wide, she felt herself fly forward, shoved out of the burning barn by the force of the collapsing roof.

Her head exploded with pain, then everything went dark. . . .

Whimpering in her sleep, Mathilda fought the darkness with the same desperate fury she'd fought death three years ago. A dream. This was only a dream. All she had to do was open her eyes. But icy fingers of fear left her paralyzed until a shrill cry pierced the layers of sleep and pulled her free of the nightmare.

Awake, Mattie turned her face into her pillow. "Not again," she moaned. Echoes of the blazing fire roared inside her head. Sweat poured off her skin. She shivered and kept reminding herself that it had been only a dream—one that for three nights running had invaded her sleep and forced her to relive the horror of being trapped in the fire that had taken so much from her.

Rolling onto her back, she rubbed her eyes as though they still stung from smoke. She'd been incredibly lucky in her escape. By some miracle, she'd managed to open the barn doors just as the roof collapsed, sending those timbers and planks down onto her. But at least she'd made it out alive.

Rubbing the back of her shoulder, she felt a patch of raised, smooth flesh—one of several patches that were lifetime reminders of her brush with death. Yet while they'd been excruciating, her burns weren't the worst of the injuries suffered that day. The blow to the head had been worse.

As had been learning that her husband of only a few hours had died trying to rescue her.

Most of what followed her rescue remained a jumble of pain, confusion and high emotion. So much pain. And grief, for the fire and death had come less than six months after her parents were murdered.

Mattie curled her legs beneath her, then ran her palms down her soft, worn quilt until her fingers brushed against a thick robe of fur stretched across the foot of the bed. She pulled the buffalo robe to her chest and buried her face in its thickness, inhaling her mother's lingering scent. That usually provided a small measure of comfort.

Her fingers dug into the thick fur as tears spilled down her cheeks. Solace eluded her. Lifting her head, Mattie stared unseeing at the small alcove that served as her sleeping quarters.

Standing, she pulled the buffalo robe around her shoulders. Reaching out, she found the edge of the washstand where a blue-flowered pitcher and bowl sat. A quick splash of cold water helped clear her mind. Using a cloth to dry her face, she stared straight into the mirror she knew lay beyond. But she saw only darkness. No reflection. No color. No shapes, for the fire that had left her a young widow had also left her blind.

Drawing a deep breath, Mattie ran her fingers over the cool porcelain pitcher. Only in her mind's eye could she see the pretty object, or any of the other familiar furnishings in what had once been her parents' sleeping quarters.

She turned and made her way over to the rocking chair in one corner of the room. Of all that her father had given to her mother, this rocker had been her mother's most prized possession. Star Dreamer of the Miniconjou Sioux had spent many hours rocking here, nursing and singing to her babies. And each evening before the family went to bed, she'd tell her children stories of The People. Her husband usually joined them, sitting on the stool at his wife's side or on the bed, surrounded by his beloved kin.

The memory of her mother's gentle, loving voice brought tears to Mattie's eyes. Star Dreamer, a young widow with two children, had fallen in love with Grady O'Brien, a white soldier. She had given up her life among the Sioux for him.

Mattie, born Morning Moon, had adapted quickly to her mother's new world. She'd loved her new father and his two daughters. Emma, the eldest, had married Mattie's uncle, and Renny, who was just a year older than herself, was now Mattie's best friend.

Closing her eyes, Mattie knew she'd have to tell Renny about the dreams. "But not yet," she whispered. First she needed to know why the dreams had returned. Did they mean anything, or was she just reliving the past?

Most white people shrugged off dreams, bad or good, but not Mattie. Life was a circle. The past and the future were connected. So it was to her Indian heritage that Mattie turned in the early dawn for answers to the horror plaguing her nights.

She rocked gently as she searched for hidden meanings in the images of her dreams. The events played out exactly as they had happened almost a year ago to the day. There seemed no hidden meanings, no warnings of future dangers. Just heat and flames, fear and the surety of being burned alive. Mattie shivered and leaned her head back.

Dreams. A reminder of the past. Not visions.

A stab of disappointment made Mattie draw in a deep breath. Visions had been a part of her life for as long as she could remember. She'd seen all things— danger, the joy of new life, and death.

A shard of bitterness pierced her heart. The visions were gone. Forever. They'd stopped the day of the fire, the day she'd lost her eyesight. In many ways, losing her gift had been harder to accept.

It had been passed from grandmother to mother to daughter, and Mattie's mother had once believed the gift of sight to be a curse. Mattie on the other hand accepted the good and the bad of what she saw. She tried to focus on the good. There were many joyous occasions like weddings and births, the return of friends, that she could predict. Most often, her gift brought joy.

But not always, for there could not be light without dark. Or birth without death. Such was the way of the world.

Mattie rocked a bit faster and shivered. She understood her mother better. The gift of sight was a double-edged sword—simply knowing the future didn't always change it. She'd known her parents were going to die, but hadn't known when or how. She'd tried desperately to see more of those visions, so she could prevent it, but in the end death could not be conquered.

Her mother had known she would die, too. Mattie gripped the arms of the rocker. They hadn't talked about it, but she'd seen the knowledge in Star Dreamer's eyes.

Mattie fought her anger, the injustice of it all. Only when her mother died had she understood the overwhelming guilt her gift often caused. Her mother had seen the death of Mattie's birth father and been just as helpless to stop it.

No, maybe having The Sight was not so great a gift after all. Part of Mattie had wanted these nightmares to be the return of that part of her, but not if it meant more lost lives she could not save.

Frustrated, she wished for her mother's wise counsel and comforting arms. Mattie stood and tossed her robe down onto the bed. It did no good to wish for what could not be. Her mother was in the spirit world now, and there was no time or place for self-pity.

There had to be a simple reason for the sudden return of her nightmares. After all, she'd been free of the haunting memories for more than six months—a blessed relief. Even the blinding attacks of head pain seemed to have finally gone away. Only the raw ache of grief remained.

Death. Her husband had died in that fire. Her gift and her sight had also been taken. Her legs shook with fear. *Please*, Mattie prayed, reaching out to steady herself, *do not let my dreams mean more death.* She couldn't handle more loss.

Mattie moved to the window without stumbling or hesitating and threw it open, welcoming the wave of cold moist air that slammed into her and burned her lungs as she drew breath. She embraced that cold, used the shock of it to regain control of her thoughts and emotions.

A soft hoot to her right stilled her. The owl was back. Three nights the bad spirits had haunted her sleep; three mornings she'd awakened to find an owl outside her window. Her people believed that animals communicated with people. All living things were part of the circle of life, but most of the people Mattie knew didn't pay attention to the Great Spirit's creatures. Was this one trying to tell her something?

A mouse running across the path of a woman from town might cause her to scream; to Mattie, the rodent's presence would be a reminder to be quiet, a message from the tiny creature to sit quietly and listen. The appearance of this wise owl had to be a sign.

"What do you want?" she whispered, though she

could not see the bird. "What are you trying to tell me?" She reached out with her right hand, moving slowly until the tips of her fingers touched incredible softness. "What am I supposed to see?"

To her people the owl was guardian of Dreamtime, and with each of these visits, she felt sure he was either trying to impart information—or else he wanted something. Owls were masters at hearing and seeing what humans could not.

Was that the message? Was she being asked to see what others could not? The air stirred to her right. She didn't need to reach out to know the bird had flown away.

She dropped her hand back to the sill, and with her eyes closed to the misty morning, sought answers deep inside. For they were there. She just had to silence her fears and open her mind. Let go of the confusion and pain clouding her thoughts so she could hear the truth.

Lost in her musings, Mattie started when a door slammed.

"Morning," a young, high-pitched voice chirped. It was her young sister of four.

Mattie opened her eyes and smiled. "Good morning, Caitie," she called out. She put aside her worry and fears, unwilling to let her sibling sense her unhappiness.

A chicken clucked nearby, and Mattie frowned.

"Oh no, they're loose again," Caitie wailed.

"Again?" This made twice this week and once last

week that the door to the coop had been left open. And yesterday the gate to the pasture where the horses were kept had been left open. It had taken her brothers and sisters hours to round up the beasts.

Mattie leaned out the window and heard the flap of wings as a chicken fluttered away—most likely evading Caitie.

"Too bad, Cat," a voice teased. "Looks like you might miss breakfast."

Tension from her nightmare and worry over the chickens getting out made Mattie's voice sharper than normal when she scolded her young brother. "Kealan O'Brien, you know the rule!"

"Yeah, no one eats until all the chores are done!" He sounded disgusted.

"That's right. When you're done milking Lilly, help Caitie or you won't eat until suppertime!"

"Aw, Mattie! Why can't Daire do it?"

"Aw, Kealan," a third voice mocked. "Can't, I'm going out to check the horses."

Mattie closed her eyes. Just what she didn't need this morning—Kealan upsetting Caitie, then Daire egging Kealan on. She loved her young siblings, but there were times when their squabbling drove her crazy.

"Don't start, Daire. Someone let the chickens out again. Go do what you need to," she ordered her eight-year-old brother.

Kealan's voice turned sulky. "*I* want to check the

horses. I'm nearly as big as Daire. Let him chase the chickens."

"Not a chance, brat." There was smug satisfaction in Daire's voice.

Mattie brushed a stray strand of hair from her face. "Daire—"

"Don't get in a huff, Mattie." Her brother sounded resigned. He addressed the others. "Come on, you two. I'm starved. Let's get them chickens rounded up, the cows milked, then we'll all go check the horses."

Mattie turned away from the window, listening as Kealan continued to argue, and she smiled. At six, the boy thought milking and gathering eggs were beneath him.

Outside the quilt that hung from the beam ceiling and sectioned off her sleeping area from the rest of the cabin she shared with her five siblings, the scent of pork frying on the stove and the thick, aromatic scent of coffee beckoned Mattie. Shivering in the cold, damp breeze, she quickly dressed. With deft fingers she brushed and braided her long, straight hair into a single black braid down the middle of her back, then walked softly across the room. Hearing quiet whispers coming from beyond the quilt wall, she stepped out into the main room of the cabin. Silence fell.

"Morning, Mattie." Her sister Renny's greeting was a bit forced. She heard her brother Matthew, but he said nothing.

Frowning, Mattie made her way to the pot of hot coffee on the stove. Something was up. Renny was usually the first outside in the mornings.

"Chickens are loose and Daire's going to check the horses," she announced as she reached out and found her mug and the coffee pot in precisely the same positions that they were always placed for her. With the warm mug wrapped in her hands, she walked the six steps to her chair at the table, sat, then took a sip of coffee. The hot liquid was strong enough to sear her throat down to her stomach, then exploded into her veins to chase away the last of her fatigue.

Renny's chair scraped back. "I'd better get out there," she said.

"Wait." Mattie motioned for her sister to sit. The slow slump of Renny resettling in her chair, followed by a soft rustle, told Mattie that she was sitting with arms crossed—a sure sign that something was up.

"What are the two of you plotting?" she asked. She didn't need her eyesight to know that Renny and Matthew were exchanging glances. When neither answered, she lifted a brow.

"Well?" She refused to allow them to coddle her. If there was something wrong, she wanted to know. She heard Renny shift in her chair, pictured her sister slumped back, arms folded across her chest, booted feet crossed at the ankles.

"Matthew is leaving." Renny sounded glum.

Mattie sighed and cupped both hands around her

mug. The announcement didn't surprise her. Her blood brother, younger by two years, was not a rancher. Like her, he was Sioux; though he felt equally at home in either world, as did she, his heart and soul craved the open prairie and nomadic life of their mother's people.

She turned to face him. "Are you leaving today?" With the arrival of spring, she knew her brother would be eager to return to their Sioux family, but he usually gave them time to hire help for the spring and summer. He always returned before the harsh winter months.

He reached out to take her hand. "Not today. I wouldn't miss your engagement party," he said.

Mattie sighed and ran the pads of her fingers over the back of his hand. One finger traced a long, jagged scar from when he'd run through a glass doorway in Saint Louis. Mattie had taken to the new lifestyle immediately, but it had taken her brother a while to adjust to life in a city.

She sighed. The first part of her life had been spent on the prairie, the second living as a white woman. Unlike her brother, she hadn't been back except for short visits to see her family. "I wish I could go with you," she said softly.

Sometimes she missed being Morning Moon, envied her brother his ability to come and go between both worlds. Still, that was the way it was, and she accepted that without bitterness. Realistically, there was no way she could return to that simpler, nomadic way of life. Without her eyesight to aid her in an ever-changing landscape, she'd be even more dependent on others for survival, and the one thing she'd vowed to have in life was independence.

"Mattie—"

"Don't fret, Matthew. I'm happy here. Truly. Only sometimes do I miss that way of life." She took a sip of coffee. "You don't have to stay on my behalf. I tried to talk Paddy out of this party. It doesn't feel right to celebrate. Gil and I don't love each other— not like our parents, or me and Collin."

"I hate that!" Renny broke in. "You're marrying Gil just to please Patrick O'Leary. It's wrong. You should marry for love."

Thankfully, Mattie didn't have to meet the accusation in her sister's eyes. Buckling under the pressure of Gil's father, who was also her father-in-law, wasn't the only reason she'd agreed to the marriage. If Renny knew the true reason, she'd raise holy hell.

Mattie kept her face pointed down at her half-empty cup of coffee. "Pa would have been happy with the marriage," she said, smiling sadly as she thought of the white man who'd been a beloved father to her.

"Pa would have wanted you to be *happy*," Renny whispered fiercely.

Mattie sighed. "The Irish stick together," she reminded her sister, repeating one of her stepfather's favorite sayings. But remembering the love her parents had shared brought tears to her eyes, and another wave of doubt hammered at her mind. Was she doing the right thing by marrying Gil?

Taking pity on Renny, she glanced up. "Is it so bad to marry someone you like? Love as a friend? Not all marriages are love matches. Gil and I like and respect one another." She sipped her lukewarm coffee, more for something to do with her hands than any other reason. She hated arguing with or upsetting Renny.

She set the cup down. "Besides, Paddy wants me for a true daughter-in-law." That made Mattie smile a bit. Though her marriage to Collin O'Leary had only lasted a few hours, she was still legally an O'Leary.

Still, Patrick swore it wasn't the same. He wanted the two families joined in stronger bonds. He wanted grandchildren.

"He feels guilty for what happened to you." Renny's voice was gentle as she rested a hand on her sister's arm.

"I know," Mattie agreed softly. It had been Patrick's barn that had caught fire on her wedding day. He'd never forgiven himself for the loss of his son or Mattie's blindness.

Mattie's heart ached. There was nothing she could do about either past tragedy, but she could at least ease her father-in-law's pain. "He's done so much for us. Without him—"

"That doesn't mean you have to marry Gil."

Renny's chair scraped across the wooden floor, followed by the sound of her boots as she stomped over to the stove.

Mattie set her cup down. "There are different kinds of love, Renny." That, she truly believed. "Besides, it's not like I have much choice anymore." Not everyone accepted her Sioux blood. Or her blindness.

"Mattie—"

Pushing up from the table, Mattie took her cup to the small basin on the counter and pumped water into it. She rinsed, then dumped. "It's true, Renny, and you know it. I have more Indian blood than white in my veins." Her grandmother had been half white. "Who else is going to consider me?"

"Your mother-in-law is the worst," Renny muttered.

Mattie bit back a sigh. It was true. Katherine O'Leary was less than thrilled to have Mattie once more marrying into the family.

From some far recess in her mind, Mattie again heard her mother-in-law's shrill screams after the fire. The jumble of words weren't clear, but as she'd drifted in and out of consciousness, she heard the hate in Katherine's voice blaming her for her son's death. And in a sense, the woman was right. Collin had rushed into the barn to rescue Mattie, and had died trying.

Mattie shook off the past. "Grandchildren will help."

"I don't know, Mattie. She's always been a bit—"

Grinning, Mattie reached out to tug one of Renny's long braids. "Full of herself, you've always said. Now come on, we have a lot to do before we leave for town." She stepped sideways and reached for the tin of flour to start the biscuits.

A scream rent the air. Mattie dropped the tin. The three adults whirled as one to face the back porch. "Caitie! Something's wrong!" Mattie rushed forward through a cloud of flour that made her sneeze.

Renny brushed past her. "Stay here. Kealan probably played one of his practical jokes on her again."

Mattie ignored her sister. In the wake of her nightmare, she was expecting something terrible. Her heart pounded. Though Renny was right in that Kealan enjoyed playing pranks on Caitie, she could sense in her gut that this was not one of those times. Mattie's sharp hearing had discerned more than fright or anger from a prank in her young sister's screams. There had been terror.

Reaching the doorway, she found a chill fog closing around her. It didn't come from outside but from within her own mind. She stumbled, reached out and gripped the doorjamb.

The dark mist moved through her, shrouding all sound, enclosing her in a dark cocoon. *Death.*

It invaded her senses, blazed through her mind much as the fire had swept through the barn. She opened her mouth to cry out but nothing came. Fear held her prisoner while the screams in her head grew louder.

"Behind you." Matthew's strong hands gently moved her aside, shattering her numbing vision.

"Matt—"

"I'll be back. Wait here." Matthew brushed past, the butt of his rifle bumping her arm. Then he was gone.

Alone, Mattie felt disoriented and sick. And afraid.

Her gift of Sight *had* returned. She doubled over, feeling as though she'd just run a long distance. After a year of not having seen a single vision, the impact of the feelings that had just hit her left her weak and breathless.

Resentment and bitterness rose from deep inside to band together with the fear coursing through Mattie.

Dreams of death.

Visions of death.

It was just too much. She could not survive more bereavement in her life.

Death gives birth to life. The thought came from nowhere. And everywhere. Clenching her hands into fists, she straightened. "No!" The word torn from her throat spurred her forward.

"No more death." She tore out of the house, stumbled down the steps and headed toward the barn. Damp air curled around her ankles and swirled beneath her long skirt.

Normally she made the walk from house to barn without thinking, without stumbling, without hesitating, but fear made her clumsy and left her disoriented. Stopping, she listened intently. Somewhere up ahead, over Caitie's continued high-pitched screams, came the sound of Renny cursing.

Mattie's world shook. She hated being helpless.

The shaking increased. She realized someone was running toward her. Her stomach tightened but she held out her arms. "Kealan, what happened?" she asked, recognizing the odd gait of her brother. When Kealan ran, his right foot hit the ground heavier than his left. Caitie mostly skipped, and when she ran, her steps were much lighter.

Kealan skidded to a stop. A small spray of rocks hit Mattie's skirts. "The cows're dead. Someone killed 'em," he gasped. "Renny says they've been poisoned. Even Lilly!" His voice ended on a hitch.

Mattie's heart hammered. Her senses, heightened beyond endurance; threatened to explode. "What is happening?" Life for all of them had finally settled into a calm and quiet pattern broken only by the continual antics of the youngsters. Now, once again, things appeared to be falling apart. Rapidly.

In her mind, Mattie once again saw the flames spreading though the O'Leary barn, rushing toward her. It meant something. She feared her family's lives were on the verge of being torn apart.

Again.

"Kealan, take me to Caitie," she commanded. She could still hear her sister sobbing. Lilly had been more of a pet than just a milk cow.

21

The wisps of fog shifted around her. "I have her, Mattie," Matthew called. He had approached on silent feet.

Holding out her arms, she took her sister from her brother. "What's going on, Matt?"

"Take Cat back to the house."

Holding her baby sister tightly, Mattie felt Caitie's narrow chest jerk with each of the girl's sobs. Needing almost as much reassurance, Mattie whispered, "Matthew, please."

Her brother rested his hand on her arm. "Found a sack of grain in the middle of the barn." Fury edged his voice. "It's not ours."

The implication sunk in, and it made her sick. The livestock could have just been poisoned and left to die, but whoever had done this had wanted them to *know* that the animals had been poisoned. "Who would do such a thing?" she asked. "And why?"

The chickens and horses being let loose were just childish pranks. Up until now, they'd all believed it to be some kid from town who was angry at either Daire, who tended to be hotheaded, or Kealan, for his ofttimes ill-received pranks.

But killing livestock was no prank. Mattie's arms prickled with fear. They had enemies.

"I don't know," Matt said. He softened his voice. "Go back to the house, Mattie. There's nothing you can do."

The words struck Mattie's heart. She was blind. Useless. Never had she felt more inadequate than at that moment. Her family had an enemy, and there wasn't anything she could do to help protect them.

A hand on her arm made her jump. "I didn't mean it like that, sister," Matt said.

Mattie swallowed. "I know you didn't." And she did. Matthew and Renny went out of their way to include her in as many of the daily tasks as possible— even when it took longer than if they just did the work themselves.

Anger and despair rose in her. She hated not being able to carry her own weight. It would take Matthew and Renny most of the day to deal with the dead animals. Instead of insisting on helping when she knew perfectly well that there wasn't anything she could do to get the job done faster, she held her head high. There was one thing she could do, and despite the protests that were sure to come, she was determined to do it.

The swirling mist told her Matthew had turned to leave. "Matt," she called. "When we get to town this afternoon, we need to speak with Sheriff Tyler." The situation here was out of control. They needed help.

Steps heavy with fury approached. A wall of cold seemed to go right through Mattie. "No! We handle our own affairs." Renny's voice brooked no argument.

"Renny—"

"You heard me. I won't have *him* meddling in our affairs."

Mattie narrowed her eyes, but before she could tell

Renny that she was speaking to the sheriff regardless, Matthew broke in.

"I agree with Mattie." He paused. "Tell her everything, Renny."

Whipping her head from side to side as though she could see her brother and sister, Mattie felt another frisson of fear snake down her spine. "Tell me what? What did you not tell me already, Matthew?" Her voice turned hard. The one thing she could not tolerate was being coddled, being protected from the truth.

Caitie lifted her head. "We found candy in the barn." She hiccupped several times. "No one will let me have any." She laid her head back down on Mattie's shoulder.

"Renny?"

"Can't tell if it's poisoned," Renny said, her voice low. "But—"

Renny didn't need to say more. If Caitie, who had a sweet tooth, had found the candy; or Kealan—

Her mouth went dry. Whoever had left the sweets was letting them know they could have just as easily poisoned the youngsters. Mattie was frightened. And helpless.

Furious, more determined than ever to do what it took to protect her family, she tightened her hold on Caitie. "Renny, we *need* Tyler."

She felt her sister's hand on her arm. "We take care of our own," Renny reminded. "Caitie needs you. Take care of her while we take care of . . . the rest."

"Renny, be reasonable!" Mattie said. But her sister didn't respond. Mattie felt her whip around, felt the tip of her braid brushing against her shoulder.

"There's work to be done!" Renny shouted at Kealan and Daire as she stomped off.

Mattie shook her head. From the side, Matthew put his arms around her and Caitie.

"She is a stubborn fool at times," he said. "When is she going to forgive him for just doing his job?"

"Never," Mattie said heavily, leaning against her brother for a moment. "He tried to take Kealan, Caitie and Daire from us. She'll never forgive him for that."

"Hell, Mattie. Can't blame him or half the town for looking out for their welfare. Our parents had just been killed."

Mattie didn't reply. The older O'Brien children had been left with the three youngsters to take care of, but they'd managed. Life had been a struggle in those first months after losing their parents, and many in Pheasant Gully had feared that they wouldn't make it through the winter on their own.

Sheriff Tyler had proposed taking the younger three and putting them with other families for the winter. Renny had fought him tooth and nail. Finally, Patrick O'Leary, the O'Briens' only neighbor and later Mattie's father-in-law, had stepped in and personally vowed to make sure they were all taken care of.

And he had. New to Pheasant Gully, he'd just got-

ten his own home built. He didn't have to step in
and help a bunch of strangers, especially when he
had his own family to look after, but he had. And his
children had become friends with the O'Brien children. Mattie had even fallen for Collin.

She drew in a deep breath. Yes, they owed Paddy
O'Leary so much. He'd been a blessing in those
early days of grief.

Matt's voice pulled her back to the crisis at hand.
"We'll work this out later."

"Yes, we will." Now Mattie was determined to
make Renny see sense. She didn't want to go behind
her sister's back. After the fire, it had been Renny
who'd taken charge, seen to their needs. Mattie had
been laid up for months with burns and blinding
headaches that sometimes kept her in bed for weeks.
Renny had been the one who held them together as
a family.

She'd also kept Mattie from wallowing in pity. She
still did. Mattie figured Renny, who was a year
younger, had earned her place as head of their family. But this time she was wrong. Stubbornly wrong,
and Mattie was going to do everything in her power
to see the right thing get done. Even if it meant in-
curring Renny's wrath.

Left alone in the misty morning she could not see,
Mattie turned back to the house, carrying Caitie. As
she reached the back porch, she sank onto the bottom step, rocking Caitie to and fro. Her young sister
slumped against her breast, fatigue overtaking her.

Mattie wished she could so easily escape from the horrible truth.

Without her eyesight, how could she spot an enemy trespassing on their land? And if the enemy came onto their land, what could she do? A gun or rifle in her hands might just as easily kill one of her siblings.

Her stomach churned with worry and fear. She didn't know what was going on; she knew only that they were in danger. But from who? And why? She knew one thing: the dreams of fire and the return of her visions were tied to it.

Somehow, the past and present were merging. But that knowledge did her little good. In the past, she'd relied on her eyesight to make connections between her visions and the world. That was no longer a possibility.

Closing her eyes, she rested her cheek on her sister's soft curls. All she could do now was talk to the sheriff. She refused to allow Renny's pride to get in the way of their safety.

Chapter Two

"Mathilda. We need to talk."

The sound of her father-in-law's deep voice drowned out the sounds of celebration and made Mattie groan beneath her breath. Every time she was left alone, Patrick O'Leary—known by his family and friends as Paddy—felt compelled to press his case.

Mattie moved her empty plate to a corner of the quilt she was sitting on. Tucking her legs to one side, she smoothed her apron over her skirt. "Paddy, I appreciate your kindness—"

His voice loomed over her. "Kindness, bah! We're talking family, child. You're my daughter."

Mattie heard his knees creak as he hunkered down in front of her. He took a deep shuddering breath. "Sick with worry, that's what I am. Before, with just them chickens and horses gettin' loose, we all fig-

29

ured you were just being plagued by mean pranks. But what happened this morning is serious. It's a warning, child."

Sighing, Mattie reached out a hand that trembled slightly. Immediately it was engulfed in two work-roughened ones.

"Papa O'Leary, having all of us move in with you and your family just won't work." She gentled her voice, knowing he was genuinely worried about her and her siblings. And with every right.

The nagging ache behind her eyes made her wish for the day to be over, for the arguing to be done. Instead of this joyous celebration, fear and worry were coloring her day. She'd had just about all she could handle for the day. "Your home—"

"Spare the excuses, Mathilda. My house is big enough."

Mattie resisted the urge to grimace. The house was *not* big enough for her *and* Mrs. O'Leary. Patrick loved and accepted her as his own flesh; his wife did not. Katherine O'Leary had no use or liking for " 'breeds." She was more concerned with her social standing, and having a husband who not only insisted on moving his family west but also on homesteading land adjoining a family of 'breeds had only made her colder.

For the sake of Paddy and her own siblings, Mattie tried to tolerate her. But how to tell her father-in-law that moving in would just not work!?

"Think I don't know the real reason you refuse to

move in with us?" Patrick asked, his voice lowered. It had turned deep and rough.

Guilt slid through Mattie. "It wouldn't work. You know it wouldn't." She spoke softly. Regretfully.

Patrick O'Leary gave a frustrated sigh. "Then move into town . . . 'til we catch the bastard. If money's the problem, I can—"

"No," she interrupted. Mattie wished she could have kept their problems from her father-in-law, but Patrick had seen the smoke from the burning carcasses from his homestead and ridden over to see what was going on. And from that moment, he hadn't given her a moment of peace.

Nor had the sheriff, or her own sister who was fuming because Sheriff Tyler was being as stubborn as Patrick. Unlike Patrick, Tyler was back to pressuring them into selling and moving into town—something he'd tried to get them to do after the death of their parents, and again after the fire.

Here she and Renny were in complete agreement. They would not give up what their father had wanted for his children: land and independence. "No. We won't sell and move into town," she said, knowing Paddy was likely to take up where the sheriff had left off.

"We won't leave," she said again, more fiercely. Her father had fallen in love with the land during his military travels, and after years of living a city life, he'd brought his family here to live among the wide, rolling expanse of open prairie, streams and woods. Leaving was not an option. And not just because the land was paid for.

Out here, on the western edge, they were now much closer to Mattie's Sioux relatives. The location her father had chosen was perfect: close enough to a growing town to get basic supplies, and not too far from the larger river city of Yankton, the capital of the Dakota Territory. Bordered on the south by the Missouri River, steamboat trade flourished and made getting supplies not sold in Pheasant Gully easier.

In front of her, Patrick stood. "Whoever poisoned your cows is not playin' around, Mathilda. If you won't stay with us, at least think about staying here in town with the Jensen sisters. Just for a while."

"And who would take care of the land, plant the corn and tend the livestock?"

"You know full well that your animals—what's left of them—can graze my land. Give it thought. Might be one of the younguns next time."

Mattie felt again a tremor of panic and fear. It would be so easy for someone to poison Caitie or Kealan. Even Daire had a sweet tooth. But before she could say anything further, a soft, sweet voice interrupted.

"Pa, Ma's looking for you."

Mattie could have hugged Brenna, Patrick's youngest child.

"We'll speak more on this, Mathilda."

Listening to Patrick stalk off, Mattie shoved her bonnet off her head. She hated wearing them, preferring to have her hair unbound and flowing freely. "Brenna, where is Renny?"

"I don't know, Mattie. Would you like me to find her for you?"

"No, not if you don't see her. Don't disturb her."

"Want me to sit with you? I'll tell you what's going on." The girl's voice dropped. "Saw Jonathon kissing Mary. Behind the church, even."

Mattie grinned. "Tell me all." She enjoyed Brenna, who seemed much too serious for her age most of the time.

Brenna sat and chatted happily for a while, then she got up to get something to drink. Left alone, Mattie lifted her head to the weak warmth of the setting sun. Clearing her mind, she listened and imagined her surroundings.

Behind her, the creek burbled and babbled. Children scrambled over the banks and splashed in the shallow water nearby. Women chatted and laughed. Mattie saw in her mind the small groups, the pristine white aprons worn over the "Sunday go-to-meetin'" dresses. She picked out Mrs. Henley's high-pitched voice.

Earlier Renny had described the woman's attire, said she looked like a walking tipi in her full skirts, and she'd said the woman's husband, Mr. Henley, was a man with the poles up his backside. The nose-in-the-air couple owned the feed store, and both thought themselves above most citizens of Pheasant Gully.

Mattie grinned. Surprisingly, the pair's two daughters and three sons were a joy to be around; they hadn't yet adopted the haughty air of their parents. For a while, Mattie amused herself by "watching" others through her ears. It still amazed her just how much she noticed that others did not. Like the fact that Mr. Potts at the post office was having an affair with Miss Marley, the spinster schoolmarm.

She grinned. Oh yes, she knew. It was in their voices, the hidden meanings in their conversations. Sometimes she thought she saw more blind than she had with her sight.

A soft spring breeze filled the air with the warm, yeasty scent of fresh bread and spicy fried chicken. Hungry, Reed followed the demands of his stomach.

Buildings on either side of Pheasant Gully's main road shadowed the wagon-wheel-scarred street, and his boots crunched hardened clods into smaller pebbles that would soon be ground into the hard, packed road. A horse and rider coming toward him veered to the side when Reed made no move to get out of the way. Each step he took was accompanied by the comforting slap of his holsters against his thighs.

The sight of those twin revolvers caused most men to steer out of his path. Or maybe it was the sight of guns along with his dark, Indian looks. It didn't matter that he was half white; most folks saw only a 'breed.

Tall, dark, dangerous—it was an image that had served him well during the last year.

Still, the burn of bitterness churned deep inside him. He was as white as any of them, save the color of his skin; city-bred and street smart, yet he was treated like something wild and unpleasant.

Passing the last building at the end of town, he felt a shaft of late-afternoon sun spear him full in the face. He squinted against the sudden brightness and tipped the rim of his hat down to shield his eyes. Then, with hands resting casually on hips, Reed studied the congregated townsfolk spread before him like a flock of sheep. How fitting that the bucolic celebration was taking place in front of the church.

Out of habit he scanned his surroundings with an air of bored detachment, but that was belied by his hard, cold eyes, which missed nothing—including the gaiety and welcoming beauty that even he, a man disillusioned and bitter with life, could appreciate. After all, he had no grudge against the earth or its maker. Just a goodly number of its inhabitants.

Resentment crept through Reed. For the last year he'd spent more time traveling through towns than staying in them. Mostly because he was a stranger, and a 'breed, and because most people couldn't see that he was just a man like them; except perhaps with a driving sense of duty.

The experiences of the last year had made him tired of having to feel like he needed to beg the right to be among so-called civilized men. Reed clenched his jaw tight as two women hastily stepped back inside a shop. The look on their faces clearly said they were afraid of him—like he was going to capture them, take them to his village and have his way with them.

He grunted in disgust. Small towns and those who inhabited them made him nervous and uncomfortable. They also pissed him off, what with their townsfolk's superior attitudes and stupid prejudices. Usually he camped just outside of town, entering only to take care of business. But this time, he'd rebelled.

Especially this time.

This town.

His searching gaze spotted a lone burr oak near the riverbank a short distance from the main gathering spot. Reed strode toward it. Reaching the tree, he slid into shadows the hue of fermenting grapes, and leaned against the rough bark.

Hunger tempted him to leave the shadows for the light, laughter and tables of food spread out before him; wariness and experience kept him from giving in. Still, he eyed the mounds of roasted pork and beef, pots simmering with beans and soups and stews. Bowls, plates and platters blurred as his gaze feasted.

Damn, he could use a hot meal. Anything was better than the hardtack and even harder, dry as dust biscuits that he'd lived off for the last couple of weeks. Using one finger, he tipped the brim of his hat slightly up. The need to arrive in Pheasant Gully well before his quarry had meant long days in the saddle.

With each deep breath he drew, his stomach gave a sharp twang, urging him to walk over and help himself. The two women who ran the boarding-house where he'd taken a room had told him the entire town had been invited to celebrate this betrothal; why didn't he just do it?

But instead of giving in to hunger, Reed twisted his lips into a sardonic smile. The two elderly sisters had to be blind to have issued the invite to him, for his *kind* was never invited or welcome at such social functions.

Most viewed 'breeds with loathing, distrust and hatred, so Reed stayed cloaked in the deepening shadows. Crossing his arms loosely over his chest, he rubbed his buckskin-clad shoulder against the rough surface to quell an itch, then resumed his deceptively casual slouch as several families drifted away from the celebration.

A group of rowdies staggered toward him. One unkempt man took a long pull from a silver flask in his hand, then passed it to one of his pals. The sour stench of booze hit Reed like a fist to the face.

The drunks caught sight of him. One even took a step forward. "Don't like 'breeds ha-hangin' 'round watchin' 'r wo'en," he slurred.

Reed lifted a brow. "Nice friendly welcome you

boys give," he drawled. Inside, he was resigned. First night in town, and he might end up spending it in jail.

He straightened, halfheartedly jingling his holsters. Any fight he got involved in would end up being his fault, and he didn't have time to spend in a cell. Reed kicked himself for not sticking to routine, but some bit of the devil had surfaced, making him determined to stay where he pleased despite his welcome.

And once more, his foolish stubbornness would land him in jail. He sighed. With Granger's expected arrival, he didn't have time for jail, so he pulled out his meanest, darkest expression.

The other two drunks took one look at Reed, then they grabbed their pal and pulled him away. "Don't want no trouble," one of them muttered.

"Smart," Reed said as he watched the trio head off into town. He might hate being a 'breed, but he could defend himself as well or better than any man. Growing up on the streets had taught him to fight with both fist and blade. And setting out to find a gang of killers, he'd learned fast to be one of the best shots around.

He let out a long breath as fatigue washed over him. Why was he standing here, wasting his time? He could easily get himself a bite to eat—and more—at the saloon.

So leave, he told himself. Yet he didn't move, just continued to scan. Pheasant Gully wasn't any different than any other small, Western town he'd drifted through during the last year, and not much different than the town that had betrayed him. It didn't matter where he went; people were the same.

As though to prove him right, a woman standing in front of the church yanked on the sleeve of another woman, leaning in close to whisper to her. The second's gaze shifted, and the pair turned to stare into the crowd. Smiling smugly, they hurried over to join a separate group of women. Immediately, the talking behind gloved hands started anew.

Backstabbing gossips. Every single one of them. Reed would bet the bank on it. Nearby, a group of smartly-dressed men puffed on cigars. He snorted silently. Self-aggrandizing bastards.

Reed had once owned fancy shirts, trousers and suits. He'd attended school and social gatherings. He'd had everything that the son of a banker could expect to come his way. Except acceptance. No matter what he did or achieved, his heritage was still held against him. Even by the man who'd adopted him.

Shoving aside the spill of bitterness that could make a man careless, Reed pushed away from the tree. Still, his feet refused to retrace his steps. He blamed it on the rumbling of his belly. His stomach was throwing a major tantrum. Food at the saloon would be piss-poor compared to the offerings only feet away.

Of course, it was food that kept him there, a silent

watcher. It couldn't be the laughter or music that tempted him to move closer. Unlike the moths drawn to the lanterns being lit for those who wished to stay past dark, Reed resisted that temptation.

He crossed his arms across his chest. Those poor unfortunate insects would singe their wings and die. But not him. He'd do as he'd planned—head for the saloon. Didn't matter that he was in no mood for the trouble his presence was bound to cause; of his two options, it was the smarter.

Damn, he wasn't in a mood to fend off drunks who took exception to having a 'breed in their midst. Especially one who didn't touch liquor.

He'd learned the hard way the consequences of too much drink. Pain speared his heart. Drink had torn his world apart, ripped all he'd held dear from him. Drink had brought him through here a year ago, and drink was the reason he could not go home.

His hands clenched into tight fists. Home, he thought bitterly; the dream of the abandoned child he'd once been.

Surviving on the harsh streets as a child, he'd seen the worst that life had to offer. He'd fought his way out, fought to have a shot at what most kids took for granted. And he'd gotten it. A home. And a family. He'd held on to it, taken what he wanted, what he'd needed and craved for all of his miserable life. Then, in one drunken moment he'd lost it all.

The pain of loss stabbed him deep, making him bleed all over again. He closed his eyes. *Soon*, he thought. It would be over soon. Determination to right the wrongs of his past gave him the strength to continue. He allowed nothing, not even his own bitterness and despair to interfere with what had to be done. Righting the wrongs could not bring Anne back, but he prayed it would return him his soul.

Out of nowhere, a ball flew at him, tearing him from his dark thoughts. His sharp reflexes allowed him to catch the brown sphere before it could smack him in the head. Lifting his hand to toss it back to the group of boys he'd seen kicking it around earlier, he slowly lowered his hand, bringing his other palm up to frame the ball between his hands.

A lump formed in his throat as he remembered another ball from another life—a past that seemed a lifetime away. The group of boys chasing the ball stopped a short distance away to stare at him warily.

One boy with a wild shock of red hair stepped forward. "Good catch, mister." He held out his hands for the ball.

The boy's bright and eager blue gaze brought a sharp twisting pain to Reed's gut.

Danny.

The boy's image swam before him, settling into a much younger child with blond curls, chubby cheeks and bright eyes the shade of a summer sky.

His firstborn. His pride. His Danny boy.

In his mind's eye he saw himself tossing a ball to the child, felt again that burst of pride when Danny's short arms shot out in a wide hug to catch

41

it. Reed heard his son's triumphant shout before the red ball came winging toward him in a wild throw.

A wave of longing speared through Reed, leaving a path of bitterness and a pain so intense he couldn't breathe.

"Mister? My ball?"

The hesitant voice shattered the memory and yanked Reed from images of yesteryear. The past was best left alone. Although not forgotten—not until he'd righted those wrongs.

Hardening his heart, he tossed the ball from his left to his right hand, then flipped it to the boy whose grin had faltered. "Be careful," he growled. "Could've hurt someone."

"Yessir," the boy answered. "Sorry, mister." Slowly he backed away, his blue gaze flicking to the guns dangling from Reed's hips. Then he was gone.

A long shadow moved to his right. Reed caught the gleam of metal on a man's broad chest. His senses went on alert; his body tightened with tension. With a deceptively casual move, he crossed one ankle over the other, then folded his arms across his chest.

"Sheriff Tyler." It took effort to keep his voice disinterested and cool.

The lawman stopped a few paces away. Eyes narrowed, mouth set in a grim line, he nodded. "Been a long time, Reed. Didn't think you'd be foolish enough to return."

Chapter Three

Reed eyed the law of Pheasant Gully. The man was an inch or two taller than he was, broad as the side of a barn and had eyes hard as flint. He also wielded a mean punch that could knock a man out cold, Reed knew from experience.

Wearing black from head to toe, Sheriff Tyler presented a formidable obstacle. Any man walking on the wrong side of the law would be a fool to tangle with him. Unfortunately, Reed walked a very thin line.

"Well?" Menace rumbled deep in the lawman's throat.

Reed folded his arms over his chest, keeping them far from his guns. "Just come for a hot meal, *Sheriff* Tyler." A year ago, the man's title had been deputy.

Deliberately, Reed slouched farther against the tree, giving every appearance of being unconcerned.

But deep inside he was fully alert. Here stood the one man who could stop him.

Sheriff Tyler narrowed his eyes. "Don't see you eatin'. Gut tells me you're here for more than food."

Reed thumbed his hat back an inch. "Not breaking any laws by standing here." He lifted a brow.

The sheriff gave a slight nod. "And . . . after you eat—if you decide to eat?"

Reed's hungry gaze was pulled back to the tables of disappearing food. Oh, he planned to eat. Damned if he wasn't going to help himself to a nice home-cooked meal. He was here, and a man had to eat.

"Depends." His gaze roamed the peaceful meadow where the festivities were taking place. In the center of it all sat the whitewashed church. Men smoked a respectful distance to one side, while women bustled back and forth: some going inside, others coming out and still others obviously in charge of keeping food on the tables.

The scene spread before him gave the appearance of a close knit community filled with law-abiding, loving citizens. But appearances were deceptive. In many cases, smiles and laughter hid the dark side of man: scorn, contempt, hate, greed. And somewhere out there, a man walked with blood on his hands.

Reed's gaze found the group of boys. The only innocents in this town, or any other town, were the children. He deliberately ignored those.

Tyler moved, blocking Reed's view. The sun behind him cast his features in shadow. "Last time you rode through, a man died." Tyler's voice had turned harsh, warning that if Reed wasn't careful, all hell would break loose between them.

Food forgotten, Reed straightened, planted his feet apart and met the formidable accusation in the sheriff's gaze. "Four," Reed spat bitterly. "If you're going to toss it in my face, toss it all!"

Four lives lost, and he was responsible for each of them. He hadn't pulled any triggers, but the death of his wife, the previous sheriff of Pheasant Gully and an innocent homesteading couple rested heavily on his shoulders. They filled him with bitter remorse.

His gaze traveled back to the boys kicking their ball across the meadow. Unbidden came the image of his own children, screaming as they were taken from him. The weighty guilt he carried threatened to crush him into the ground. His stupidity had cost so many so much.

He said, "Let's cut the chitchat. It's a free country. If you're going to throw me in jail, at least let me eat first." He half-expected to spend the night in jail no matter what he did. There was no love lost between he and the sheriff. The lawman killed two years ago had been Tyler's older brother.

Damn, Reed was too tired for this confrontation. Exhaustion that was as much emotional as physical swept through him. So much depended on what happened in the next few weeks. He'd either vindicate himself, or he'd forever lose his chance to clear his name.

"Might just do that if you don't tell me why you're here." Tyler's voice was deep, quiet, authoritative.

At the threat, Reed relaxed and got up the nerve to smile, amused. "You won't. Another man of law might—has, just because he could—but not you."

Reed knew firsthand that Tyler was a fair man. Hard but fair. Reed was alive today only because the man had prevented his unjust hanging. Back when Reed had been blamed for the deaths of Tyler's brother, along with those of the man and woman who'd been unlucky enough to have been in the path of the Granger gang, Tyler had put a stop to it.

Reed figured he at least owed the man an answer.

"Don't want no trouble."

Trouble.

That one word summed up Reed's life. As a boy, he'd been trouble to his whoring mother who just dumped him in the street to fend for himself. Growing up on the streets he'd been trouble to those he stole from to survive, and to the lawmen trying to lock him up.

Later, after Reed found a home with a man who adopted him, he'd figured his troubles were over. Reed had thought the man loved him, accepted him, but when he'd fallen in love with the man's daughter, he was back to being a 'breed. Not a son.

A thread of bitterness crept unbidden into his

tone. "Don't always get what you want. You ought to know that, *Sheriff.*"

Seeing the man's jaw tighten, Reed winced inwardly. Damn, if he didn't hold his tongue, he'd end up in jail as sure as the sun rose in the east.

Sheriff Tyler glared furiously at him. "Heard you paid for a month's stay with the Jensen sisters." He tossed his cigar to the ground, then crushed the butt beneath his heel.

Deciding it was better to keep silent, Reed returned his attention to the celebration. It was winding down.

"You're here because of Leo Granger."

Reed didn't bother to agree to or deny the statement. The bounty was high for the Granger gang, dead or alive. Reed had already brought in three of the five, dead. And another had died here, in this small Western town.

His lips twisted. Four for four. He should feel avenged. But each life taken, though sanctioned by law, was just another reminder of the mess he'd made of his life.

He turned his attention back to the sheriff. "Figured you'd want the bastard who killed your brother."

Sheriff Tyler gave him a long, considering glance. He rubbed his chin with three fingers. "You plan to turn him over to me?"

Reed shrugged. "Don't have to. Wanted *dead* or alive."

Leaning in, the sheriff lowered his voice. "And the money? Heard it was never recovered. If you're here and Granger's returning, that means the money's still here. Somewhere."

"Give the man with the star a hand," Reed joked, glancing around. He didn't need anyone overhearing them. While it had been no secret that the posse chasing the Granger gang hadn't recovered the money stolen from Reed's adoptive father's bank, it was generally assumed it had been divided by the gang before they'd split up. Yet Reed knew from capturing three of the gang that the money had been stashed while they were on the run. With the posse hot on their heels, they hadn't had time to split it. Only one man knew where it was, and that was the man Reed was here to find.

Unfortunately, he had no idea of the man's new identity or what he looked like, just that his trail led here. He shoved his hands into his pockets. There was only one man who knew who Malcolm Arthur Clemmings was: Leo Granger, his partner.

Leo would lead Reed to "Mac," the mastermind behind the bank robbery and the death of Anne, the love of Reed's life.

Reed held out little hope of gaining forgiveness from his adoptive parents or regaining custody of his children, but he was determined to recover the money and restore his father's reputation.

And maybe he could regain a bit of his own honor, though nothing could put to rights what that night of foolish temper and drink had done. Reed drew in a deep breath. "Sometimes a man has to do the right thing."

He stared sightlessly out toward the flowing stream, noted the glow of the lowering sun on its surface.

Anne. Her hair had been golden, like ripe wheat at sunset, with just a hint of fire in it. How he'd loved her hair.

Sheriff Tyler took off his hat and smacked his thigh with it, startling Reed. "Damn it, Reed. Don't need this kind of trouble. If Granger is coming back to find the money, then every thief in the territory will be hot on his heels."

Reed didn't care about them. He didn't even really care about Leo Granger. The man was as good as dead. It was just a matter of time. There had been many opportunities over the last year when Reed could have taken the man out. But he hadn't. Reed needed him alive, and had even made sure the law hadn't gotten their hands on him.

Reed would never forget that day at the bank: the fear of those around him during the robbery, and his own shock upon seeing Leo Granger, his drinking buddy, as part of the gun-wielding men demanding the newly arrived railroad payroll being held at the bank for safekeeping before it headed westward.

Then another man, masked and heavily disguised, had stepped forward. He'd ordered Anne brought to him, and before Reed could reach her, he'd shot her in cold blood.

A daughter for a daughter. The words uttered by the man before he pulled the trigger haunted Reed day and night.

Feeling the past closing in on him, Reed glared at the sheriff. "If you don't mind, it's been a long day." He walked past, toward the tables laden with food.

Sheriff Tyler reached out and stopped him. "You were a hothead with something to prove a year ago."

Reed smiled grimly. "Still have something to prove, Sheriff." He turned and walked away. Appetite gone, he still headed for congregated people.

He was a stubborn fool with something to prove all right. Right now he'd prove he could go where he wanted, be where he wanted, and it didn't matter one damn bit whether folk wanted him around or gone. Reed was here to stay until he found justice for his wife. For his children. For that boy he'd once been, who'd thought he'd found it all, and for the grown man who had nothing.

Heaven. Leaning his hip against the edge of the abandoned table, Reed used his teeth to tear off another hunk of meat from the drumstick gripped in his one hand, then took a bite of the thick bread slice he held in his other. He felt as though he was in heaven as he stuffed the rest into his mouth.

"Hey, 'breed!" a voice from behind him called out.

Reed froze, then lowered his drumstick. He turned slowly. Three young men swaggered toward him, eyes full of contempt, bodies tense with challenge and recklessness.

"Don't want your kind eating food our ma fixed. Go hunt yerself a rabbit."

Shifting, Reed tossed the chicken leg down, reached out and took another. He kept his eyes trained on the foolhardy boys and deliberately ate more of the tender, juicy meat. Without taking his eyes off them, he finished it and tossed the bone down. Immediately a dog scooted out from beneath the table to take it. The first bone was already gone.

Whipping his hand behind him, Reed pulled out his hunting knife, watched the boys' three pairs of eyes widen. In one quick flash, he whacked off another hunk of bread, then used his knife to scoop butter out of a wooden container.

No one spoke as he continued to eat.

When he was done, he lifted a brow. "One of your mothers baked this fine bread?"

The same boy who'd spoken before stepped forward. "Yeah. Mine. And she don't want no 'breed eating it."

Reed met each boy's gaze. One by one each looked away. "Best I've had in a long time," he said, scooping more butter from the bowl and using his knife to spread it on another slice. Speaking as if they were having a normal conversation, he shoved his hat back with the tip of his blade. "Be willing to bet that

51

a woman who bakes as good as this wouldn't want to see her son do something stupid."

He stepped away from the table. Waiting until each pair of eyes slid down to his twin holsters, Reed smiled as the trio of troublemakers shot nervous glances at him.

One by one they faltered, giving each other scared looks. "Maybe we don't want no trouble," one muttered.

"I should say not!" agreed an angry voice. A woman marched forward out of nowhere. "William Henry, you got mush for brains?" She whipped out a cloth from the basket she carried and smacked the young man. He lifted his hands to ward her off.

"Ma," he squealed. "Not here!"

"Don't you speak, William Henry! You get yourself home!" She turned to the other two. "All of you. And don't think I won't be telling your mothers what fools they've raised! Go!"

Without uttering another word, the trio of troublemakers fled. The woman turned to Reed. "I apologize, sir," she said, fire in her eyes but nervousness in her voice.

"No harm done, ma'am."

She nodded as she picked up her crock of butter. "Take the rest of the bread." With that, she stalked off.

Reed watched as she caught up to her son, gave him a shove toward town. The other two boys quickly moved off on their own.

Reaching down, Reed decided it was a good time

to leave, himself. Most of the guests had already taken their leave; only a few families remained. He scooped up the remaining loaf of bread.

A young couple walked past the tables. The young woman had her hand secure on the arm of her beau. They walked close, talking softly. Reed watched as they bumped against one another, so engrossed in their conversation that they seemed oblivious to everything around them.

Unexpected flashes of memory of him and Anne walking exactly the same way, talking with heads close, wrapped up in each other's presence, struck his heart like bolts of lightning struck the trees on the prairie. The food in his belly churned. Though their life had been hard and the separation from her father had devastated her, they'd been so happy, so in love. Like this couple.

He had to get out of here before the past rose to crush him with its dark fist of grief.

"Make a pretty couple, they will," came a slurred voice.

Startled, Reed slid his eyes to the man suddenly standing beside him. Involved in his thoughts, he hadn't heard him approach. Which was stupid. Not to mention unforgivable. A man unaware of his surroundings often ended up dead.

The old man swayed and grabbed the table to steady himself. *Great. He was a drunk.* The only thing worse than a young hothead was a drunk. Nodding personably, Reed started to move off.

"Damn shame about her first husband, though." The drunk took out a silver flask, tipped his head back and swigged. "Killed in that fire. Left the woman a widow on their wedding night. Damn shame, if you ask me—a man don't even get his wedding night."

Reed shook his head. "Yep. Damn shame."

Watching several people go over to speak and shake hands with the young man, Reed realized that this was an engagement the town was celebrating. The young man shook hands, puffed up like a peacock, looking exceedingly proud.

Reed's eyes widened as the boy stared at his fiancée like a smitten pup. Hell, he couldn't blame the young man. She had an amazing body, and shiny strands of blue-black hair hung past her waist in a glorious waterfall. Every movement of her head sent the shimmering strands into a sensuous dance.

She turned her head, and Reed felt like he'd been punched in the gut. Holy hell! She had a face that made him think of warm honey and silk. This was the most strikingly beautiful woman he'd ever laid eyes on. And his awe turned to surprise as his eyes traveled over her exotic cheeks and into eyes that were rich, dark pools of amber.

He'd bet the loaf of bread in his hands that the young woman was Indian. Pureblood. It wasn't just her raven-black hair, or even her warm, dark skin. Her noble heritage showed in her face: prominent cheekbones, the proud line of her nose, the gentle slope of almost almond-shaped eyes.

Undeterred by his silence, the drunk took another gulp of liquor. He offered the flask to Reed. "Gal's right lucky to find herself another husband."

Reed refused the flask by shaking his head. He glared at the drunk. "Why? Because she's got Indian blood?" His voice was low, tight. If the drunk made even so much as a disparaging comment about 'breeds, squaws or Indians, he would be tempted to knock him on his backside.

Stopping himself, Reed took a deep breath. He tried to be rational. Starting a fight would land him in jail for the night. It would just give Tyler an excuse to have him watched and followed.

The drunk blinked, taking a good look at Reed, then backed away—which left Reed feeling slightly disappointed. In one short hour, his emotions had been rubbed raw—by that kid, the sheriff, the young men and by the memories of his wife. A good fight would have wiped out the blast of unwanted emotions.

But it wasn't to be. And a good thing. Getting himself run out of town would not help his quest for justice. Deciding it would be wise to simply return to his room at the boardinghouse, Reed turned to go.

A light laugh stopped him. It was the woman, enjoying some joke with her friends and betrothed. He turned. Like the damn moths fluttering against the heated glass of the nearby lanterns, he felt drawn to this young beauty. He moved closer.

The woman's loveliness drew him, yet there was more. Something deeper. Though she smiled, laughed and chatted with those surrounding her, he sensed the shadows she hid within herself. It was there in her eyes, and in the slightly drooping corner of her mouth as her smile faded. Absently, Reed leaned against a table. Lost in the woman's haunting beauty, he ignored several wary looks thrown his way.

Without warning, the woman swung her head toward him. Something invisible flared between them hitting him right between the eyes. Reed felt as though he'd been speared by her wide, dark gaze. He waited until her eyes met his, waited for a reaction to his presence. It didn't come. Her gaze was on him, yet it seemed as though she were looking right through him.

She gave no indication that she'd seen him, or that he was at that moment staring into her eyes. Still, there was something powerful and compelling being exchanged between them. He found it unsettling. He willed her to acknowledge him. To see him.

Around her, the group of well-wishers laughed. But she'd gone still. Her smile had faded completely. Her haunted look deepened, and she looked incredibly sad.

Reed took a step forward before he realized what was happening. Unnerved by the strange potency of those eyes, he backed away, following the edge of the table. Then, cursing beneath his breath, he turned and walked off. His steps quickened, but he felt her eyes burn twin holes into his back, one finding his heart, the other his soul.

He shook with fear. What was going on? Cursing, he lengthened his stride. He'd walked away from his share of fights, but he'd never run like this. And he sure as hell had never run from a woman.

Scowling, Reed reached into his pocket and fingered a gold coin. Leo Granger would arrive soon; he'd seen to that. After tracing the murderer to this region, he'd made sure that Leo knew where to find the man who'd organized the bank robbery. With any luck, Leo would find Malcolm—or whatever name Malcolm went by now. And Reed would be right behind him. The man who'd killed Anne was as good as dead.

Still, revenge wouldn't bring back Anne. It was too late for her. And him. Revenge wouldn't give him back his children, and his adoptive father had made it clear that Reed would not be allowed to return for any reason. But at least his children would not have to live with their father's shame.

He clenched his hands into fists. This time, he wasn't going to leave justice to men who pinned a shiny star to their chest and proclaimed themselves the law. This time, justice would be served. By his hand. And that, he told himself, was where he was going.

Unbidden, the woman's image returned, blinding him. Reed cursed, his steps quickening. He'd never run from trouble before. But deep inside, he knew he was doing just that: fleeing the unknown.

Mattie's heart slammed against her ribs. A pair of startling blue eyes had just pierced the shadows of her mind and captured her mind and body in a way she'd never experienced. The vision had been strong, powerful, compelling.

For once she was thankful she didn't have her sight, for being blind meant she could close her eyes and no one would think anything of it. Counting each beat of her frantically racing heart, she retreated into her mind to examine what had just happened.

She'd felt him. Seen him! But she didn't know who *he* was. Still, the vision had told her two things: the spirits were truly returning her gift, and somehow, the man she had sensed would play an important role in her life.

She didn't know how she knew this; she just did, for she'd never felt so strong a presence, and she'd never, ever, felt a sensation of leaving her body to merge with another. She'd definitely felt herself going to him, felt him welcoming her, and most of all she'd felt safe within those strong arms. Mattie closed out the chatter and activity around her and focused deep inside her mind.

At first she'd felt like a deer who sees a hunter, bow drawn, arrow poised to fly, and then a whisper of warmth had engulfed her—liquid sunshine mixed with the softness of downy feathers and an elusive, woodsy scent.

Then, to her shock, she'd felt herself drawn into a pair of strong arms, and in that brief moment she'd felt wanted. Cherished. Loved. The shock of it still reverberated through her.

Frightened and excited, Mattie opened her eyes. She scanned the darkness, searching for him, but he was gone. She wished she could escape, be alone. She needed time to think and examine everything that was happening to her. There was so much.

Visions had been a part of her entire life. She'd embraced the gift, accepted both the good and the bad, the weight of responsibility and the rewards. And she'd accepted that the blow to her head had destroyed both her eyesight and her gift of Sight. But apparently not forever.

Her world for the last year had lacked color. Only in her dreams and memories did she remember what it was like to live among all the radiant hues of the world. Until now. Her chest tightened. Did this mean her eyesight would also return?

For the first in a long time since the fire, Mattie admitted how much she missed being able to see, both physically and spiritually. The accident had destroyed the very core of Mathilda Morning Moon O'Brien, leaving her confused, unsure of who she was and her purpose in life.

Without conscious thought, she pulled away from Gil and rubbed her arms.

"Are you cold, Mattie?" he asked.

She felt him shift beside her, and forced a smile to her lips. "Just tired," she said. What did this mean for Gil, and her marriage to him? What of the vision of death she'd experienced earlier that morning, and her dreams?

Her heart jumped. Not Gil. And please, not the stranger whose eyes had just pierced the darkness of her world. Do not let them die! Once more confusion swept through her mind. Concentrating on what was going on around her, Mattie swatted an insect away from her face. Gil and his father were talking to her left; her mother-in-law stood across from her, foot tapping impatiently on the ground.

Behind her, Mattie heard Renny chatting with one of the Jensen sisters: Martha—her voice was just a bit softer, her speech more hesitant, shy even. It was getting dark; Mattie felt the coolness of the breeze, heard the buzz of mosquitos drawn to the oily heat of the lamps and the rhythm of grasshoppers along the river.

A hand touched her arm. "Good night, Mattie," a loud voice called. "Got to get home. Early day tomorrow."

"Good night, Miss Marley," Mattie replied softly. She smiled. Was she the only one who heard the hidden excitement in Miss Marley's voice? *Have a good rendezvous with Mr. Potts*, she added silently.

She was without her eyesight, yes, but she was not senseless. She heard more than what was said in voices, could tell when someone was not really paying attention, and she even knew when someone was staring at her. She heard the whispered words of pity or gossip from those around her who somehow assumed she'd lost her hearing along with her eyesight; that if she couldn't see them, she couldn't hear them.

She chuckled softly. If they only knew just how much she saw.

"You're having a good time?" Gil asked.

Mattie smiled at him. "Yes. And you?"

"Of course."

Mattie narrowed her eyes. His voice sounded strained. Forced. She felt his head turn. His shoulder brushed hers. Without turning her own head, Mattie listened intently and heard soft whispering. Beside her, Gil tensed. No one would see the movement, but she felt it.

"Who's coming toward us?" she whispered. The buzz of conversation was winding down, the scent of food fading, and she heard the cry of tired children being gathered. People were leaving.

"Josiah." Gil hesitated, just a fraction, then added, "and Francine."

While the two men shook hands, Mattie accepted a hug from Francine. "You are fortunate," the other woman said. "I wish you well, Mattie."

Mattie smiled. Francine was a year younger and

had always been friendly toward Mattie and her family. But tonight her voice held an edge—a tenseness that matched Gil's as he accepted congratulations and some back-slapping humor from Josiah. Josiah, on the other hand, sounded pleased as he announced he was walking Francine home.

She turned to Gil when the young couple walked away. "Gil—"

A hand on her shoulder startled her. "It's just me, Mattie," Matthew said. "I've got Caitie. She's nearly asleep. Why don't you take her back while I round up the others?"

Beside her, Gil agreed. "I'll let Pa know that you're leaving. Wait, and I'll walk you back."

Mattie frowned but said, "All right." In truth she was eager to leave and get back to the boardinghouse. She was sharing a room with her sisters, but it would at least be a place where she could think, and if what she suspected was true—that Gil and Francine were in love—then she *really* needed to do some thinking.

Taking Caitie's hand in her own as Matthew set her down, Mattie started toward the boardinghouse. She didn't wait for Gil; Caitie could guide her as well as anyone.

That morning, they'd all looked forward to this night in town—a night away from their ranch and the smell of death. But now she just wanted to be alone. *Truly* alone. Around her, low voices drifted past: other couples and families also headed back toward their homes. Horses pulled wagons; dogs padded down the road after their masters.

"Lead me to the boardwalk, Caitie," Mattie said after feeling a wagon rumble past, a bit too close for comfort.

When Caitie slowed and hesitated slightly, Mattie did the same, then stepped onto the plank walk that ran past the bank, newspaper and sheriff's office. Tired and drained, she stumbled, catching her foot in the hem of her skirt.

Without warning, the wooden post to her left exploded. Splinters flew around her as the loud report of a gun deafened her to all other sound. Screaming, Mattie jerked back, lost her balance on the edge of the wooden walk, and fell into the street. Her head struck the edge of the boardwalk, and all went still.

Chapter Four

"Mattie! Mattie!"

The high-pitched screams pierced the fog of pain in Mattie's head and pulled her out of the hostile grip of unconsciousness. She lifted her head. She lay in the road, feeling the damp from the recent rain seeping into her chest.

Confusion sounded everywhere: men shouting, women screaming, and the ground beneath her shaking with the vibrations of running feet. Worse, chaos reigned in her own mind.

She felt a crowd grow around her: feet scraping the ground, bits of dirt pelting her arms and face, petticoats rustling as women gathered around her.

Mattie rubbed her aching temple, then winced at both the pain and the sticky feel of blood. Her fingers trailed down, finding several slivers of wood embedded in her cheek. Immediately the sound of the gunshot, the feel of the wood splintering returned with the realization that someone had shot at her. Terror skittered through her.

"Caitie!"

She used her hands to feel around, searching, praying that her sister was nearby and unharmed. Her fingers scrambled over the uneven ground, scraping against dirt and rocks. All familiarity of her surroundings had fled, leaving her in a dark void.

Scared, vulnerable, she got to her knees. A sudden weight on her back knocked her back to the ground.

"Mattie!" Caitie clung to her, small arms wrapped tightly around her neck, skinny legs gripping her waist.

Relieved that her sister sounded unharmed, Mattie reached behind her and pulled Caitie into the security of her arms; then she sat, her skirts twisted beneath her.

"Caitie!" Her throat seized, turning her cry into a croak. Ignoring everything but her frightened sister, Mattie ran her hands through the child's tangled red curls. "Are you all right? Are you hurt?" She cursed her blindness as she felt carefully over Caitie's small body, searching for injury.

The child tucked her face into the hollow of Mattie's neck. She trembled uncontrollably. Panic returned to Mattie. Where was she? Even with so many people around, she had no idea where the bank was, which way led back to the Jensens' boardinghouse. Was she in the alley beside the bank, or out in the street in front of it? Why did no one speak up? Why did no one help?

She opened her mouth to ask, then stopped. Shame mingled with anger. She hated the loss of her independence. Reaching out, she hoped to find the edge of the wooden boardwalk from which she'd fallen. Her fingers brushed against crisp fabric.

She hastily pulled her hand back. Close to tears, she sat silent, surrounded by townsfolk. But instead of feeling safe and secure, she felt confined. Trapped. She couldn't even attempt to stand in case she bumped into someone. Her breathing quickened. She fought the urge to scream.

"Renny," she gasped. "Someone get my sister. Please."

She listened, heard some shuffling, the scrape of cloth against cloth. Scents clinging to silent watchers invaded the small bit of space where Mattie and Caitie sat—acrid smoke from the open fire pits where slabs of beef had been roasted, dust from hems of skirts, stale drink, the sourness of clothing worn without being washed.

Mattie's nose twitched. Someone to her left had stepped in something unpleasant. The air was suddenly thick. She couldn't breathe.

"Give them room," a deep voice barked. "Move aside."

At the sound Mattie's panic eased, which surprised her, for she didn't recognize the commanding voice at all. People moved, however; and a breath of fresh air edged in, bringing with it a new mixture of scents—leather, sun and something she had no word for.

"You all right?"

The voice was male. Deep, a bit gruff, a bit angry, yet gentle. Mattie's heart quickened, and without reason she felt weak. Dizzy.

"I think so," she whispered. The voice was new, as was his scent. Her rescuer was a stranger. But instead of frightened, especially considering she'd just been shot at, Mattie felt strangely calm, as though she knew this man, as though she already trusted him. He stood close, his eyes on her—his rich, summer-sky blue eyes—and she didn't need to see to know; she felt it.

"Let's get you out of here. Away from these damned gawkers." Strong hands gripped beneath her arms, effortlessly lifted her to her feet.

Then the man paused. "Damn it, people, move! This isn't a damn circus. We need a doctor!"

Trembling, Mattie continued to clasp Caitie tightly to her. This was the man she'd seen earlier, in her vision—the man who'd held her. Somehow she recognized the feel of him, the scent of him.

She didn't need to touch him to know that he was tall. His voice and his breath brushed the top of her head. She felt the broadness and the strength of his body near hers. His warmth cloaked her, shielded her, protected her. With each breath she drew, she drew in his scent. And felt more safe.

A flurry of skirts and pounding steps came at her. "Mattie! What happened? You hurt?" Renny's voice was fraught with worry.

"No . . ." She broke off at a twinge of pain from the gash on her temple and the slivers of wood buried in her cheek.

"Let me take Caitie."

Grateful for Renny's arrival, Mattie handed over Caitie, then brushed her hands down her skirts. Her elbow bumped against the stranger. She froze, embarrassed, yet was unable to move for she had no idea where to step.

Without the sun, she didn't even know which direction she faced. She was totally turned around. The crowd had moved back, and with the arrival of the stranger, they had begun talking; some in whispers, others in loud voices. Mattie knew she'd be the topic of much gossip come morning.

"Renny? Take me back." She spoke low. Desperate.

"No. Someone fetch the sheriff."

The command came from the stranger. He was standing beside her, and Mattie's growing panic fled as she was reminded of his presence. A feeling of security took over. For just a moment, the horror of being shot at faded. There weren't many people who made her feel comfortable, and the situation confused even as it comforted her.

Beside her, Renny stiffened. "We don't need—"

"Right here, Reed. Somebody want to tell me what happened?"

Mattie sniffed, recognizing the scent of Sheriff Tyler's tobacco. She gave a startled yelp when he took her arm in his. "Let's get you inside."

He pulled her away from the crowd. Away from Renny and Caitie. Away from the stranger. And Mattie felt cold and alone.

"Step," he warned.

Mattie stumbled, barely having time to step up onto the plank walkway. She turned her head. As nice as Tyler was, he was a big man, with a big, rough, stomping stride.

"Renny?" she called. She couldn't keep the panic from her voice. Too much was happening, too much was out of her control. Her voice shook.

"Hold up, Sheriff," came the stranger's call.

Mattie was jolted to a stop. She felt like a rag doll, being swung to and fro. Then she felt *him*— the warmth of his hand on her arm, the soft breath of air, then the comforting feel of his arms around her as he swept her up into his embrace.

"She doesn't need you dragging her behind you," he chided Sheriff Tyler.

Then, once more, they were moving; this time smoothly, with no stumbling in the dark. Mattie should have felt embarrassed, but she didn't. She should have been afraid of this stranger. But she wasn't. He could be the one responsible for the harassment, the threats, the poisoning of her family's cows. But, inside, she knew he wasn't responsible, because every part of her recognized him as the man from her vision. As the man who would play a big part in what was yet to come.

And that frightened her more than the fact that someone had tried to kill her.

The woman lay stiff as a board in his arms. "Relax," Reed ordered gruffly. He shifted her slightly. She sagged against him. Her cheek rested against his pounding heart. Someone had nearly killed this woman.

He tightened his grip, drawing in her sweet scent of spring grass after a gentle rain. Inhaling deeply over and over, as if he couldn't get enough of her, Reed felt something shift deep inside. His life for the last year was like the harsh, cold winter—bleak, dead, hopeless. But the first time he set eyes on this woman, he'd felt as though a ray of warmth had speared through the coldness of his world. Holding her, he felt the promise of spring. Of hope.

Disgusted with his fanciful thoughts, Reed shoved away that hope. This was just a woman who'd been shot at. Nothing more, nothing less. He just happened to have been close by.

At least that's what he kept telling himself. He conveniently ignored the fact that he'd seen her leave, had been curious and followed. He'd left the celebration but was still hanging around the buildings, observing each man who walked past, waiting to see if anyone recognized him.

He'd seen the woman and young child walking

toward town, passing him where he stood in the shadows. His world had spun crazily when he'd heard the shot ring out and saw her fall.

All color had faded, and he'd felt gut-punched. He had run as fast as he could, dodging wagons and horses, feeling as though he were moving far too slowly—like swimming though a thick mire—to get to the woman.

So what? So when he'd heard the shot, watched her fall, he'd done what any man would do—go to her assistance.

Then why did you not leave when the sheriff arrived? he asked himself. *Why are you carrying her now, involving yourself?*

Reed tried to ignore the insidious voice, taunting him in his mind.

He did not like this turn of events. He'd had a plan. Helping a woman who turned his insides to mush was not part of it.

For the last year his life had revolved around one thing: clearing his name. How many women had he noticed in that time, in distress or not? None. He'd neither felt attraction nor paid much mind to what went on around him. The truth was, a week ago he'd have let someone else deal with this woman and her situation.

In the graying dusk, Reed's gaze traveled over the woman's features. Her eyes were open, wide and staring. Her arms were crossed protectively against her breasts, her fists tucked beneath her chin.

Stoic. Yet vulnerable. The fact that she was trying to be brave made her so damn fragile. She was like a scared child putting on a brave front. The need to protect, care and love exploded out of him. He cursed.

Her gaze latched onto his. One again Reed felt himself drawn to her—into her. He couldn't look away. Instinct warned him to stop, to hand her over to the sheriff and hightail it away from here as fast as he could. And in that moment Reed knew she could up and ruin everything.

"In here." Sheriff Tyler's hard, furious voice was like a lifeline to Reed. He entered the lawman's office, ready to hand over his burden. But it was not to be so simple.

"Stay with them, Reed. I'll be back," Sheriff Tyler said, edging out the door. He moved past the red-haired woman carrying the sobbing child. But before Reed could protest or even set down the woman in his arms, the door burst open. In strode a dark-haired man.

"Mattie! Are you all right?" The young man strode toward Reed.

Reed knew at once that the two were related. Both had unmistakable coloring and features proclaiming Indian blood, and they had other shared facial similarities, down to gentle dents in their chins.

"I'm fine, Matthew." The woman in Reed's arms shifted.

Reed carefully lowered her to her feet. He was

torn between the need to set her down as far from him as possible, and the desire to sweep her back into his arms and never let her go.

He should leave. He didn't. He kept a supporting arm beneath the young woman's elbow—and not because Tyler had ordered him to stay. Foolishly, even had the sheriff told him to leave, Reed would have refused.

He'd seen the splintered wood where the bullet struck, had noted that it was mere inches from the top of this woman's head. She'd been incredibly lucky. He'd been struck with fear and panic when he'd heard the shot and seen her fall. He'd thought for sure she'd been hit.

Killed.

Turning to the woman's brother, he narrowed his eyes. "Someone tried to kill your sister," he said, sucking in his breath against the despair the thought engendered.

"Who are you? How do you know we're related?" The man moved closer, looking every bit as dark and dangerous as Reed knew himself to be. The two men stared unflinchingly at one another.

"For heaven's sake, Matt!" The young red-haired woman stepped forward. "You and Mattie look like twins! Only a blind man wouldn't see that you were related." She wrinkled her nose. "Sorry, Mattie."

Beside him, Reed felt the woman called Mattie draw in a deep breath. "It's okay, Renny," she said. She turned to her brother. "I'm fine, Matthew." Her eyes roamed the room but obviously took in nothing. She bit her lower lip and hugged herself tightly. "Where are the others?"

"Don't worry, Mattie. They're here." Renny was staring at the doorway where two red-haired boys were watching.

Reed frowned as he felt Mattie's sigh of relief. She was facing the door, staring at the boys even as she asked for their whereabouts. One of the two slouching in the doorway was the same he'd spoken to earlier. The boy clutched his ball to his narrow chest like a shield. He tipped his chin up and moved forward.

"I seen you before," he said to Reed, his voice full of suspicion.

"Yeah. You nearly took my head off with that ball." Reed stared at each of the people crammed into the small, closet-sized office. Who were they? What were they to the frightened woman standing so close to him he could feel her warmth through the sleeve of his shirt?

"Perhaps you all should wait outside until Sheriff Tyler returns." He didn't want his charge feeling crowded.

The young boy with the ball ran forward. "You can't make me leave my sister!" He glared up at Reed then kicked him in the shins.

"Yeow!" Reed choked.

"Kealan," the redhead beside him scolded. "You apologize for kicking Mister—"

"Reed. Just Reed," he growled, glaring down at

the youngster, who had put muscle behind that kick.

"Reed, then. You mind your manners," she finished.

Surprised, Reed glanced at her. The woman's hands were now resting on her hips. She had color in her cheeks as she glared down at the child.

Beside Reed, Mattie sighed. "I apologize for my brother's lack of manners, Mister . . . Reed." She turned away from him. "I'm fine, everyone. I'm fine."

"Someone said you'd been shot at!" The older of the red-haired boys pushed into the cramped office. His hair was darker.

Reed found himself pinned by the child's gaze. Deliberately, the boy stared at the twin holsters dangling from his hips.

"I don't shoot women or children," he snapped. Damn, where was Tyler?

The redheaded woman stepped forward. "Don't mind them. We appreciate your help and concern. I'm Renny O'Brien, and this is Caitlin." She jerked her chin toward the girl in her arms. Then she motioned to the boys. "Those two are Daire and Kealan. And next to Mattie is Matthew. We're all brothers and sisters."

Reed inclined his head toward each of the O'Briens. "Any reason someone would take a shot at your sister here?" he asked after a moment.

Silence fell. Reed glanced around the room. The

two young boys exchanged frightened looks, Renny suddenly refused to look at him, and Matthew firmed his lips and stared blankly at the wall.

Even Mattie refused to look in Reed's direction. Only the little girl met his gaze. She blinked and rubbed her eyes. "Someone killed Lilly," she said, tears streaming down her cheeks. She buried her face against her sister's shoulder.

"Who is Lilly?" Reed asked. What was going on here? Why was he concerned? And, damn it, what was keeping the sheriff?

"Our cow," answered the boy with the ball.

His older brother—Daire, Reed remembered— smacked him hard in the arm. "Shut it," he warned.

Kealan yelped, then clamped his mouth shut and lowered his eyes.

Frustrated, Reed was about to address the woman standing beside him, but the door flew open again. A large man charged into the room. "Everyone all right?" he asked. His voice boomed through the room.

Reed looked him over, then locked eyes with the man. He had dark hair, almost brown, but there were glints of red in it.

"Your father?" he asked. Outside the door, he saw others waiting, but this office was crammed full.

"Papa O'Leary, we are all fine," the blind woman said. Her voice sounded weary.

Reed frowned as yet another person squeezed into the room. He recognized the young man as the one he'd seen walking with Mattie earlier—the groom-to-be.

The young man made no move to stand next to Mattie, though. He remained near the door—which was fine with Reed. He wasn't ready to hand Mattie over to anyone.

"Jesus Christ! Out, all of you!" Sheriff Tyler appeared just outside the doorway, other townsfolk pressing in behind him. He had his hands on either side of the door, effectively blocking it had anyone decided to listen to him.

But unsurprisingly, no one budged. "Don't think anyone's going to leave, Tyler," Reed called out. He was feeling rather closed in himself.

"We're family. We aren't leaving," Renny snapped, glaring at the sheriff.

A soft, quavering voice came from the doorway, and a white-haired woman peered from beneath the sheriff's arm. It was one of the Jensens, who ran the boardinghouse where Reed was staying. "Sister and I heard about the trouble. Might we invite you to use our parlor, Sheriff? Much more room."

Tyler ran a hand through his hair. "Good idea, Miss Martha."

She nodded and turned away. Reed heard her rather shrill voice add, "Sister, come along. We must fix the poor dear a cup of tea." Reed watched the sisters hurry past the window.

"Okay, let's go," Sheriff Tyler barked. "Out." He waited until everyone had filed from the room.

Reed ignored the cold, hollow feeling that came over him as Mattie moved out, her brother holding her arm. He realized he had no part in whatever discussions were to come, and he decided not to follow to the boardinghouse. This, whatever the problem was, had nothing to do with him. He had his own mission. His own goal. His own life to straighten out. He had no time to get involved in the troubles of others.

"You too, Reed."

"I'm not family, Sheriff. Don't want to intrude." Reed lifted an eyebrow. "Unless you think I had something to do with this."

Tyler jammed his hat down onto his head, hard. "If I thought you were behind this, you'd be locked up in that cell right now." He hooked his thumb over his shoulder. He sighed heavily. "But like it or not, Reed, you're involved."

Reed leaned against the wall. "Don't think so," he said. He was not involved. Not even the tiniest bit. His moment of playing the hero was over and done with. It was time for him to concentrate on his reasons for being in Pheasant Gully, and the haunting beauty of one arousing woman who needed protection had no place in his mind or heart.

Sheriff Tyler rubbed the back of his neck. "You remember the couple killed by the Grangers?"

A chill ran down Reed's spine. He straightened. "Seeing how I was nearly hanged for their murders, I'm not likely to forget." If not for the sheriff letting him go with an order to get the hell out of town, Reed would have been strung up by the angry crowd who blamed him for their deaths.

"They were the parents of these kids. Seems someone has a grudge against them."

"Are you still blaming me?" Fury rose in Reed, mostly at himself. One mistake, and four innocent people were dead. He might not have pulled any triggers, but it was his fault they had died nonetheless. And damn it all, wasn't that the reason he was here? To end it? To bring the killers to justice and clear his name once and for all?

For how much more could he be held responsible?

All of it, a voice whispered in his heart. *All of it.* Each death brought on by his enemy was another burden heaped over his shoulders. Each link in this chain of killing is his fault.

Images of the woman named Mattie swam before him—her dark beauty, the aura of sadness he'd noticed at the celebration. His mind and body had reached out for her, yearned to take her into his arms and hold her. Her scent, which he had absorbed as he held her, made him want to run after her and scoop her back into his arms where she belonged.

He growled with frustration. The woman was engaged. She wasn't his.

But her life was now in his hands. Swearing, he strode out after the sheriff.

Chapter Five

Renny paced behind a moss-green settee in the Jensens' boardinghouse. Mattie sat in its center, Caitie curled in her lap. Kealan and Daire flanked her. Kea sat back, his legs sticking straight out, arms crossed tightly in front of him. Daire sat forward, feet planted on the rug, hands gripping his knees. Both brothers wore grim expressions that matched Renny's own.

Little warriors, she thought, staring at them. Her baby brothers were growing up quickly. Watching Kea trying to be brave, the realization also infuriated her. He was entitled to the innocence of childhood, and in the last year, much of that had been stolen from him.

Mrs. O'Leary sat ramrod straight in a chair designed for looks, not comfort. With her head erect, her eyes staring unblinkingly and her nose in the air, displeasure screamed from every line in her face.

Sitting at her mother's feet with her legs tucked demurely to one side, Brenna still wore her dark cloak and gloves. The young woman always looked fragile, but the yellowish orange flames in the fireplace gave her pale features a sickly cast as she stared blankly into them.

Glancing at the door, Renny turned impatiently on her heel and strode over to the frilly-framed window. Where were the others? She glared out into the night. Someone was after her family. Her fists clenched, her lips tightened and the blood roared inside her head. She'd lost her parents. She refused to allow any harm to come to her brothers or sisters.

Spinning around, Renny decided to go find out what was keeping the men. If they were attempting to exclude her and the other women, she'd put them straight. The Troll—Sheriff Tyler—might think he knew what was best for them, probably thought he was protecting the "fragile" women and youngsters, but if he thought he could shield them from the fact that someone was out to get them, he was wrong.

Her pa had never shielded any of them. They were a family, and family meetings were a part of their daily lives. Decisions were made after everyone had their say, and if the sheriff thought he could butt in once more and change all that, he had another think coming.

She reached the doorway but stopped as the men

arrived. Turning, she went back to her place behind her sister. Gil slid to the side of the door. Paddy O'Leary stormed in, then hesitated as he stared at the remaining chairs. Each seemed too fragile to support his weight. He backed away, his hip nudging a small round table covered with delicate glass objects. A tall figurine teetered dangerously. Then he moved to join Renny behind the settee where there was more space to move.

The sheriff came in next and moved to the fireplace. The mantel, strewn with glass figurines, seemed to baffle him as he tried to find a place for his elbow; then he gave up.

The stranger, Reed, followed, stopping just inside the room and clasping his hands behind his back. Renny's brother Matthew stood beside him, his features a cold mask barely hiding his fury. Renny almost expected him to shed his white man's trappings for breechclout, bow and arrow.

Her own mouth firmed. She was with him in spirit. Whoever had taken a shot at Mattie would pay. Her brother might dress as any other townsman while living as a white man, but in his heart Matthew was all Sioux warrior.

Renny slid a quick look at the stranger. Standing next to her brother, Reed's similar Indian heritage was obvious. Only his startling blue eyes bespoke mixed parentage whereas Matthew's white blood from his grandmother remained hidden.

The packed room was silent except for the echo of

boots; Renny's and Patrick O'Leary's as they each paced behind the settee.

After several minutes during which no one spoke, Mattie demanded, "Well? What did you find?" The men had seen that Renny and the rest of the females and children were settled safely, then had left to return to the site of the shooting. Renny wanted to know what they'd learned.

"The shots came from the roof of Harry's place. Barrels were stacked behind his store, which made for easy access to the roof—hop up, then down. In the confusion, no one saw a thing." The sheriff shook his head in disgust. "Found a shell, but it won't tell us much. Harry sells them. Could have been anyone in Pheasant Gully."

His gaze swept the room. "And no, it didn't come from Reed's guns—if anyone was thinking that. It was a shotgun, and whoever did the shooting was a *damn* good shot."

Mrs. O'Leary stiffened at the sheriff's language, and he let out a long breath. "My apologies, ladies," he added.

Renny, long used to the woman's difficult nature, ignored her in order to sneer at Tyler. "Come on, Troll. The bastard *missed*." She wiggled the fingers of her right hand. Given the chance to get even, she wouldn't miss! Not with gun or arrow. She was an expert at both.

Tyler narrowed his eyes. "Wrong, *Renait*. Whoever took those shots had a perfect view. I think our shooter missed on purpose." The sheriff paused to study each of the O'Briens.

Renny hastily dropped her gaze. Lifting her eyes slightly, she saw Tyler pace in front of the fireplace. The silence in the room grew uncomfortable. Sheriff Troll, as she unfondly thought of him, reminded her of a large bear—a ridiculously large and clumsy bear, especially in this fussily cluttered room that looked as though it belonged in Victorian England.

"Well?" Impatience made Tyler's voice harsh.

"Not your concern, Sheriff," Renny said, finally breaking the silence. "We take care of our own."

"Wrong!" Tyler whipped around and strode over to her. "As the law around here, it *is* my business." He crossed his arms and stared down at her. "You weren't going to tell me, were you?"

"Tell you what?" Renny glanced at Mattie. It did not do any good to glare, as her sister wouldn't see it, but she did so anyway. "*You* told him!"

"Some," Mattie admitted. "But he has the right to know, Renny, and whether you'll admit it or not, we need help."

Renny backed away and leaned against the windowsill. "No one was hurt. There's nothing he or anyone else can do."

Oppressive silence filled the small room. Tyler went to Mattie and knelt down in front of her. "Mattie, earlier you said you were having problems with the livestock. You didn't mention any threat to anyone's life."

Mattie sighed. "There wasn't time to go into it, Tyler. That's why I asked you to come see us before we left in the morning."

"It's not his concern, Mattie," Renny broke in. She rushed to stand behind her sister, her hands on Mattie's shoulders. Her furious gaze clashed with Tyler's. "We don't need his kind of help. Not after the last time."

"Dammit, Renait! I am the *sheriff*."

"As if any of us can forget." Scorn laced her voice. "Sheriff Trowbrydge Tyler Thompkins Tilly, master and ruler of Pheasant Gully. Well, Sheriff *Troll*, we don't need your brand of help. I'm not giving you a second chance to try and split us up."

Inside, she seethed. Stunned with grief when their parents were murdered, the O'Briens had welcomed his gesture of help, his vow to find the killer. Unfortunately, his offer of help had included a plan to take away the three youngest O'Briens and farm them out to other families. Renny would never forgive him. Ever.

"*Renait*." Tyler's voice had gone soft and cold.

Mattie's hand rose to cover her sister's. "Renny, please."

Hearing Mattie's distress, Renny held her tongue.

From the open doorway, the stranger who'd assisted Mattie spoke up. "I don't know what is going on, but someone shot at your sister tonight. The sheriff is right. It was a clean shot—even considering that it was nearly dark. Whoever did it might not choose to miss next time."

Renny glared first at Tyler, then at Reed. "Fine. The sheriff can try to find whoever shot at Mattie, but he'd better not interfere with my family. Never again." She tipped her chin at Sheriff Tyler as he stood.

He moved as close to the couch as possible, leaning over Mattie and Caitie. "One of these days, Renny, you and I will have this out once and for all."

Renny leaned forward. "I have nothing to say to you. Now, or in the future." Beneath her breath she added, "Troll."

Reed noted the tiredness, worry and exhaustion on Mattie's face and stepped toward her. He deliberately tried to stay out of affairs that did not concern him, but he couldn't ignore the fragile-looking woman sitting beneath what looked to be a war in the making.

And something else about her drew him. He held out his hands. "Obviously there is no love lost between the two of you—can't blame you there," he couldn't help but add as he met Renny's startled gaze. "But despite his lack of tact, social skills and manners, I'd trust my life to Tyler. Owe him it, in fact."

Reed held Renny's gaze until she folded her arms across her chest and leaned a hip against the back of the settee. Then he glared at the sheriff, who stood with hands on his hips. Watching the two try to stare one another down, Reed swore there was enough heat in their eyes to ignite the room.

Interesting, especially as he knew so few people who could rile Tyler—or who were foolish enough to deliberately use the man's given and much hated name, let alone any unpleasant play on it. Fireworks were to come later, he was sure.

"It might help everyone concerned, whether they want to be involved or not, if we knew everything that was going on." He directed his voice to the dark-haired woman, who was chewing on her lower lip.

Once again he was drawn by her beauty. He willed her to look at him, to see him. But as she had all night, her gaze gave no sign of recognition or any other emotion. Right now her eyes were aimed at him, filled with fear and concern, yet they stared blankly through him.

Reed found the sensation unnerving. He turned away. The soft sound of her voice made him turn back.

"Renny, he's right. They're all right." She stared at him—through him—as she began her tale. He listened while she told everyone what had been happening up at their homestead, starting with the trouble with their chickens, the horses being let out, and just that morning, the poisoning of their cattle.

Agitated, Patrick ran his hands through his hair. "Mattie, child, surely after what happened tonight you can see that the best thing for you all would be to come stay with us until this is all sorted out."

Mattie shook her head. "There's no room."

Patrick went down on one knee before her. He took her hands in his. "Nonsense. We'll make room. We're family. You could have been killed tonight."

Silence fell heavily in the room.

Reed kept his gaze on Mattie, unnerved by her blank stare yet unable to glance away. "That wouldn't necessarily solve anything. It'd just put the rest of you in the same danger."

Tyler spoke up. "I have to agree. Sounds like you and your family have an enemy."

Just the thought of someone harming the beauty sitting surrounded by her family yet looking so lost and alone left Reed's knees weak.

Gil moved to stand in front of Mattie, breaking Reed out of his thoughts. "Who are you?" he accused. "What do you know?"

Reed avoided the sheriff's sharp gaze and stared out the window. Darkness had fallen completely, and the glass reflected the glow of the fire and lamps around the room. "Too much," he said quietly. And unfortunately, he did know too much. In his gut, he accepted that Sheriff Tyler was right in saying Reed's past was involved. The strange thing was, whoever had taken a shot at Mattie had missed on purpose. But who and why?

There was one answer that maybe made sense.

Someone wanted her off her land, and Reed could think of only one man who'd want it that badly: Malcolm Clemmings. But Why?

Malcolm Clemmings—the man who in cold blood had robbed Reed's father's bank and killed Reed's wife. He wouldn't let a bunch of youngsters stop him from getting what he wanted. Especially not recovering a hidden cache of money, if it happened to be buried there. Reed drew in a deep breath. He couldn't reveal all that he knew, not even to Tyler, but he had no choice but to do what he could to prevent more deaths.

Mrs. O'Leary stood. "This is not suitable talk for children or delicate young ladies. Brenna is getting quite upset. I am taking her to bed." She eyed Kealan and Caitie. The children didn't budge.

"They are part of the family. They stay," Matthew said.

Disapproval filled her features. "Very well." Her gloved hands were as tightly pressed together as her lips.

Reed didn't really think she was as upset as the rest of the O'Learys and O'Briens, but he did note that her daughter indeed looked pale and upset by the events. A linen handkerchief was threaded like a ribbon between her fingers, and she worried the scrap of fabric. At her mother's command, she stood and smoothed her skirt.

"You don't mind, do you, Mattie?" She asked in a hushed whisper.

"No, of course not, Brenna. Good night, Mother O'Leary," Mattie added.

Without a word, Mrs. O'Leary hustled her daughter from the room.

Reed found it curious that she hadn't spoken directly to Mattie all evening. She hadn't even asked if the girl who was her daughter-in-law was all right, or if she needed anything.

The sheriff glanced around the room, his gaze settling on the three youngest O'Brien siblings. "I don't like this, Mattie," he said.

Mattie leaned her head back and closed her eyes. "None of us is exactly happy about any of this, Sheriff Tyler. But until we know who is behind it all, there's not much we can do."

Her comment immediately started the arguments: Patrick insisting the O'Briens come to live with him, the O'Briens refusing, the sheriff wanting them to move to town. Only Gil and Reed remained silent.

Reed stared into the fire, trying to keep out of family business that had nothing to do with him. Though he was involved, what decisions the band of siblings made were theirs to make. Malcolm Clemmings. No doubt about it. The murdering bastard was here, in Pheasant Gully. And Reed would find him.

This was the break he needed. All he had to do now was wait for the man to show himself. Then Reed would turn him in, find and return the bank money, and restore his father's reputation—and his own honor.

Yes, things were definitely looking up. When Reed had ridden into Pheasant Gully earlier that day, he hadn't been sure that his information was correct. The trail that led here was sketchy at best. Now he was vindicated.

He glanced at the sheriff, who lifted a brow, conveying he also understood the significance. The bank robbery money was somewhere on O'Brien land. Reed gave a subtle shake of his head. He didn't want anything said. The family was upset enough.

Yet having them off the property seemed wisest and smartest. The lives of these people wouldn't mean a damn thing to Malcolm. Or to Leo Granger, if he showed. Reed was pretty sure that Leo was on his way. Especially as Reed had let it be known that Malcolm was hiding in the area.

Willing Mattie to look at him, Reed spoke. "You'd be smart to take your family and leave. If someone is after you, staying with friends or family in the area isn't going to help. Surely there is somewhere safe you can all go."

Seeing the sparks of denial ready to burst into flame all around him, Reed hastily added, "Only until we find out what is going on." He winced inwardly when he realized he'd said "we."

But hell, wasn't he already involved? Before he could analyze whether the woman sitting so silent and still across from him had anything to do with his willingness to get involved, all hell broke loose.

Mattie felt disconnected from the arguing and angry shouts that exploded around her the moment the stranger suggested they leave the area. Her siblings had closed ranks all around—Renny behind, her young brothers on either side and Caitie in her lap, clinging tightly.

Strong hands clenched her shoulders. They were Matthew's, who'd moved in his silent way to stand behind her. There was no way any of her family would leave. She sighed. Her siblings were each quick to anger and to speak—all but Matthew who, like her, tended to remain silent and watchful, preferring to wait until their hot-blooded siblings wound down.

The loudest shouts in the small parlor came from Renny and Tyler. Mattie leaned her head back and sighed. Sheriff Tyler meant well, but he just didn't understand. The house and land represented their father's dream, his desire for a new life for them all, a place where social standing and breeding mattered less than the honor inside a man.

Living in St. Louis, he'd hated the way his friends and neighbors treated his wife and his adopted children. That was why he'd moved them out West—closer to their own world. He'd embraced the idea of starting over, taking pride in building a home for his family and working the land to provide for them.

A soft voice broke through the loud protests. "Is a bit of pride worth more than your lives?"

All evening the voice of the stranger had drawn her, touching something deep inside. And she'd felt his eyes on her often, just as she did now. She couldn't see their color, hadn't had time to ask Renny to describe him, but she knew with certainty from her earlier visions that they were a brilliant blue—brighter than a clear, cold winter sky.

"You don't understand," she said, turning her head toward him. In the midst of chaos she felt him draw near. She inhaled. He was close. His voice when he spoke again came from in front of her. The creak of leather sounded as he knelt down, his knee brushing hers.

"Maybe not," Reed said gently. "But is it worth dying over?"

Mattie tightened her hold on Caitie. The lives of her siblings were more important, far more important, than pride. Yet the land was their life. It gave them food, shelter and, up until now, a semblance of security and safety.

"We have nowhere else to go," she murmured. Beside her, Kealan shifted. Mattie held up her hand, warning him not to interrupt. "Reed . . ." His name rolled off her tongue easily. "We can't be sure someone really shot at *me*. It could have been an accident."

"Do you really believe that?"

Mattie sighed. "After everything else that's been going on, no."

"It was no accidental shot," Reed said. "Though I don't think your enemy meant to kill you. Just to scare you. You, and the rest of your family."

"I agree," Renny said, leaning down over the couch. "After this morning, we can't allow ourselves to believe anything else." The room fell silent as the others stopped their arguing to listen.

"Then see reason, Renny," Sheriff Tyler snapped in frustration. "What happens when Matt leaves? A bunch of youngsters and a blind woman don't stand a chance." He paused. "Sorry, Mattie, but it has to be said. You can't work the farm or protect them."

"Blind?"

Mattie shifted her blank stare to the stranger kneeling at her feet. "You did not know?" She assumed everyone knew of her blindness.

"No," he whispered. "You don't . . . act blind . . . helpless."

"That's 'cause she ain't," Kealan shouted.

"Kea, enough. Mind your manners," Mattie scolded gently. "I don't need your pity, or anyone else's," she said to Reed. It wasn't hard to imagine the pity in his eyes. She heard it, felt it all around her whenever she went to town.

She tried to pretend that she was no different than anyone else, yet each time someone rushed to open a door, to move a piece of furniture out of her path or to speak loudly as though her hearing was also damaged, she was reminded that to most, she truly seemed weak and helpless.

And on those occasions when she tripped and fell, and in the horror-filled and awkward silence that followed, Mattie longed to give in to the need to yell, scream and rant against her dependence upon others. Imagining the stranger's reaction to be typical, she felt like crying right then and there.

But now wasn't the time to fall into a round of self-pity or recriminations for something she could not go back and undo. Before another round of angry shouts could begin, Mattie lifted her hand.

"Sheriff, you mean well, and we appreciate your concern." She ignored the rude sounds Renny made behind her. Then, Renny leaned down the back of the settee, her breath stirring the air near Mattie's ear. She wanted to talk privately.

Mattie reached up, found her sister's face and tipped her head back to whisper to her. "I think Tyler and Reed have a point, though. The danger to Caitie, Kealan and Daire is great. Our enemy proved to us this morning how easy it would be to poison not just the livestock but the children."

Renny pulled away. "We *aren't* sending them to strangers."

"Mattie, we aren't strangers," Paddy O'Leary said, a wealth of hurt in his voice.

"Paddy, until we know who the enemy is or what he wants, no one will be any safer there. Besides, what about Brenna, Gil and your wife?" Mattie shook her head.

"What do you have in mind, Mattie?" This came from Renny.

Mattie smiled. Her sister and friend knew her so well. "We send the children to our family—we take them to Wolf and Jessie for the summer."

Kealan and Daire were protesting, waking Caitie who added in her protests—though she didn't know what she was protesting. Behind her, Renny and Matthew sounded off in agreement.

Mattie glanced down. The strength of Reed's scent, and the hint of warmth where his knee nearly touched hers told her he hadn't moved. "My brother and I are Sioux," she explained. "Each year Matthew returns to our mother's people."

She almost said the words defiantly, as if trying to use her Indian blood to keep this strange man of her visions at a distance. Something about this man made her nervous. She didn't like the way his voice soothed and calmed, or the warmth she felt when he looked at her. She didn't need eyesight to know he watched her. Even his physical closeness drew her, tempting her to lean into him—to fall and let him catch her.

Daire jumped up from the settee. "I'm not leaving. I'm grown. I can handle a rifle just as good as Matt and Renny!"

Kealan, never one to be less than Daire, followed suit by stating that if Daire stayed, then he too would stay.

Tired, needing some quiet to step back and look at all that had happened, including the return of her nightmares and visions, Mattie suddenly felt too exhausted to argue.

Tyler's voice broke through the argument. "Better if you all went away for a while, Mattie." He paused, then continued in a frustrated tone. "Though I know that won't happen."

"No, it won't. But at least the children will be safe. Matthew and Renny will take them. Tomorrow." She wanted them all away, safely.

A voice from the doorway asked, "What about you, Mattie?"

"Brenna, what are you doing back down here?"

Brenna stepped back into the room. "Mama's asleep. I snuck back down. I think you should go too. Stay with your family. Someone tried to shoot you, not anyone else. If you stay away for the summer, whoever it is will surely give up."

Mattie shook her head. She'd never be able to stand being away. She needed the familiarity of the cabin, her independence. "No, I won't lead my enemies to our tribe." It was an excuse, lame though it was.

The events of the evening were catching up with her. Now that the shock of the attack was over, she needed action. She felt hemmed in, but in a strange room, she couldn't stand and pace to work off the restless energy coursing through her. All she wanted was to escape to the chamber they'd rented and to try to make sense of what was happening.

Renny moved around the settee and settled on its arm. "Us taking the younguns to Wolf and Jessie is a good idea. But you can't stay here alone." She reached out to touch her sister on the arm. "You'll have to come with me and Matthew. Then the three of us can return here to deal with the problems."

Knowing Renny was right didn't make the truth easier to swallow. Even if there wasn't the threat of their enemy, she couldn't stay in their cabin alone. But she also knew her sister well enough not to be fooled. She wouldn't put it past Renny and Matthew to leave her at Wolf's with the youngsters. After all, what could she do about it if they just left?

Tyler cleared his voice. "Reed is passing through. Perhaps he'll agree to stay at your place and watch over things while you're gone."

Mattie lifted her brow. Tyler's suggestion sounded reasonable on the surface, but she picked up on an underlying tension in his request. To her ears, it sounded more like he was giving Reed an order.

"This isn't his problem, Sheriff Tyler. It's ours. We can't ask a stranger to put himself at risk." She turned her head, seeking the stranger's presence. She'd felt him move away.

"You'll stay with us, Mattie," Patrick said, sounding determined. "Then Gil and I can see to your place."

Mattie kept her distaste at the suggestion from her features. Mrs. O'Leary would throw a fit, but she didn't see another choice. No matter how much she hated the idea of being under the same roof with her cold, biased mother-in-law, she'd do it in order to get her siblings out of harm's way.

Tyler offered her a second choice. "I can vouch for Reed, Mattie. He's a good shot. He's a bounty hunter. He can take care of himself and your property."

"A bounty hunter? Cool!" Daire exclaimed. "We could all stay."

Reed spoke up. "It'd be no problem, Mrs. O'Leary," he said. "As the sheriff said, I'm just passing through. If I can be of service, then it's my desire to help."

Frowning, Mattie wished with all her heart she could see him, but instinctively she knew that had she been able to see his face, his features would not give away what she'd picked up in his voice—an edge of steel that matched Sheriff Tyler's. Something was going on, something none of them knew about save the two men.

Why would Tyler ask a stranger to stay at their place? She trusted the sheriff with their lives—despite Renny's harbored resentment, she knew he'd only been looking after all their best interests a year ago when their parents were murdered—but why would he place so much trust and faith in a stranger riding through town? She made up her mind to learn what was going on.

In the meantime, she said, "If Reed agrees, then I will stay."

Protests rang out around the room. Mattie stood, letting Caitie slide down until the girl was standing in front of her. Her fingers slid through the young girl's soft curls.

"Reed, it is my desire to hire you to protect both myself and my land. Will you accept?"

A blaze of blue smacked into her mind—brilliant colored eyes that seemed to pulse with life as Reed's soft voice drowned out all protests.

"I accept."

"It's settled." She ignored the complaints, the comments that it wasn't proper from Gil and his father, the worry from her siblings, and even Brenna's concern about staying alone with a strange man.

"There is much to be done before Renny and Matthew leave in the morning. We need to return home tonight and pack." She started to move forward, toward the doorway, but the bursts of color behind her eyes darkened, beat against her mind with fury like a storm about to unleash itself.

The sensation of anger was strong. Mattie swayed slightly. After a year of no visions, the return of her gift hit with enough force to make her feel ill to her stomach.

Strong hands beneath her elbow steadied her. "It's been a long day. Let's get you and the others home." Reed's voice pulled her back from the black void of her vision. As he led her out of the room, she felt safe and protected once more.

And something else. But what that something was, she had no idea.

Standing outside in total darkness, Mac clenched his fists. All his careful plans were about to be destroyed. It had taken him nearly three years to plan that robbery and to get his new identity in place. He'd paid attention to details, found the perfect place to move, and now, the presence of this 'breed threatened everything.

Anger slid deeper into his heart. Harold E. Robertson, the 'breed's adoptive father, had killed his little girl, but the man had paid.

A life for a life.

A daughter for a daughter.

The money he'd taken couldn't bring Laura back. Nothing could. But it was his, payment for the void in his life. That, and the knowledge that Robertson would go through life filled with misery and grief as he'd done. Mac's nostrils flared.

Shutting out the pain, he concentrated on what to do next. It should have been so easy: Bury the money, lose the posse and return for the cash later, when it was safe to do so. But it had taken him longer to return to this area than he'd expected.

Mac kicked a rock in frustration. He'd chosen his site carefully—or at least as carefully as he could with a posse riding his tail. He'd memorized the landmarks and measured the distance from the river, but in the time he'd been gone, a prairie fire had scoured part of the earth, burning the trees and shrubs that had marked the place he'd buried the money.

Then, a few weeks ago, the river had flooded during a storm, taking away a good deal of the bank and changing the course of the river. For all he knew, the money was beneath.

No! It wasn't. It couldn't be. He just needed time to search the area, which meant the kids had to go. He feared another storm could easily take away more of the bank and make retrieving the money impossible.

And that wasn't the worst of it. The 'breed was now here to add to his trouble. He grinned. There was some good news. He'd come face-to-face with the 'breed and hadn't been recognized. He sneered. Of course, the 'breed hadn't known him, hadn't known what his adoptive father had done to him, so why would he recognize Mac—a man he'd never met except for that day at the bank.

Although, he admitted to being a bit worried. If the 'breed was here it was because he'd traced the name of Malcolm Clemmings to the area. Which meant Mac hadn't been as careful as he'd thought.

Mac gave the man credit for persistence. He even admired it. After all, he himself had waited years for his own retribution against Robertson.

A twinge of guilt ate at him. He'd felt true regret

for the 'breed's pain at losing his wife. But no one had cared that Mac had lost his daughter.

Fury lengthened his strides as Mac stormed down the middle of the road.

Damn. Things were going to hell in a handbasket. It should have been so easy, but his previous attempts to gain the land had all failed. Who'd have figured that a bunch of half-breeds would cling to their farm like parasites!

What to do? He couldn't risk searching during the day, and nights were impossible. He'd tried. But the glow from his lantern was far too great a risk, especially when Matthew was home; he often went riding at night. The boy had nearly caught Mac on his land once.

Mac sighed. He'd already killed Grady O'Brien and his wife, the parents of these kids. He didn't want to kill any more of them if they caught him digging on their land. But he had to do something. If the river again rose or changed course he might lose all chance of retrieving the stolen money. Or he might be found out by one of the kids.

He sure hadn't figured on nature taking such a turn against him. Whirling around, his mind went into action. He wasn't beat yet. If he couldn't drive them off the land, he'd force them into giving it to him. Fair or foul, it didn't matter. He would have his money and complete his revenge.

Chapter Six

Darkness ruled the night. It surrounded Mattie, existed within her. Eyes open or shut, it didn't matter; she was now as at home in the dark as she'd once thrived in the light. There was no light or color for her. Not even in her visions, for she hadn't had a single vision since becoming blind.

Until today. Or rather yesterday. She didn't need to see out the window in her bedroom to know dawn approached. It had been quite late when they'd all tumbled into their beds for a few much-needed hours of sleep.

Mattie rubbed her eyes. She needed sleep but each time she tried, the vision that seemed to be hovering somewhere at the edges of her mind crept closer, seeking audience. She refused.

"No. I can't do this. Not ever again," she whispered, tears streaming down her cheeks.

Once, she'd been proud of her gift. It had been second nature for her to see things. To know things. She'd never understood her mother's resentment and reluctance to embrace the same. Now she did. The pain of seeing death, then of being unable to do a thing about it still consumed her with anger and fear when even she let it. So she didn't think about it. Yet she hadn't had to think of her failures much, for the visions had faded into the darkness of her world like a severed arm.

Until tonight.

Now that part of her had returned to haunt and mock her.

At first, she'd been shocked. Then pleased. The blue of the stranger's—no, *Reed's*—eyes had soothed her, and his arms offered solace. She'd welcomed those bursts of warmth and color into her mind's eye.

But she was paying the price for those brief moments of pleasure, paid with the visions that were now creeping around her conscious mind. They weren't the stuff of daydreams; they were dark, filled with turbulent emotions, hate and anger.

Dropping her head onto her knees, Mattie wondered if she was going crazy. But she knew the truth. Her eyes remained blind but she could see what was happening. No! Squeezing her eyes tightly, she refused to believe.

As if to mock her feeble ability to refuse the will of the Great Spirit, a violent burst of light and color exploded across her mind. She cried out, muffled the sound with a fistful of bedding. Her stomach twisted and roiled, and she broke out in a sweat as she beat the vision back.

When it faded, she opened her eyes. Over and over she fought the demands of her gift. Finally, she slumped over her knees in exhaustion, resigned that she'd not be able to hold her Sight at bay any longer.

"Where is your control? Your courage?" she whispered to herself in the darkness.

Always she'd taken in stride what was to be. She'd prided herself on her ability to handle the difficulties her gift often brought, such as pain and death and fear, because good was also part of her gift; the ability to foresee the birth of a niece or nephew, a blossoming new love, the arrival of friends and loved ones.

"You want your independence, then take it!" she hissed to herself.

Mattie controlled her breathing—deep and slow. She listened to her heart, slowed its rhythm, and waited.

Her mind cleared, became a grayish slate waiting for the future to be written upon it. A tiny bit of dark color swirled inside—as if hesitant to show itself. Gasping, Mattie panicked, once again opening her eyes.

She couldn't do this. She couldn't invite the vision into her. Fear of what she'd see, what she'd learn, and the knowledge that she might not be able to change the outcome frightened her.

"No," she moaned. "I can't do it. Not again. Not ever again."

Her greatest fear was that she'd lose another loved one. Yet, in realizing that fear, Mattie found courage. She stretched out on the bed. The fear had given her strength, for there wasn't anything she wouldn't do for her family.

No matter the cost to her sanity.

Reed paced restlessly in the barn where he'd elected to bed down. He'd told Matthew that he hadn't wanted to intrude on the family. All the way home, one or another of the youngsters had been crying over their early-morning departure. Reed's excuse had sounded good. Reasonable. But he'd lied.

During that long ride from town, he had had to resist the urge to take young Caitie in his arms or pull Kealan, the shin kicker, onto his horse and hold them tightly while trying to comfort them.

And then there was Daire. The boy rode in the back of the wagon with his shoulders set stiffly, his head held high. No tears from him. But Reed saw his tightly clenched jaw, and he knew the boy was trying his best to set an example for the younger O'Briens.

Reed rested one hand on the frame of the barn door and stared out into the night. In a matter of a few minutes, all his carefully built barriers had crumbled, leaving him vulnerable.

He'd vowed the day Anne died that he'd do what-

ever it took to set things to right. That meant finding
the bastard who'd shot her, taking down the last of
the Grangers and clearing his name. Now Caitie's
tear-streaked face slid across his mind's eye, followed by another small girl's teary features.

"Lizzie," he whispered. He hadn't seen her in
more than a year. His baby girl would be close to
two years old. Danny, nearly four.

Twice since having his children taken from him
Reed had gone back to see them. The fighting with
his father—no, the man who'd adopted him then de-
nounced him—and the tears of his adoptive mother
were hard to take, but he would have withstood
them and more in order to see his children. But he
wasn't able to handle the wrenching tears, screams
and pleas that came from his children when he had
to leave.

During his last visit to see them, as he'd ridden
away with Danny screaming for him, Reed had
vowed that until he had his life in order he would
not go back. It wasn't fair to any of them. By the time
he saw her again, Lizzie wouldn't remember him.
The thought made him sad, and angry, but he had
only himself to blame.

He consoled himself with the thought that when
this was over, whatever it took he'd find a way to be
a part of his children's lives. It only helped a little to
know they were loved and cherished by their grandparents despite their mixed blood.

But not by their father, a voice whispered in his

mind. *Not by him.* Not now. He's not allowed to cherish them.

"We will be together," he vowed. "A family."

Until today, he'd never believed it possible. He'd been ready to settle for living close enough to visit sometimes. But that was no longer good enough.

Something had happened to him today. After a few short hours with the O'Brien youngsters, he knew he could never settle for less. For them. For him. *For Anne.* He would find a way to make them all a whole family once more.

Spinning around, Reed dropped down onto his bedroll and used his linked fingers for a pillow. The first step was taken: he'd learned the name of the man who'd murdered Anne.

A daughter for a daughter.

His adoptive father had told him of the man who'd come, begging for a loan to take his daughter east to seek medical care; had felt regret to this day that he had not loaned the man the money he'd needed. He'd certainly paid dearly for making a business decision.

Reed's lips twisted. Malcolm Clemmings. Hell of a lot of good it did him to know the name of the bastard, or even to know the reason behind the robbery and murder. What good was it without knowing what the man looked like? So he planned to draw him out. He'd get the man to reveal himself.

He smiled grimly. That was where Granger entered the picture. As soon as the outlaw arrived in

Pheasant Gully, he'd lead Reed to Malcolm. And to the gold. The only flaw in the plan was the O'Briens. They were innocently in the middle of this dangerous game. Neither Granger nor Malcolm would hesitate to kill any or all of them. And that was the last thing Reed wanted: more innocent blood.

Reed reached for his rifle to be sure it was close at hand, as were his revolvers. In just a few hours it would be light, and Renny, Matthew and the children would be on their way to safety. Then it would just be him and Mattie. That would be better.

But would it? Her haunting beauty made him groan. "Don't think about it," he warned himself. "You're here to protect her and nothing else." But her sad eyes and soft mouth made him want to scoop her into his arms and ride away with her into the sunset. Just to keep her safe.

He snorted at his nobility, then admitted to himself what a liar he was. Truthfully, he longed to carry her away from her fiancé and claim her as his own. Maybe he was no better than a savage.

His lips twisted. For the first time in his life he was tempted to give in to that side of his heritage. Except, he knew nothing about the Indian part of him. Not even his father's name or tribe. Where would he take a woman he wanted for his own?

Closing his eyes, he tried to put thoughts of Mattie from his mind. But as he drifted off to sleep, it was to sweet images of him doing exactly what he wanted—taking her away from her fiancé to claim her as his own.

The sound of shattering glass drained the pleasant drowsiness seeping through him. Leaping to his feet, he grabbed his weapons and ran toward the house.

Pulled from the frightening grip of her vision, Mattie sat frozen in bed, afraid to move. Something heavy had crashed through the window to land with a thud on the floor at the foot of her bed. Her cheek stung, hit by . . . a shard of glass? Lifting a shaking hand, she felt the wetness of blood.

To her horror, she gave an uncontrolled laugh. Between the gash on her head, the rawness left by the removal of several slivers and now this, she was going to look a sight.

Voices rose in the quiet house. "What happened?" Renny burst into her sleeping quarters.

"Careful," she called out, her voice shaking. "Glass."

"Matt! Candles. Quickly."

"Move. I've got shoes on," a strong voice ordered.

Mattie felt strong arms go around her, and she knew it was Reed who scooped her out of bed and carried her through the curtain wall. Glass crunched beneath his boots. Feeling safe and protected, she wrapped her arms around his neck.

"You seem to be carrying me around a lot," she whispered.

Normally she hated being coddled. She prided

herself on her independence, especially in her own home. But something told her she could get used to having this man's arms around her, could truly enjoy it. To her disappointment, she felt him bend over to set her down.

"Wait here. I'll go have a look," he answered.

"Found it," Renny called, following them out of the bedroom. "Someone threw a rock through the window."

Reed whipped around with Mattie still in his arms. "What's that tied to the rock!"

"Nothing," Renny snapped, her voice low and fierce.

Mattie pushed at Reed until he lowered her gently to her feet. She turned to face her sister.

"Renny, what is it?" She knew that tone; Renny was trying to hide something from her.

"Mattie, it doesn't matter."

She said nothing, just waited.

"Fine," Renny burst out in disgust. "It's a dead bird."

Mattie shivered and hugged herself. "What kind?" she found herself asking.

From behind her, Reed spoke. "Looks like a blackbird."

Mattie gasped. Stepping back, she tried to escape the omen she couldn't see.

"More death," she whispered in horror.

Renny swore again. "Mattie, that's what someone wants you to believe. It's just a dirty trick to scare us."

"It's working," Mattie said. She reached out her hand, searching for a chair. Having been carried into the kitchen, she wasn't quite sure of her position. She heard the scrape of wooden legs, then felt a strong hand close over her hand. Reed guided her to the chair.

"Sit," he ordered. He drew forth another chair, and the wood groaned as he sat. "Get rid of that," he ordered Renny softly.

Mattie heard the soft pad of her sister's bare feet across the floor, then the squeak of a door opening. "Matthew?"

"Here, Mattie. Renny is right."

"Matt, you know as well as I do that this warns of danger. It's an omen." Shaking, Mattie buried her head in her hands. On top of the visions, the dead bird could only mean the death of her loved ones. There was no escape.

"You don't truly believe that?" Reed's voice was filled with disbelief.

Matthew spoke up, his voice quiet. "You should know that our people take omens and spirits seriously. Whether it was done only with the intention to scare us, it's still an omen. A bad one."

He brushed past Mattie, his fingers trailing gently across her shoulders. He stopped behind her, his words aimed at Reed. "I find it curious that you were on hand when Mattie was shot at earlier, and now this."

Hearing the accusation in her brother's voice,

Mattie turned her head. "Reed isn't behind any of this, brother. I'd have felt the darkness in him. My visions have returned, and I see only the beauty of the sky surrounding him." She kept to herself the warmth and feelings of security that Reed gave her.

She turned toward him. "You cannot understand the significance of this warning, but I cannot ignore it. Not with the return of my Sight."

"You can see?" Reed sounded confused.

Mattie smiled sadly. "Not with my eyes. With my mind. The spirits bestowed the gift of Sight to me as a child. When I lost my eyesight, they took that gift away." Tears welled in her eyes. "But now it has returned. The visions come once more."

"Visions?" Reed's voice was full of doubt and skepticism. "I'm afraid I don't hold much belief in such things, Mrs. O'Leary. I believe what I see, and only what I see."

"What is your tribe?" Matthew asked, disapproval heavy in his voice.

"Tribe?" Mattie turned. "You're one of . . . us?"

Reed's chair scraped back from the table. "If by 'one of you,' you mean a 'breed, then yeah, I'm one of you."

"Then you know the importance of spirits."

"Sorry, ma'am. The man who sired me gave me his Indian looks but that's all. I know nothing about him or where he came from, and I don't believe in all this talk of spirits and omens. Only facts. And the fact is, someone is succeeding in scaring you. That's it."

Mattie reached out with her mind. She'd never been able to call a vision to her but to her surprise, she found she could reach out and touch this man. It happened with an ease that frightened her. His features remained hidden, all but the blue of his eyes. Yet even those seemed to blur—just a shimmer of color that wiped out all else.

It seemed odd. They were opposites. Her world was dark. His was light. She couldn't see with her eyes, only her mind. Perhaps his mind was blind, though he saw with his eyes.

She opened her eyes and faced him. She didn't need his sharply in drawn breath to confirm she was before him. She felt him, found his presence by following the trail of color in her head.

"You *will* see," she said, as a darkness she hadn't sensed deep inside him seeped out. In her mind's eye she saw him struggle to free himself, but the more he fought, the farther from the light he strayed.

"You walk a lone path of darkness. You fight what is inside you. Open your eyes and see. Accept what you are, who you are, and you will be whole."

•Chapter Seven

Owl shook out his wings, then folded them back. Already the sun was burning through the gloom. Soon, it would be clear and bright. It would be dawn. He twisted his head, searching the heavens. *Mahpiya!*

A small sliver of light speared through the gray. *Why do you call upon me, Owl?*

Owl tipped his head, showing the spirit of the heavens his respect. *The humans leave soon.*

A whisper of wind ruffled Owl's feathers, and *Tate*, spirit of the wind, joined them. *He knows,* Tate said.

What help does he give? Owl asked boldly of both spirits. He blinked sleepily. It was time for him to find his tree and rest.

In answer, Tate whipped the leaves of the tree, while the spirit of the heavens called forth clouds and blocked the light of Sun.

Owl had to be content. He wished he could do more for the humans but his place was here, with the woman. For the truth lay in her dreams.

Kneeling in the center of a prayer circle, Mattie lifted her head. The scent of sage and sweet grass surrounded her—her offerings to the spirits. She felt helpless; a prayer at that moment seemed so little, but it was all she could do.

A breeze caressed her cheek. Something soft tickled her nose. Reaching up, her fingers closed over a soft, downy feather. She glanced up. "You *are* there," she whispered. A soft hoot confirmed that the owl had returned.

She wasn't sure whether to be reassured or not, for his presence meant more dreams. And dreams had recently meant pain, uncertainty and fear. Still . . .

Bowing her head, Mattie clutched the bit of fluff to her heart. "I will listen, and learn what it is you are trying to teach me, *Hinhan.*"

Tucking the feather into a tiny leather pouch hanging from her neck, she got to her feet and left her prayer circle. Without stumbling, she made her way to the back of the house. Stopping near the steps, she drew a deep breath of cold air into her lungs. Normally she loved mornings; the freshness and newness, the gift of life each day represented.

But not today. Uncertainty dulled her joy. Were the O'Briens doing the right thing in separating? Mattie closed her eyes.

Pretend the children are just going for a short visit, she told herself. They'll be back. The sheriff would soon find the enemy, deal with him, then once again it would all be safe. And they'd be together. Still, uncertainty ate at her.

A brisk wind tugged at her hair and sent it flying about her head—a reprimand from the spirit of the wind? Mattie sighed. She could not help the fear she felt. Or the resentment. If only she had the use of her eyes.

Combined with her visions, she'd surely learn the truth much faster if she weren't blind. And she'd be more able to protect her loved ones by recognizing where danger lay. Using one hand, she gathered the long silky strands of her hair and took a half-dozen steps forward.

The jangle of harnesses and restless pawing of hooves guided her to where her brother and sister were preparing for their journey. With one hand slightly lifted, she took several more steps, guided now by the soft snuffling of one of the horses.

Her heightened senses picked up the softer sounds of the animals, the strong smell of horse and even the heat of the beasts. Seconds before a nose was thrust into her outstretched hand, she felt the current of a warm exhalation.

Mattie ran a fingertip over a small crescent-shaped scar on the nose. *"Sunghinhota winyela kin,"* she said. *Old Gray Mare.* "Renny," she called out. "Why are you taking Sun? She is old. Slow. Take Raven. She is fast." They had four horses total. If Renny and Matt took Raven and the two strong grays, they'd make better time.

Renny brushed against Mattie as she walked around the horses. "Raven stays with you. Our uncle trained her for you, and she responds to you better than the others."

"But Sun will slow you," Mattie protested. "Sorry, Sun," she said. But it was true. Sun had once been a fast animal, but age had slowed her greatly. Hearing a grunt, she turned, following her sister.

"You may need Raven," Renny argued. "We'll leave Sun and the other two horses with Wolf and Jessie when we get there. Wolf will have horses that we can use to return."

After a moment, she huffed out a breath and added, "Mattie, come with us. I don't like leaving you here alone."

Mattie sighed. She'd lost track of how many arguments with her siblings she'd had since leaving the Jensens' last night. "I won't be alone, Ren. Reed will be here, and Paddy is only a short distance away."

"Mattie, Reed is a stranger!"

Just thinking about Reed gave her visions of blue clouds and warm light. It was strange, but she *wanted* to be alone with him. "He's no stranger," she said. "I'll be safe." And she believed that. Somehow, they were connected. And she couldn't fight her visions.

Renny grunted. "People are going to talk. It's not proper for you to be here, alone with him."

"I'm a widow!" Mattie laughed.

Renny scoffed. "You and Collin didn't share the marriage bed."

Mattie felt a twinge of pain. She'd loved Collin, had looked forward to becoming his wife. "I'm still a widow. And people will talk no matter what."

"What about Gil?" Renny put her hands on Mattie's shoulders, gently moving her out of the way.

Mattie didn't say anything. She was remembering the picnic; the tenseness of Gil's shoulders pressed close to her, the strain in his voice as he'd greeted Josiah and Francine. Before she could say anything, Kealan and Daire ran up, followed by Matthew and Caitie.

The next few minutes were torture for all of them, as the children were hoisted up onto horseback and all the good-byes were said. Everyone was ready, but Renny still stood in front of Mattie. She clasped her sister in a tight hug.

"We'll hurry back, Mattie."

"Renny . . ." Mattie frowned and rubbed her temple. What could she say? How could she explain what she'd sensed more than seen in her nighttime visions? She felt uneasy, frightened, scared. And not just for herself but for the others. But this was what had to happen. Pulling back, she tipped her chin up bravely.

But . . . there was something in the air. She couldn't see or touch or define it, but it was there. Unfortunately, she didn't know whom to warn. Herself? Most likely, for all the attacks seemed directed at her. But what if she were reading the signs wrong? What if it was one of the others in danger? She opened her mouth to tell Renny of her unease . . . then changed her mind.

Renny would insist Mattie go with them if Mattie let on that danger was closing in. Mattie needed the reassurance that her three young siblings were away from any danger. Especially if it was directed at her.

"Mattie, what is it?"

Ever since losing their parents, Renny had taken on the responsibility of taking care of their family— including her—whether she wanted it or not. And thank the spirits for her sister's tenacious spirit and determination. It had kept their family together. Once more, Renny was doing what had to be done. So must Mattie. She shook her head. "Nothing. Just be careful."

A long silence fell between the two women. They were sisters who shared not blood, but a friendship that went much deeper. Mattie turned away. "Be careful."

A hand gently grasped her elbow and turned her. Mattie felt Renny's searching gaze, though she could not see it. Her sister said, "Mattie, I hate leaving you. Come with us. I promise that you will return with Matt and me." She paused. "I promise not to leave you behind. Please don't stay here alone."

Mattie lifted a hand to her sister's face. To her

shock, she felt tears trickling down Renny's cheeks. Her own eyes watered and spilled. "I have to stay. You'll go faster without me." And the threat would also stay behind with her.

Her fingers slid down to rest against Renny's lips as the woman's mouth opened in protest. "Don't ask me to endanger the children," she said. Inside, she felt torn. The last thing she wanted was for Renny, who seldom gave in to tears, to worry. Her sister carried enough weight on her shoulders.

"That's as good as saying that you *do* think someone is trying to kill you." Renny's voice was fierce.

"No. I think someone is trying to scare me. And they are succeeding. Now go." She dropped her hands to her side and hurried back to the porch.

Facing her family, steeling herself against Kealan's nearly silent sobs and Caitie's hiccuping sorrow, Mattie prayed for their safety. Unable to handle any more tearful good-byes, she turned and made her way back into the house. Alone, she sank into a chair at the table and dropped her head onto her folded arms, letting her own tears of helplessness wash down onto the scarred wooden table.

Without warning, a black wave rose from deep inside her and clawed at her mind. She gasped, feeling physically ill. Hate beat at her. Fury lunged at her, held her prisoner. In a flash, like a tornado dropping down from the sky, it worsened. Swaying, dizzy in its malevolent grasp, Mattie gripped the table and fought the nightmarish hold. Everything around her was black. Not just dark and colorless, but heavy, thick, oppressive. She felt terrified.

The storm in her mind thinned, rose from the ground to reveal the image of riders on horseback. It was her family—riding away from their home, unaware of the danger at their backs.

Each breath came fast, furious and painful. As the psychic storm rose back to the clouds from whence it had come, relief set in. The vision, Mattie thought with relief, was over.

But like *Iktomi*, the spider spirit of her people's lore, playing one of his cruel jokes, the whirling black funnel cloud came back out of nowhere and with a suddenness that stopped her heart, produced a vision of her brothers and sisters scattered dead across the ground like dry, crumbling leaves in the fall.

"No!" Mattie jumped up, sending her chair crashing across the floor. She shouted, screamed against the vision, cursed her sightless eyes. But when the storm of hatred in her vision again grew faint, she willed it back, clung to it, tried to force it to reveal more.

Who wanted to hurt them? Who hated them? She had to know.

Show me. Show me.

"Mattie!" Strong arms caught and shook her.

"No! It's going! Got to get it back. Let me go!" She shouted. She almost had the answer. Fighting Reed, she searched her mind. But the vision fled.

Grabbing Reed by the shirtfront, she sobbed. "Stop them," she cried. "Stop them. Go after them. Bring them back. Danger. They are in danger." Her voice broke as horror overcame her.

"What have I done? I should have told Renny. Danger. Should have told her more." Then Mattie's knees gave out. This was her fault. She'd told Renny and Matt to take the youngsters away.

Too late, she realized that sticking together they were stronger.

"Damn!" Reed had gone to the house right after Renny and Matthew left. He'd hoped to talk to Mattie, for he knew nothing about the needs of a blind woman and wanted to find out what was expected of him. At the door he'd seen and heard her tears of grief, and like a coward, he'd wanted to flee. Tears from a woman could bring any man, no matter how tough, to his knees. Bad enough that he was already in above his head.

His straight-and-narrow path of vengeance and justice had taken so many twists, he felt dizzy and disoriented. Not once during the last year had he strayed from his set course. Now, in the space of a day—

No, in the space of a single *heartbeat* everything had changed. Emotion had replaced cold calculations, and the tears and suffering of one woman promised to be his undoing.

Holding the struggling woman, Reed scanned the kitchen but saw nothing amiss.

"Renny! You have to stop them. Get them back. We have to stay together!" Mattie's voice came in short gasps. Her knees gave out. Reed swept her into his arms.

Relief shimmered through him as he sat and cradled the woman. Nothing had happened. She'd just panicked. "It's all right, Mrs. O'Leary. Nothing will happen to you while I'm here." And it wouldn't, he vowed, staring down into her wild, unseeing gaze.

She struggled to her feet and held out her arms to keep him from pulling her back down. "You don't understand. Danger. They are in *danger*. We have to stick together! We have to go after them. Stop them." She turned, found the table with her fingers and followed it.

Reed shook his head, then realized she couldn't see his response. "No. The young ones will be safer away from here." He jumped up as she stumbled over her tumbled chair. But before he could help her up, she'd regained her feet and was out the door.

Swearing, Reed crashed through the door behind her, amazed to find Mattie already down the steps and running down the path to the barn.

"Damn it, woman," he muttered, taking off after her. Catching up, Reed wasn't sure whether he should reach out and grab her or try to talk sense.

He decided to do both. "Hold on, Mrs. O'Leary."

126

He reached out and grabbed her arm. To his surprise, she whirled on him, a spitting, fighting she-cat.

"Go get them. Bring them back!" Her voice was fierce, commanding.

Reed ran a hand through his hair, his gaze searching her. But there wasn't anyone or anything to help him deal with this distraught woman. Damn Tyler for doing this to him!

"I can't. There's no way in hell I am leaving you alone."

Mattie spun around, stopped, her head lifted as though to the sun. Relieved that she seemed to have calmed, Reed folded his arms and waited.

And watched, which wasn't hard to do. Mattie—Mrs. O'Leary—was incredibly beautiful. Her full skirt billowed in the wind and long silky strands of hair whipped around her face. Standing close to her as Reed did, those soft strands brushed against his cheeks, luring him closer.

Lifting a hand, he let her hair brush against his fingers, drawing him to her. He closed his eyes, needing that incredible feeling of being connected to her. The sky above them darkened, the wind shoving and pushing, but all Reed could see was the woman he'd promised to protect. She lifted her hands, palms faced outward, and turned in a slow circle. Head back, eyes closed, hair flowing freely around her, she became one with the elements.

Born and raised in a city, Reed was fascinated by the transformation. He'd never seen anything so beautiful or compelling. Mattie looked every bit the savage his kind were accused of being. Her lips moved silently. His heart sped up. Caught up in the sight of her, he could do nothing but watch.

When she at last stopped, her eyes flew open. She seemed to be looking right at him. "You have much to learn," she whispered.

Then she broke the spell by putting two fingers in her mouth. Her shrill whistle tore through the air.

Startled, Reed glanced around. Massaging the back of his neck, he groaned. Surely she didn't think to call her family back with a whistle? Did she not realize that, at the pace they'd rode out of here, they were long gone?

The thundering of horse's hooves had him whirling around. A huge black horse came charging toward him. He dove aside, rolling off the path onto a damp patch of grass.

"What the hell are you doing?" he shouted, jumping to his feet when he saw her jump onto the back of the animal.

She stared down at him, almost as if she could see, her hands tangled in the horse's long black mane.

"If you won't help me, I'll find someone who will," she shouted.

Reed lifted a brow and crossed his arms across his

chest. "And how are you going to do that? You are *blind*," he retorted. He hated to be cruel, but if she thought she could forget the fact, she'd soon learn otherwise.

Relaxing, feeling a little more in control, Reed couldn't help but add, "Don't tell me. You can find your way around by using your visions."

Her chin came up a notch. "Do not mock that which you do not understand."

Feeling like a heel for being so mean, Reed stepped toward her horse. "Look, you're not going anywhere. You know it, I know it, so let's just go back into the house so you can fill me in on what needs to be done around here."

A wave of desperation crossed her features, darkening her earth-brown eyes to nearly black. Her lips trembled then firmed as she closed her eyes and appeared to be gathering strength from an inner well. When she opened her eyes and un-erringly seemed to latch onto his own gaze, he felt the impact of that determination and strength. Blind she might be, helpless in this situation even, but the woman towering over him was not a weak woman.

Great, just what he needed on top of his other worries—a stubborn ward!

But a very appealing and desirable one. Used to seeing proper city women, Reed found himself irresistably drawn to this woman of the earth and spirits. Silence stretched between them. Reed felt a bit uncomfortable with her eyes fixed so intently on him.

"Your eyes are blue. A brilliant blue—that of a sapphire surrounded by diamond." Mattie smiled grimly at him, as though she could see his stunned expression.

Reed gawked up at her. Anne had always loved his eyes. She'd called them her jewels. She'd never wanted the sapphires he could have bought her, said she already had two of the best.

He folded his arms across his chest. "Nice try. Anyone could have told you the color of my eyes. That doesn't mean you can see—"

"No one told me the color of your eyes, Reed. Scoff at my words. At my beliefs. But you'll learn. My visions are truth. Not everything that is can be seen with the human eye." She paused, her eyes going blank for an instant. Then she asked, "Would you like me to tell you what I see?"

"What I'd like is for you to get down and stop this nonsense." Reed reached out, but her horse shied away. Afraid Mattie might fall, he stopped.

The woman closed her eyes. "I see a brooch. It's old. Two plumes. Feathery blues and greens." She lifted her hands to form a cup. "Surrounding a posy of flowers—violets. Pinks. In the center . . . no, top . . . a tiny bird with a long, narrow beak and a green stone for his eye."

She opened her eyes. "That is why you are here. To find it. And the peace you seek."

Stunned, Reed stared at her. "How—"

"You *will* believe."

Then she whirled her horse and shouted, "Go! To Paddy's place."

Chapter Eight

Reed ran for the barn where he'd left his horse. Damn the stubborn, hell-bent woman! Was she trying to kill herself? Reed threw open the stall door, jumped on his gelding's back and swung the horse around and out of the stall. He didn't bother with a saddle—there was no time, if he was going to keep Mrs. Mathilda O'Leary from breaking her beautiful neck!

He eyed a coil of rope on the ground, thought about scooping it up. The way his luck was running with what should have been an easy assignment— keeping one blind woman safe—he might need it to tie her up and bring her back.

Riding around the back of the house, Reed followed the narrow worn path that he'd spotted earlier that day. He now realized it led to Mattie's in-laws, and to the home of her future husband.

He scowled. Maybe he should just leave her there and let them deal with her. They would keep her safe. That would give him free rein to find Malcolm and Granger. Reed had no doubt the man who'd been the leader of the gang would arrive in the area any day. He'd made it impossible for the gang leader to resist coming.

But right now he had this woman to deal with. This beautiful, wild, tempting woman.

Churning the earth as he urged his horse to go faster, Reed also determined to get some answers. How had she known about the brooch that belonged to Anne? It had been torn from the collar of her dress by Malcolm Clemmings, right before he'd shot her in cold blood.

Mattie heard Reed closing in on her. She didn't slow, just let Raven have her head as she galloped down the worn path toward Paddy's homestead. Tears stung her eyes. She hadn't expected Reed to understand; how could he? But all the same, it hurt that he didn't even try.

But Paddy knew her. He'd believe her and go after Renny, Matthew and the others. He'd bring them back safely. She sniffled and admitted that it was time to put aside her own personal feelings and accept the help that Patrick offered. Renny and the others would protest, but all that mattered at the moment was keeping them safe. And to do that she'd

NAME: _____

ADDRESS: _____

_____

_____

TELEPHONE: _____

E-MAIL: _____

_____ I want to pay by credit card.

__ Visa   __ MasterCard   __ Discover

Account Number: _____

Expiration date: _____

SIGNATURE: _____

*Send this form, along with $2.00 shipping
and handling for your FREE books, to:*

Historical Romance Book Club
20 Academy Street
Norwalk, CT 06850-4032

*Or fax (must include credit card
information!) to:* 610.995.9274.
*You can also sign up on the Web
at* www.dorchesterpub.com.

Offer open to residents of the U.S. and
Canada only. Canadian residents, please
call 1.800.481.9191 for pricing information.

If under 18, a parent or guardian must sign. Terms, prices and conditions
subject to change. Subscription subject to acceptance. Dorchester
Publishing reserves the right to reject any order or cancel any subscription.

put up with her mother-in-law's sullen silences and sniffs of haughty disapproval.

"Hold up," Reed called out, riding up alongside her.

Mattie veered her animal slightly so Reed couldn't grab the horse's mane.

"Damn it, woman! You're going to break your neck!"

Tired of his assuming that because she was blind she was helpless, Mattie whirled her horse around. The sound of his furious curses as he had to pull up short to avoid crashing into her made her smile grimly. She heard the snort of his horse, felt the shadow of the animal as it reared. She didn't move. When all movement stilled but for the harsh exhalations coming from Reed, she lifted a brow.

"Seems you're more at risk for that than I am, and you have your eyesight. Sometimes it doesn't do to rely on only one sense." Turning, she nudged her horse on, and continued on her course though at a slower pace.

"You're a load of trouble," Reed grunted as he once again caught up with her. "How do you expect me to keep you safe if you go riding off on your own?"

"I can take care of myself," she shot back. The fact that it wasn't really true only made her angrier. She hated not being totally independent. But as long as she had her legs, her arms, her sense of smell and her sharpened intuition, she would do as much for herself and those she loved as was possible.

And that meant bringing her family back and keeping them together and safe. Mattie closed her eyes to keep from crying. Once more her life was undergoing rapid change. So much had happened in just a day that it left her feeling sick. Her family was in danger; she herself was engaged to a man in love with another woman, and now she feared that she could lose her own heart to this stranger with incredible eyes and an empty heart.

Empty? Yes. The piece of jewelry she'd described to Reed had come from the woman who held his heart. That shouldn't hurt, but it did.

"Right. I should just leave you right now." Reed's voice was a challenge, pulling Mattie back to the struggle between them: his desire to control her, her need to get her family back together.

She pressed her lips tightly together. She hated the fact that she couldn't manage on her own, but faced with a disagreeable man who didn't believe in the gifts of their heritage or a mother-in-law who hated everything about her Indian birthright, Mattie was willing to pick the lesser of two unpleasantries.

She slowed her horse to a walk. "So, you do not believe in visions. Have you no tribe?"

Reed snorted. "I told you. I know nothing of my father or his family. Or of his life."

"Yet you have made no effort to learn about your

heritage. Have you not sought to be adopted into a tribe of your choosing?"

Reed was silent. "Why should I have done that? If the whites don't accept me, why should Indians?"

"Because we don't see blood. We see what is inside a man. Honor is more important than the color of their skin."

Reed snorted. "Right."

Mattie tipped her head to one side. "You've been hurt."

"It doesn't matter," Reed said shortly. "The past is past."

"Yet you are here because of the past." Mattie stopped her horse and waited.

"What makes you think that, Mrs. O'Leary?" He sounded bored. Or tried to.

Mattie smiled. "Did you know you call me by my married name only when you seek to put distance between us?"

"That does not answer my question, Mrs—Mattie."

Stroking Raven's neck, Mattie softly clucked. She heard Reed's horse follow hers. "I may not have the use of my eyes, but my hearing is sharp. I listen—not just to words, but how the words are said." Tones, inflections. She thought of the schoolmarm and Mr. Potts, of other things she'd discerned. "Often what is *not* said is the true message behind words."

Reed remained silent. Mattie sighed. "It was clear

that Sheriff Tyler trusted you from the beginning. He left me with you. He ordered you to stay and brought you to the Jensens'."

"That doesn't mean anything," Reed said.

Mattie heard the scowl in his voice. "It says it all. Tyler is very protective of all of us. Someone shot at me. You're a stranger in town. Why would he not suspect you?"

"He's a damn fool," Reed bit out.

Mattie laughed. "Sheriff Tyler is many things, but—"

"Yeah, I know. He's no fool." Reed's tone indicated he begrudgingly agreed.

"Then you do know each other. You're not just passing through." The air was turning moist. A single drop of moisture landed on her cheek, and she shivered. She lifted her head to the wind. In the distance she heard cattle. They were nearly to Paddy's.

"We've met," Reed muttered.

Nodding in satisfaction, Mattie relaxed her hold on Raven. "You have a reason for being here, Reed. One that is somehow connected to us. I've heard—"

"That's a lot of hearing you've been doing, Mrs—"

Mattie gave a soft laugh. "You'd be surprised at what I know. People assume that because you can't see, you also can't hear. How wrong they are."

"I'll remember that," Reed grunted. He fell silent.

"You do not ask how I know I'm right." Mattie didn't wait for his reply. "Actually, with that; it's not so much what I heard but what I've seen."

Reed gave a snort of disbelief. "Nice try, Mattie. But I only believe what *I* see. Or what it's possible to see."

Reed's attitude didn't upset Mattie. He would believe eventually. Everyone did.

"You showed up the same day my visions returned." She turned her head toward him, called to her mind's eye the blue of his irises. She lost herself in them. "Never before have I been able to call a vision to me. Yet, with you, I can do so with ease. I see the blue of your eyes and feel your warmth."

"How about we don't talk about this nonsense," Reed suggested. "In fact, let's just turn around and get back to the house before the storm hits."

Mattie felt the difference in the ground: pasture had given way to the hard-packed earth of the O'Learys' yard as the path between the two properties ended.

They were to the left of the barn. Below her, Mattie heard the squawk of a chicken. She stopped. "We are already caught up in its eye," she whispered.

"Darkness surrounds you as well," she continued after a moment. "I feel the gathering of hate. Tell me, Reed. Is it within you, or does it follow you?" As soon as she put into words what she'd felt, she knew she was right.

The darkness of hate, the warmth and beauty of Reed—the visions were connected. She'd thought she was seeing only blue when she called her visions of Reed to her, but the darkness that she'd assumed was her normal sight was actually another force surrounding Reed.

Good and bad. Beauty and hideousness. Love and hate. Where there was one emotion, the other was not far away. A thread of unease slid through her. If only she had use of her eyesight. But she didn't, so she would have to use whatever resources she had available—including Reed—and that meant learning why he was here.

"So . . ." He broke into her thoughts. "Can you see me?"

"You're changing the subject."

"Maybe. Maybe I'm curious about what you know." Reed reached out and smoothed back a strand of hair caught in the corner of her mouth. She felt him move closer. "You said you saw me. Felt warmth. What does that mean?" Mattie heard the doubt mingling with curiosity in his voice.

She turned her head, calling his image to her. A ribbon of blue swirled before her eyes. She knew right where he was. Not only did she see the blue of his irises, but she felt the warmth of his presence.

"Safe," she said. "I felt safe when I first saw you. Protected." She left out the most important emotion.
Loved.

She'd felt warm, safe and loved during that first brief vision of him, that vision when she'd felt his arms around her.

Hearing a door from the O'Leary house slam,

Mattie nudged her horse forward. If Reed didn't believe her, then that was his problem.

Mathilda O'Leary. She unnerved him, downright scared the pants off him, and intrigued the hell out of him. And when fired with the wild passion of her beliefs, she drew him as no other woman ever had.

Reed dismounted and went to help Mattie down, but Gil had come out of the barn and was already helping her. A surge of jealousy ripped through Reed. He joined them, deliberately standing close to Mattie, invading the man's space.

"What are you doing here, Mattie? Is something wrong?" Gil asked. His eyes narrowed on Reed. "Something wrong?"

Mattie reached out. Gil took her hand. "Gil, where is your father? I need to see him. Right away. Renny and the others left, but I need them back here. My visions warn of danger. If you and your father leave right away, you should be able to catch up with them by nightfall."

Hearing the distress in Mattie's voice made Reed want to pull her into the safety of his arms.

Safety?

He suddenly felt ill. He hadn't been able to protect Anne, couldn't stop his in-laws from taking his children from him, so how could this woman who knew nothing about him feel safe around him? And why was he trying to protect her? Damn Tyler! Of all men, he knew Reed and Reed's past. What would Mattie say when she learned that he was responsible for the deaths of her parents? She couldn't already know.

Her rejection, the horror that would surely appear in her beautiful eyes nearly brought him to his knees. But her quietly stated confidence made him determined to right those wrongs. No one else would die from his stupidity. He'd give his life to protect her and hers. And when the time came, he'd accept her hate as part of his punishment.

"I can't get him," Gil replied. "Pa went out. Said he was going to see Mr. Brown about a new bull."

"Guess that's that, Mattie. Let's go." Reed turned and saw the girl named Brenna standing behind him.

She stepped forward, into their group. "Momma's fit to be tied, Gil. People are going to talk." She walked around her brother, Reed and Mattie as if strolling casually through a garden.

Gil glared at his sister. "Shut it, Bre. This is none of no one's business but our own."

Brenna shrugged and clasped her hands behind her back. She sent Reed a sly look beneath her lashes. "Renny and Matthew are going to be gone how long? A week, maybe two?"

Gil stared over her shoulder. "I trust Mattie," he muttered.

Reed narrowed his gaze. Last night, Brenna had been so quiet, seemed a mouse among the hot-tempered lions. Now he saw that assumption was wrong. "What do you suggest, Miss O'Leary? Your sister-in-law cannot stay with your family. It'd put you *all* in danger."

Gil shoved his hands deep into his pockets. "I'm good with a rifle," he argued.

"Not as good as I am," Brenna said, smiling broadly. She rubbed her nose against Raven's.

Mattie jumped in, "Yes, you always were the best shot of us all. Used to make your brothers mad." She laughed.

"Still do." Brenna looked sad. "Although Collin hated it even more than Gilly."

Seeing the redness creeping into Gil's face, Reed stepped in. "This is getting us nowhere. What do you want to do now, Mrs. O'Leary?" He deliberately used Mattie's married name. There was no sense in aggravating either Brenna or Gil.

"You can stay here if you want," Gil offered.

Reed narrowed his eyes. He was not going to let Mattie out of his sight. "If she stays, I stay."

Mattie shook her head. "No," she said. "I won't put you, your mother or Brenna in danger," she decided at last.

To Reed's relief, she turned back to her horse. Before Gil could offer, he had his hands around her waist and had lifted her onto her horse.

"They'll be okay, Mattie," Gil said. He sounded too cheerful.

Nodding her head, Mattie swung her horse

around and let her mount follow Reed. As soon as they were out of the yard, he dropped back. "Glad you've come to your senses," he said.

Mattie kicked Raven into a gallop. "They will be fine—because we're going after them."

Here he went again! Why he was surprised, he didn't know. Had he really expected Mattie to meekly accept the fact that she was going to just have to wait for her brother and sister to return as planned?

Yes, he thought as he urged his horse faster. He'd actually figured that Mattie would finally act sensibly. Yet here she was, riding like the hounds of hell were at her heels.

The damn woman was blind—why didn't she act like it!?

A lone oak rose up in her path. He sucked in a breath. "Tree in front of you," he shouted. No sooner had the words left his mouth than her horse veered. Instead of being relieved, Reed was furious.

He rode up alongside her. "Slow down," he ordered. "You're not going anywhere." His voice was firm, his decision final. He'd taken on the responsibility of protecting this woman, and he would. Even if it was from herself!

As he'd commanded, Mattie halted her horse— but without warning.

Reed cursed the air blue as his horse nearly plowed into hers. He leaned forward, dug his fingers into the mane of his steed and fought to keep his seat. But the horse, unnerved by the tide of high emotion, refused to calm. The chestnut gelding pawed the air, then twisted, throwing Reed.

Reed expected to hit the ground flat on his back. Instead, he landed against something incredibly soft. And moving.

Stunned and confused, he struggled. "Hold still," Mattie's soft voice ordered.

Astonished, he realized he'd landed on Mattie's horse. Right across her lap! She'd reacted quickly, wrapping her arms around him to keep him from tumbling off.

The soft croon of foreign words washed over him. He didn't understand the softly spoken phrases, but whatever she was saying seemed to be calming her horse. He remained still, not wanting to risk having her mount panic and send them both flying.

Glancing around, Reed saw his horse bolting for home. Or at least what was his temporary home. "See if he gets any oats tonight," he grumbled.

"It's not his fault," Mattie chided. She expertly brought her animal to a halt.

"No, it's *yours*," Reed blurted. He tried to sit up straight. How was he supposed to take this woman to task when he was all but cuddled in her arms? Her soft, gentle, yet strong arms. When her horse shifted nervously, he stilled.

A soft laugh came from above his head. He felt her breath, breathed in her sweet scent. "Which of us has eyes that see?" she mocked.

145

"That was a damn foolish stunt. We both could have been hurt," he snapped. He wasn't sure he liked their positions. *She* was supposed to be in *his* arms. Though, he had to admit he liked the feel of her arms around him.

Fool, a small voice in his head taunted. You don't just like this. You're in heaven. Shut up and enjoy it.

He did. He felt the softness of her breasts, saw every inch of her face as she stared down at him: the tiny mole on the side of her neck, the strong line of her jaw, the soft curve of her face, the gentle slant of her nose, the rich, smooth fullness of her lips.

His heart nearly stopped as he stared at her mouth—a mouth just made for kissing. His mouth went dry and he lifted his gaze to her eyes. In a million years he'd never have believed her blind, for the intensity of her eyes boring into his surely saw all the emotions not only on his face but those hidden deep inside him.

"Mattie—"

"Shush, Reed," she ordered softly. "I want to see you. Please?"

Reed swallowed hard. What was he supposed to say to that? "Uh, Mattie, I wish you could, but I'm no miracle worker. You're the one with the visions."

Visions? Yeah, right. But he really did want Mattie to be able to see him.

"You are handsome?"

That made him feel awkward. "Well . . . never heard no one complain about looking at me."

"Your hair?"

"Black." His eyes closed on a sigh as he felt her fingers comb through his hair.

"Curly. Soft." She bent forward. "And clean. Fresh."

Reed rolled his eyes. "I do bathe. Daily even." Damn, he was out of his element! What was a man to do or say when a woman talked this way?

Humor edged Mattie's voice. "You'd be surprised how many do not even keep their hair clean." Her fingers trailed down the side of his face to his shoulders. "I know you're tall. I saw you—in that first vision. And you're strong. I feel your strength." Her hands were sliding across his shoulders.

Reed felt as though his entire body had turned to butter. At this rate he'd slide off the horse into a puddle on the ground. "Think we'd better get back to the house. It's too open here. We're sitting ducks."

He had only a knife tucked into his boot. He tried to move, to jump off and lead her horse home, but that made him nearly snort with laughter. The woman didn't need leading. He was just now realizing just how capable she was.

"Wait." Her hands gripped his shoulder. "I need to see . . ." Her hands lifted slowly and traveled up the column of his neck, cupped his jaw in her palms, her fingers lightly resting behind his ears.

He covered her hands with his own. "Mattie." Her name was torn from him. It'd been a long time since he'd reacted to the touch of a woman. Not since

Anne. He hadn't even been able to bring himself to pay for pleasure since her murder. His abstinence was just one more way he punished himself.

Yet in Mattie's arms, he felt rising from his prison deep inside him the shadow of the man he'd once been. He fought the return of that part of him. He had a job to do. A past to atone for. A murderer to catch.

"Please?" Mattie sounded hesitant. Vulnerable.

He stared into her face. Her full mouth was slightly parted, her dark lashes sweeping the softness of her cheeks. The wind billowed through her long hair, curtaining him and her in their own private world.

He reached up and ran his fingers through that black silk. "How can you see me?" His voice turned to a hoarse croak as she touched his face.

"Like *this*." Her fingers traveled up his jaw, feeling every inch of him. Her touch was soft as a feather, and incredibly sensuous. He fought a shudder of desire as she traced his mouth with her fingertips. His lips came apart on a sigh.

"Mattie," he whispered.

"Shhh," she responded. Her finger trailed down the straight line of his nose, over his cheeks and forehead. He watched her lashes flutter closed, her head fall back and her brow crease in concentration.

Reed couldn't resist. Taking his hands, he lifted them to her jaw and cupped her chin. Her eyes flew open. "I want to touch you, too," he said. "To learn the feel of you." He held her gaze—rather, she held his as his fingers slid up and over her smooth hon-eyed skin.

"To see you as you see me," he continued.

Reed had never experienced anything so erotic in his life. His blood stirred, his body hummed with need. But it wasn't just sexual release he sought. He needed the gentle touch, the sweet smile, the soft dreamy glow—all that was Mattie at her best.

Her finger slid over his eyelids. "Then close your eyes. And see."

Reed did as ordered. He closed his eyes and for-got about everything but the feel of her beneath his fingers.

He started at her jaw. His fingers felt rough and clumsy, but her fingers kept him from opening his eyes. Reaching her ears, he smiled as he traced their curves, felt the soft lobes. In his entire life, he couldn't remember touching a woman's ears with the same desire and need—to see with his other senses.

His thumbs trailed down over her cheeks, his fin-gers moving into her hair, then traveling over her head to feather across her brow, then her eyes. "Your lashes are long. Soft," he murmured.

Her fingers stroked his closed eyelids. "As are yours," she whispered.

He learned the slope of her nose, the satiny-feel of her face, then his thumbs caressed her mouth. "Sweet," he said.

Her lips parted in response. He cupped her chin, his thumbs playing over her mouth, touching and smoothing as if he couldn't get enough of her.

"Mattie, I think I *have* to touch you."

"You are," she said, her voice breathless.

"Not with my fingers. With my mouth." Then he opened his eyes, reached up to cup the back of her head with his hands, and drew her close.

Chapter Nine

The wind roared through the meadow as Reed wrapped one hand behind Mattie's neck and pulled her down until her lips hovered just above his. The storm brewing around them was nothing compared to his need for a kiss. Never could he recall needing anything as much as he needed Mattie.

The stroking of her fingers, the feel of her fingertips sliding across his face—lingering, exploring and *seeing* him as no one ever had before—set him on fire. He inhaled deeply, filling his lungs with her sweet scent as the moisture of her breath fanned his mouth.

Draped across the horse in front of her, he felt her trembling anticipation. Even his own body seemed to freeze; the moment before their lips touched seemed to last a lifetime.

Reed resisted to urge to pull her down, to slant his

mouth across hers and take and taste her furiously. Waiting was torture, but it was sweet—sweeter than honey, more exciting than anything he'd ever felt.

And then her lips brushed his.

Reed groaned, parting his lips and capturing hers. Both he and Mattie froze, became one, the breath of one becoming air for the other.

Mattie sighed. Reed drank the exhalation.

"I think I like this touching," she whispered. Her lips moved against his, two of her fingers sliding down the lines edging his mouth.

Thrusting his fingers through her hair, Reed wrapped the long strands around his palms. "Let's touch more," he whispered. Then he opened his mouth and covered hers again. Like a starving man, he learned the shape, the feel and the taste of her mouth. He nibbled, tracing the smooth curve of her full lower lip, the path of her upper.

Each soft, breathy sigh drew him closer, deeper into her. He was drowning in her sweetness, in the darkness that fired the light that had dimmed deep inside him. The feel of her fingers brushing over his face drove him wild, yet the very gentleness of that touch, the shy, hesitant manner, told him she was taking her time and he kept himself in control.

Normally, kisses didn't stay sweet and pleasant for long. Kisses were the gate to other pleasures, deeper needs to be met, but Reed found himself content with this slow exploration. Mattie lifted her head slightly. He stared at the wonder in her face, the drowsy drooping of her eyes and the moistness of her lips.

Protectiveness, need, contentment. He felt all these things. And Reed felt as though he could have stayed cradled against her forever. Shaken by the range of emotions coursing through him, he tried to draw back and sit up.

Yet what did he think he was about? "Mattie—"

"You are beautiful," she whispered in awe.

Reed groaned, and he reached up to take her exploring fingers into his hand. "We have to stop."

"Not yet." This time she used his own hand to cup his face, her palm over its back, her fingers stretched out atop his. Reed's head fell back, his chest constricted, his pulse pounding.

He groaned. "You're going to kill me."

Mattie chuckled. Wrapped in the heat and warmth radiating from the man in her lap, she forgot about everything but the color and wonder Reed had brought back into her life. She lowered her head.

"Soft," she murmured. "I never thought a man's mouth would be so soft."

She touched the tip of her tongue to each corner of his mouth, then let her lips merge with his. She aped his earlier movements: tracing his lower lip, feeling the rough edge where pink flesh gave way to the start of stubble. Her upper lip felt the roughness of his skin, while her tongue found only smoothness.

Mattie pulled away. She liked very much what she'd "seen" and felt and tasted of Reed.

"Not yet," he whispered, taking back control as his mouth slanted over hers. "We can't stop yet." At his gentle urging, her lips parted and Mattie sank into the most incredible sensation—floating in a sea of pleasure.

But then all gentleness fled. Reed kissed Mattie without reserve. He nipped, licked, stroked and suckled. When the tip of his tongue slid into the corner of her mouth, she parted her lips, having an idea what he intended. And it wasn't gentle.

She'd seen her parents kiss—they'd been in love and not a bit ashamed of showing that love. But Mattie had had no idea how wonderful a rough kiss could be. She felt weak yet strong. She could do anything, be anything.

Deeply she drew Reed in, tasted him, felt the roughness of his tongue, its slick underside as she used her own to taste, feel and learn this very intimate part of the man that she somehow knew would be her future. Time stood still—until a sudden clap of thunder above their heads startled them apart.

Reed shot up. Caught off guard, Mattie fell back. Raven shied violently, both from the thunder as well as the sudden movement on her back.

Mattie shrieked as the horse jerked forward. She reached out, her fingers latching onto the front of Reed's shirt, but it was too late. The horse did a quick sidestep, and they both tumbled off.

* * *

Reed hit the ground, wrapping his arms around Mattie and rolling, trying to bear the brunt of the fall. Unsure of where the horse was, he covered her body with his in protection.

A glance over his shoulder made him sigh with relief. Her horse had not reared out of control as his had, but had just startled and shied. She was looking at him as if in wonderment at what he was doing on the ground.

Turning his attention to Mattie, to be sure she was unhurt, he stared down into her startled face. "Your horse did not flee as mine did," he said.

Mattie's hand slid from his shoulders to his chest. "Raven is trained to stay with me. She will not leave unless I give the command for her to do so."

Reed pushed up onto his hands. "The storm is about to hit. Let's get back."

But he stared down into Mattie's face. Her eyes were dark—twin pools with a shining like moonlight dancing deep in their depths, and her hair was a black cloud spread out beneath her. A storm of her making raged inside him. He lowered his head, unable to resist. This time his body melted into her softness, her breasts pillowing his chest, her hips a welcome cradle for a part of him that he'd long thought dead and lifeless.

Mattie.

He'd been dead until the touch of this woman who saw so much she scared him.

She fascinated him.

Their kiss deepened. All else was forgotten. Danger, visions, the past—nothing existed but this. Him. Her. *Them.*

A sudden drenching cold shocked him. Above his head, the clouds had burst open. Rain pelted his back; he felt a faint tremble beneath him and assumed Mattie was cold lying on the ground. In seconds, they'd both be soaked. A rumble spread across the heavens, followed by a bright flash of light.

Reed jumped up and pulled Mattie to her feet. To his surprise, she was laughing. She stumbled into his arms.

"I think I like kissing you," she gasped. Her palm cupped his cheek.

"I like kissing you, too, but we've got to get out of the storm." Staring down into her face dripping with rain, wreathed in mirth, he felt something tumble deep inside of him.

"What are you doing to me?" he whispered. With a shaking hand, he scraped her hair back from her face.

She sobered, reached up and drew his head down to her. "Giving you life," she said, and kissed him. Once. Briefly. Too briefly.

Reed closed his eyes. The impact of that kiss meant more to him than the longest, deepest, most intimate of kisses. Or perhaps it was the words she'd whispered that loosened something precious he'd thought lost to him—hope.

A soft whistle cut through his thoughts. Reed jumped out of the way as Raven nosed him aside, trying to reach her mistress.

Mattie swung up onto the back of the horse.

"We must hurry," she said. "If we leave right away, we may catch up with my family by tomorrow morning."

Reed's mouth dropped. "I thought we settled this. We are *not* going anywhere."

Mattie tipped her chin up and stared off into the distance. "You still don't believe me about what I saw?"

"It's not a matter of whether I believe or not. I was hired to do a job."

Her eyes flashed. "Was kissing me part of it?"

"Dammit, Mattie, kissing you had nothing to do with the job."

"Then believe me; take me to find my siblings before it's too late."

Reed approached her horse. "Look, let's talk about this tomorrow," he said, sure she'd see reason after she had time to think clearly.

As though she could not only see but could cow him with her furious glare, Mattie sat taller. Her hair billowed around her, the wind pulling at her skirts and her face gleaming with rain. She looked part of the elements, not a victim of this spring storm.

"You have learned nothing," she said, her voice low and tight. "You speak words meant to deceive me, but I hear the truth. You do not trust me."

Her horse shifted. Reed wiped the rain from his face. "If it's trust you want, then *you* have to trust *me*."

"How can I trust a man who is blind?" she asked bitterly. Whirling her horse she shouted, "Home, Raven."

Reed ran after her. "Mattie! Come back here!" he shouted. She didn't listen.

He slid in the mud and landed on his backside. Standing, coated with grime, he stalked back toward the O'Brien homestead, his mood as dark, dangerous and savage as people always assumed him to be.

Brenna lay flat in the grass, a pleased grin on her face that the wetness of the storm couldn't diminish. A scolding, even a punishment from her mother for soiling her dress so badly, was worth what she'd just seen. She'd followed Mattie and Reed, watching from the brush along the river a short distance from the meadow separating the families' two parcels of land. She'd been hoping to learn something incriminating, as Mattie could not be allowed to marry her brother. It was too dangerous. For all of them. She'd been hoping to see something she could use to make Gil jealous and angry enough to call off the wedding. Her pa wanted the marriage between the two families. Wanted it as badly as Brenna couldn't allow it.

And she had learned something. When she'd seen Mattie and the bounty hunter stop, she'd moved in and watched. She'd been worried at first, for Mattie and Reed were arguing. Then she'd seen him fall. Then they'd kissed. For a long time.

Her gaze grew dreamy as she thought of the one man she herself longed to have kiss her. But he wouldn't. The man didn't even know she wanted him like that. It was her secret.

It had to be a secret. The risk of him learning, of anyone learning, what she knew was too great. Besides, Matthew never saw her—not truly. And that was by design. People didn't see her because she didn't want them to.

It was better. Safer. For she had secrets—knew some terrible things that ate at her soul. She was better off alone, and now Gil and Mattie would be apart too.

Chapter Ten

The morning storm gave way to blue skies and a bright yellow sun the shade of corn silk. Anticipation hummed through the land as the air warmed.

Deer nipped at the tender, wet grass, their young frolicking in the meadow; and rabbits stood on their hind feet, ears twitching as they washed the last of the storm from their fur. In the pasture, a mother horse and foal raced along the fence, heads and tails arched high.

Even the birds rejoiced in the warm afternoon, rewarding all who took the time to listen to their birdsong. But there was one who didn't appreciate the beauty of the day.

Reed didn't see the emerging creatures or heard the songs floating on the gentle breeze. He didn't feel the peace of spring. Inside him a storm still raged. Grabbing another log, he set it on a stump, lifted his axe and brought it down with all the built-up frustration and anger coursing through him. His bare torso gleamed with the sweat of labor, and his eyes burned with fury. Hefting the axe over his shoulder he glared at the house. At *her*. The log split cleanly in two as he brought the axe down.

The pile of firewood to his right grew. His muscles bulged, tiring, but he kept going. If he stopped, Reed feared he'd stomp up those damn steps and kick the damn door down.

She'd locked him out. He'd knocked on the door, but she'd refused to answer.

He'd pounded, he'd shouted. Silence was her reply.

Splitting another log, he tossed the pieces to the side. One went too far and landed in the water trough. Burying the blade of the axe in the stump, he walked over to the rippling water and fished the firewood out.

He'd refilled the trough after returning, carrying bucket after bucket of water from the river up to the yard. Then he'd filled the water barrels, which had for some reason been covered during the storm. Two hours had passed. He'd tried to talk to Mattie again. Same results. If he wouldn't take her and go after her brothers and sisters, she had nothing to say to him.

Women! Damn them.

Kneeling, Reed plunged his head into the cold water of one barrel. Standing, he shook his hair, sending droplets of water in all directions. The rivulets running down his chest and back cooled the heat of the sun on his flesh, but they did nothing to ease the torment of Mattie's words.

"How can I trust a man who is blind?"

Blind? Hell. He knew manipulation when he saw it. At least she hadn't used tears. His insides shifted. Anne had used tears very effectively. Reed had never been able to handle her tears—not when she'd been a young girl, his adoptive sister, and not later when she'd become his wife.

It had been her tears that had made him run off and marry her when her father, his adoptive father, refused to allow it. Her tears had kept him working for the man. In fact, for all the years he'd known Anne, her tears had brought him to his knees.

Except at the end. No matter how much she'd cried, he'd refused to swallow his pride and make things right between him and his father. Not even for her would he beg forgiveness.

Then it had been too late. His tears had mingled with hers when she'd died in his arms. Taking the axe back up, he grabbed another log. The sound of metal slamming into wood echoed around him but couldn't drown out the turbulence inside him. He couldn't even drive it from his body.

Another hour passed. He stopped to glare at the closed-up house. "Damn, stubborn woman," he shouted.

He waited. Nothing. Not even the flicker of a curtain at the window.

He wiped at a bead of sweat running down the side of his face. "Fool," he muttered.

Not like she's going to be peeking out to see who's shouting. He was the only one here and she was doing a pretty good job at pretending otherwise. And that was pissing him off.

Picking up an armful of split wood, he carried it to the woodpile and stacked it. One trip became two. Then three. Loading up the fourth load, he dropped the wood when he saw the approach of a rider. Wiping the sweat from his face, he waited.

Recognizing the sheriff, Reed didn't relax. Instead he stalked down to meet the man. "What do you want, Tyler?" he asked. Here was the source of all his frustration.

Sheriff Tyler must have noticed Reed's dark mood. He stopped but didn't dismount. His gaze swept the yard. "Where's Mattie?"

"In the damn house." Hands on hips, Reed glared up at the lawman. "What's the matter, don't trust me?"

Lifting a brow, Tyler stared down at him. "If I didn't trust you—though you've given me little reason—you wouldn't be here now."

Reed narrowed his gaze. "Why?"

Tyler dismounted. "Not sure why you're in a fight-picking mood, Reed."

"Answer the question. Why the trust?"

The sheriff started leading his horse up the drive to the O'Briens' tidy yard. "You could have disappeared a year ago and walked away from this damn mess. You didn't. You went after the Grangers. Got three."

"Four," Reed corrected.

"Counting the one killed here. The point is, you didn't walk away once I let you go. You've put your own life on the line to avenge my brother's death, and gone after those responsible."

"Revenge, Sheriff," he barked. "That's not so noble."

Tyler led his horse to the trough. "Yet you returned. Got involved." He speared Reed with a considering look. "And you played quite the hero last night."

The words dropped like a stone in Reed's gut. "Hero, hell. You and I both know I'm probably responsible for the crap that's been directed against these kids."

Tyler nodded. "Yep. But you're here. Doin', not waitin'."

Reed wanted arguments. Hell, he wanted a good round of pounding fists. He gathered up the load of wood he'd dropped. "Don't make me out to be a saint. I'm here because of guilt—and my own need for revenge." He stalked back over to the woodpile.

When he returned for another load, Tyler stepped in his path. "Did some checking by wire. Know you've returned more than half the stolen money. Even refused the bounties you were owed. Seems to me that speaks of more than guilt and revenge."

"Yeah? What does it say of me, Sheriff?"

"Says you're a man of honor."

Reed dropped the wood. Honor wasn't even in his grasp. Yet. Once, the need to regain what he'd so foolishly lost had been his sole reason for surviving. Now he knew even that wouldn't be enough.

"Honor won't bring Anne back. Or your brother." Reed jerked his head toward the house. "It won't bring back their parents either. But I'll sure as hell die trying to stop anyone else from being killed."

He thought of Mattie and his refusal to let her do what she wanted. The plan to take the youngsters to her other family was good. She'd see that, and when Renny and Matthew returned, he'd go into town and see if Leo had arrived. Leo, who would lead him to Malcolm.

"Where's Mattie?"

Reed scowled. "In the house."

Tyler narrowed his eyes. "She okay?"

"How the hell should I know? The woman won't let me in!" His frustration flew out of him.

"What'd you do to her?"

Looking up at Tyler, Reed sneered, "Where's all that trust you were talking about?"

"Reed . . ." The sheriff's voice was a low growl.

"She's in a pisser of a mood. What do you know about these visions and things?" He gave Tyler a brief rundown of the events of the morning—omitting the kiss, of course. Hell, he hadn't allowed himself to think of that kiss, and he refused now to do so. It had been a mistake. A very distracting mistake that none of them could afford.

"You know, now that you mention it, seems I heard Mattie talking about knowing her parents were going to die."

At Reed's look of disbelief, Tyler shrugged. "She was pretty torn up with grief after their murder." He sent Reed a sharp glance.

It was like a punch to the gut. Though Tyler didn't say it, Reed knew the sheriff was also grieving the death of his brother. And it was all his fault.

"So . . . you believe that nonsense? Her knowing ahead of time? Visions and stuff?"

The sheriff shook his head. "Hell, that's more in line with your own heritage. Why are you asking me?"

"Because she believes her brothers and sisters are in danger now," Reed ground out. "She rode out of here on her own because she believes it." He kicked a hunk of wood into the air. "And she won't come out or let me in until I believe it and agree to take her and go after them."

Tyler spun on his heel. "We'll see about that. She'll let *me* in. I'll make her see sense."

Reed watched Tyler run up the stairs and knock on the door.

No answer. Tyler tried to open the door. Still locked.

Grimly satisfied, Reed spread his feet and crossed his arms across his chest, listening as Tyler bellowed like a thwarted two-year-old. He chuckled, thinking his own son Danny had lungs that could raise the roof!

Annoyed, Reed cursed and ordered himself to think only of today. Not yesterday. Not the past. Not even the future. He scowled as the front door opened. For a few minutes, Mattie and Tyler talked. Reed strode closer, saw the sheriff shaking his head, heard the tears in Mattie's voice.

Then he saw her bow her head, step back and shut the door. Not slam it. She just closed it and them off from her. Part of Reed felt vindicated. Had Tyler gained entrance, he would have been furious. Hurt, even though he was essentially a stranger.

But the shadow of their kiss blurred his thoughts. *No two people could be strangers after sharing such an incredibly tender moment as in the meadow,* a voice whispered in his head.

"Mister Sweet-Talker himself, aren't you," he said when Tyler tromped back down the stairs.

"Shut up, Reed." The sheriff sounded frustrated. "I happen to agree with you. She's better off here where you can protect her."

"And if she's right about her family?"

"You think there's a chance about all that nonsense?"

Reed shook his head. "I only believe in what I see, Sheriff. But she obviously believes that she's having visions or whatever. Maybe—"

Sheriff Tyler grabbed the reins to his horse. "Keep

an eye on her. If she won't let you in come dark, you go in. I don't want her alone. I'll be back tomorrow afternoon."

Reed watched the sheriff ride out of the yard. Great. He'd hoped that Mattie would be over her sulking come nightfall. But Tyler's interference had probably just made her mad all over again.

Picking up another load of firewood, Reed stalked back across the yard to the woodpile. "Women!" He shouted the word loud enough to be heard inside by Mattie.

"Fools! Cain't do nothin' right!" Leo Granger kicked his cousin Jasper. "You were supposed to lay low and watch, not open yer trap."

Jasper yelped and hopped on one foot. "Ow! What ya kickin' me fer?"

"Yeah, wha'd we do?" Jasper's brother, Bart, jumped hastily out of Leo's way.

"Ya screwed up," Leo said. Fury rode him. There was a time when he'd given an order and it was followed. Those days had been taken from him, one brother at a time.

"But Leo, the old geezer said it was easy money. Like takin' candy from a baby." Jasper and Bart snickered.

"It wasn't what I ordered the pair of you fools to do," Leo spat. God, he hated his cousins. Stupid idiots, both of them. But with all his brothers dead, he didn't have much choice. Family was family. He eyed them. And they were expendable after he got what he wanted.

Jasper edged around him. "Don't see the harm in it," he sulked.

"Ain't payin' either of ya to think." Leo whipped around, ignoring both the pain in his leg and the protests coming from his cousins, and stared out at the horizon. It held a spreading sheen of gold.

He was here for one thing: the money he'd stolen from the bank. Leo looked around him. Nothing seemed familiar. But then again, the last time he'd ridden through here, he hadn't been checking out the scenery; he'd been evading a posse.

He spat on the ground. It should have been simple. Rob the bank, run, hide out for a while, then live high. He shoved his hands deep into his pockets and stalked off to stare into the growing dusk. The 'breed would pay. With his life. When he'd first learned that Reed was after them, he'd laughed at the thought of the drunk city boy taking on him and his brothers.

But he'd underestimated Reed. The man had proved to be a cold, formidable enemy, and a deadly shot, but he still didn't know how to keep his mouth shut. That would be his downfall. It was Reed's own loose tongue that had brought Leo back here, and maybe to the man who'd cheated them all out of their share of the loot in the first place.

The number of men in the posse had made them split up. He and Mac—Malcolm—were to meet back and split up the loot. Half for Mac, half for Leo and his brothers. But Mac had never returned.

Leo had been double-crossed.

Bart approached and handed Leo a brown wrapped package.

"What's this?" Leo asked.

"Payment. The old man said it was half. The rest comes after we do the job." His eyes glowed with greed. "Lot of money to pass up, Cousin. Easier than robbin' some bank."

Leo silently scoffed at the idea of robbing a bank with these bumbling idiots. He unwrapped the bills and stared in disbelief at the paper banding them together; it bore the mark of the money they'd stolen a year before.

He laughed as he fanned his finger over the edges of the bills. Not only was this a lot of money, it was the money he was after. Excitement raced through Leo. He tossed the banded stack from one hand to the other.

"Ya know? Maybe I'm bein' a bit hasty here."

"Mattie! Open the door!"

Sitting at the long kitchen table, Mattie ignored Reed. His fist pounded on the door. She grimaced, her head pounding with each thud.

"Dammit, Mattie, answer me!"

Mattie shivered, pulling her woolen shawl more tightly around her. Getting up, she went to the door.

"Only if you promise that we leave at first light," she called, leaning to one side.

A long silence followed. Steps scuffed back and forth outside. "No."

Putting her hand on the door, she spread her fingers. "Then that too is my answer." She felt his rage in the ensuing quiet.

"At least let me light a fire for you. A lantern." A pause followed. "Scratch that. You don't need a lantern." A slight creaking at the window told her he was trying to see inside, but she knew it was as dark in here as out.

Sighing, Mattie returned to the table, her silence her answer. A fire would be nice. But lighting the wood stacked in the fireplace for warmth, or the stove to cook, was something she could not—would not—do while alone. Her fear of fire was too great.

Within minutes, Reed started pounding and shouting all over again. It would have been so easy for him to break a window or even to kick the door in, but he didn't. He alternated between swearing, threatening and pleading, but the words she needed to hear from him did not come.

She needed to hear him say he trusted her, believed in her.

Too sick with worry and exhaustion for food, and too cold to sit at the table, Mattie stood and wandered. Her bare feet went from the cold, hard flooring to a soft carpet. It was small, fit to the small sitting area, which made that the coziest part of their small home.

Two chairs crowded the area, one for each of her parents. She and her brothers and sisters had been more than content to sit or lie on the thick carpet her father had given their mother after building this house.

Above the chairs was the loft where they'd all once slept crammed together—boys on one side, girls on the other. Mattie paced across the house. It was small, especially in comparison to the three-story townhouse in St. Louis. She still remembered her awe on arriving at her stepfather's house when she was but a child of eight. Years ago, now.

Years. A sad smile flitted across her face. Winters, years. She now thought of the passing of time in the white man's manner; had become more white than Sioux. But deep inside, where it was important, she'd not lost her heritage.

Which included listening to spirits. And to her own intuition. Right now, all that she was screamed for her to ride off and find her siblings. But she couldn't. Not alone. Entering the small alcove where she slept, Mattie drew in a sharp breath at a blast of cold air. She'd forgotten about the broken window. Hesitating, she closed her eyes. She'd not be able to sleep here. She felt too vulnerable.

"Mattie, it's getting late. If you don't let me in I'll kick down the door. Tyler even told me to do so, you stubborn woman!"

Her eyes flew open. Reed's voice came in the window. She heard the soft hiss of a lantern.

"You won't," she said. "Or you'd have done so earlier." She had no real idea of the passing of time—there was no light for her to watch fade. She only knew that it was dark by the coldness seeping into the house, and by the weariness of her body.

Wanting the robe she'd left on the rocking chair, she made to fetch it. Reed's sharp voice stopped her. "Glass," he warned.

"It's been swept," she said, walking toward the window. She heard his breathing, knew he was close enough to reach in and grab her. But he didn't. Mattie picked up the buffalo robe and turned away.

"How long are you going to stay locked inside there?"

"Until you believe," she answered.

"What about a fire? It's cold. At least let me come in and build you a fire," he begged.

She sighed, not bothering to tell him that she also wouldn't stay alone in the house with a burning fire. Not after the past. She took another step away from him.

"Food! You need to eat."

Mattie turned. He was starting to sound frantic. "Not as much as I need you to believe me."

She went back through the old quilt that served as a curtain, separating the room from the rest of the house. This time there was no pounding. No yelling. No curses. Just silence that pressed in on her with the same heaviness as the darkness behind her eyes, and that stole into her heart.

How could a man who made her see so much color with just his presence, feel so much warmth with just a touch, be so cold to her needs? She needed him to believe. So much depended on it. She felt it, knew it with as much certainty as she knew the darkness of night would give way to the light of day.

Climbing the ladder, she entered the loft and slid into the bed she'd once shared with Renny. For just a while, her world had been renewed. That kiss she'd shared with Reed had changed her. He was her destiny. How could he not be when he made her feel and see so much?

Closing her eyes, Mattie held her fingers to her cheeks, remembering every line of his face, the firmness of his jaw, the slope of his nose, the bushy brows, thick hair that fell over his forehead. And his mouth. His incredible mouth.

Mattie had never thought much of a man's mouth. It was just there, a part of the man but nothing special. How wrong she'd been. Reed's mouth told her much. Firm and soft and moist as the morning mist . . . Rolling to her side, Mattie curled into a ball. And stubborn, that mouth was.

Wrapping herself in her robe, she buried her face in a pillow and cried. The spirits had returned her gift, sent her a man who made her see and feel like never before. He was her soul mate, her other half, but the spirits were full of deception. How else could her soul mate not know and trust her as she knew and trusted him?

This time, the scent of her mother's buffalo robe failed to provide her much-needed comfort, for she was also surrounded by the scents of her siblings and the knowledge that she might never see them again.

It was going to be a long, sleepless night. Reed stared at the dark house. Mattie was in there, alone, cold and probably frightened. He smacked his fist into the barn door, then swore at the pain. He'd promised Tyler he'd go inside, even if he had to force his way in, but he couldn't.

Just as he couldn't make false promises for whatever Mattie asked of him. Not even in his need to protect her. He wouldn't lie to her. And yet he couldn't agree to what she asked of him.

Reed refused to be responsible for another death. His belly churned with bitter bile. So where did that leave him? He grimaced.

Cold. Hungry. Angry.

And most of all, battered.

The last year had been spent mourning his losses, kicking himself for his foolishness, regretting the pride that had kept him from giving the man who'd adopted him the one thing that would have most likely put things right—a simple apology. An apology for running off with Anne to marry her. But he'd been too young and arrogant. And it was not something he was sorry for. He only regretted that it had come to deceiving the man who'd loved him as a son. Pride had kept him silent. His wife and his adoptive mother had begged him, but he'd remained as stubbornly silent as his father.

And look where that had gotten him. Instead of losing the love and respect of one man, he'd lost it all. Had he put things to right, none of this would have happened. He'd have been home in the evenings with his family, not out drinking and trying to prove to himself that he didn't need the old man's love and acceptance.

Hell, the old man had actually tried once to apologize and make things right between them, but Reed had refused to listen. Instead, he'd allowed his bitterness to turn him into the very image he'd fought all his life—a drunk half-breed.

Then, while drunk and full of righteous anger, he'd allowed himself to be manipulated. And people had died.

He crossed his arms on his chest and glared at the house. The woman inside was trying to manipulate him, and he wasn't having any of it. He would do what he needed to keep her safe.

But what about the others? What if she's right?

What would it hurt for him to take her and go after her family? He could protect her just as well on the road as here. He stared out into the night. In fact, he might be able to protect her a hell of a lot better.

Houses could be set to fire, they could become

traps. Hell, someone could easily find her here. And there were many places for an enemy to hide on this property. Reed found himself considering the idea. He could even just ride Mattie around in circles until her brother and sister returned.

He scowled. No, he wouldn't do that to her. He picked up his rifle and started for the house. Reaching the door, he settled on the crude porch swing and stared up into the blinking night sky. The chain squeaked in the crispy cold of the night, and seemed to whisper, *But what if she's not right? What if this is the wrong decision?*

All the regrets of the last year came at him with the speed and impact of flying bullets. He felt the wounds—each and every one of them—and felt the blood pour out of him.

His vision turned red. He saw her, his Annie, lying on the hard, polished floor of the bank, her new daffodil yellow dress stained with blood. Her eyes were glazed, fearful. Tears streamed out as the blood pooled beneath her.

"My babies. Promise to take care of our babies."

Reed heard the echo of his own voice promising that she'd be all right, that he'd make everything all right again. But things weren't all right. There was still blood. Lots of it. Too much. His hands were slick with it.

He glanced around. There were bodies strewn all over. The dead sheriff, each of the Granger brothers except Leo. An older couple.

Surrounding them, he saw their children. They stared at him. Silently. Accusingly. One by one they fell, dead; their eyes still trained on him.

He lifted his head and cried out against the injustice of it. And this time, when he looked down at Anne, he got a shock. It was Mattie on the floor, cradled in his arms.

It was Mattie's face, not Anne's. Her eyes were wide open. Dark and unseeing. Horror filled him as he pulled away. When he stared at his hands, he saw the blood covering them. He jumped up to run as far and as fast as he could from the vision of death.

Chapter Eleven

Reed's eyes shot open as he tumbled down the porch steps. He landed with his face flat in the dirt. "What the hell?" He pushed himself up onto his elbows, completely at a loss as to how he'd fallen.

A dream. A damn dream, he thought. A chill slid through his body as he recalled the horror of it. No, it had been real. Yet not. Still caught up in the horror of all that blood, he dropped his head and rubbed his eyes with his thumb and forefinger. Anne's blood. Mattie's blood. *So much* blood.

His eyes shot open. The images played over and over, just like in the dream. Was he still dreaming? The pain in his aching body said no. The surrealness of it all said yes. Reed feared he'd finally lost his mind. He felt helpless as he lay there, paralyzed, unable to escape whatever was happening to him.

The sudden shriek of a bird startled him. He

flipped over and stared up into the wide eyes of the largest owl he'd ever seen. It sat above him, on the railing, staring down. It lifted massive wings and spread them.

Reed blinked. Now he knew he was dreaming. Owls didn't come this close to humans. The great night bird flapped his wings and let out another shrill cry.

Reed lifted his hands to protect his face, but the bird didn't come at him with those razor-sharp talons. Instead, it dug into the wood. Torn between the need to scoot away and to reach up to see if the bird was real, Reed did neither. He held his breath and waited. He'd never experienced anything so wildly beautiful. His dream had taken a twisted turn.

It's no dream.

The voice seemed to whisper in his head. Reed blinked slowly. Man, he was going crazy. His nightmares had turned into his own personal hell.

Find the answer in your dream. The voice was as soft as the down on the owl's chest.

"Oh, man." Reed closed his eyes. "Wake up. You gotta wake up," he muttered.

He opened his eyes cautiously. The owl was gone.

Sitting, Reed ran a hand through his tangled hair. "Some dream," he breathed. Standing, he brushed off the front of his shirt and pants. His hands froze when he saw the single, soft, downy feather.

"Holy sh—" He broke off as he glanced up into

the sky. The dawn was just streaking across the clear heavens.

No, it hadn't been real. It couldn't have been. He held the tiny feather between his thumb and forefinger. At the bottom of the steps where he'd landed, Reed examined the rail. It wasn't light enough to see, but he felt the deep grooves in the wood. He pulled his hand away. Fresh slivers clung to the pads of his fingers.

Backing away, Reed stumbled. From inside his mind, he heard the softly spoken command again. *Find the answer in your dream.*

"What answer? What is the question?" Reed stared at the brownish feather, noticed the faint ripples of darker color. He'd been dreaming. He glanced once more at the sky. He'd fallen asleep. His gaze traveled back up the steps to the swing. Slowly, he returned to it and sat.

His dream. No, not a dream. A nightmare, and the mother of all nightmares. Reed hunched over, his elbows on his knees, his head bowed as he sought answers to what was happening to him. He really didn't want to learn he'd lost his mind, so he tried to remember each sickening detail.

The part with Anne—that was the same as before. And him holding her, her blood washing over him. Same with each innocent person who'd died: the sheriff, the couple.

The Granger brothers were part of it too. Though he killed them out of revenge, and had the law behind him, each of their deaths added to the pool of blood collecting in his dreams.

"God," he moaned. The worst thing was, this time, his nightmare had included Mattie and her siblings.

"No!" He couldn't handle more deaths. Not innocents. He'd give his own life rather than live with any more guilt. He felt the air shift around him, heard the soft swish of wings.

He didn't look up. He knew the owl was back. "How much more do I have to bear?" he asked wearily. "How many more will die?" Everyone, his gut said. His dreams were of death. His heart and soul were coated with it. And if the dreams were right, he'd have more death heaped on his shoulders. How could he tell Mattie that she'd been right, that her family was dead?

It is within you to stop it.

This time, Reed glanced up. The owl was there. And so was his answer. Previously all his nightmares were of deaths that had already happened. He glanced back at the house. Mattie had been in his arms. But she wasn't dead. She was in there, alive.

And that meant that her family had to still be alive. He had time to stop more tragedy. Jumping to his feet, he ran to the door. It was still locked.

Leaping down the steps, he ran around to Mattie's bedroom window. He'd taken out all the glass and nailed a piece of canvas over it. He ripped that off and climbed inside.

"Mattie," he called. She wasn't asleep in the bed.

He entered the rest of the cabin and stopped. It was cold, dark and gloomy. His gaze pierced the shadows. "Mattie!" He raised his voice and called again.

Hearing a soft moan, he spotted the loft. Climbing quickly, he entered the small area and located her on the bed.

"Mattie, wake up. We have to go." Reed reached out to shake her gently. She rolled toward him. He sucked in his breath. Her eyes were wide. Blank. Empty.

"Did you hear me, Mattie? I believe you. You were right. We need to go. Now!" Desperation made his voice sharp.

Mattie closed her eyes. "Too late. We're too late."

Mattie had heard Reed shouting, calling, begging for her to come back to him, but she was so tired. So alone.

"Mattie, it's not too late."

It was. "The river turned red," she whispered.

"What river?" Reed shook her.

Mattie turned away from him. "Leave me," she begged. All she wanted was to sleep. To escape. To hide—from him, herself and her own failures.

The bed dipped as Reed sat on the edge of the straw mattress. She felt his arms go around her, and felt him lift her into his arms. Gentle fingers stroked the hair from her face.

"Look at me, Mattie." Strong hands cupped the side of her face.

Mattie did as ordered. But . . . "I cannot," she whispered. Still, she opened her eyes and stared at where she knew his face to be.

The blaze of blue she saw struck her so hard it almost hurt. But she clung to it, used it to wash the red away. Slowly, the warmth of Reed's body seeped in and chased the cold from her bones.

"Listen to me. I had a dream—"

"You do not believe," she whispered, fighting to hold her own dreams at bay.

"I do. Hold out your hand."

Weary, wishing he'd just leave her alone, Mattie held out her hand. "You do not have to do this. I accept that you cannot believe." That he didn't trust her. A soft moan escaped his lips. How could she expect him to trust her when she no longer trusted herself?

Reed took two of her fingers in his own and pinched them together. "Feel this." He guided her hand with his.

Mattie felt something soft brush against her check. "Reed—"

"Mattie, it's the feather of an owl. I saw an owl."

Mattie went still. She'd heard the cry of the owl earlier. It had drawn her from the grip of another nightmare, herself. "You found it outside?"

Reed leaned down and brushed his lips against the top of her head. "No. The owl came to me. He was so close. So beautiful. And he spoke to me."

186

Slowly, hesitantly, Reed told her about his dream, about the owl. Then he waited.

Mattie felt tears slipping down her face. Her fingers gripped the tiny feather he'd given her. "Then it is too late." She wanted to be angry with Reed and blame him, but she couldn't. He now believed her, but it was too late.

"No. You don't understand. I've only dreamed of those who've already died. Not those who haven't."

Reed's breath fanned her face. She sank deeper into him. She was cold. So cold. "You said you saw them—me—dead."

"Mattie, you're not dead. I'm holding you, talking to you. But in my dream, you had replaced Anne."

"I don't understand."

"Anne was my wife. She was killed in a bank robbery." He told her about his recurring nightmare with Anne, and about each person who'd died.

"There's something you have to know. I came here with that posse a year ago. We followed them into Yankton, then out here. Tyler's brother died when we cornered one of the robbers." He paused, explained his part in it, then finished. "Two more people died. They were found on their land by their children."

Mattie's heart stopped. "My parents," she said.

"Yeah. I believe that they came upon one of the robbers, maybe even the leader, and were killed. It also means they died because of me. I see them in my dreams as well. Their blood is mingled with Anne's."

187

He took a deep breath. "You have every right to hate me, Mattie. I wish I could go back and change things."

Mattie reached up and put her fingers over his mouth. "No. This is not your fault. I saw their deaths months before it happened. I could not have stopped it. Nor could my mother." She explained about their shared gift. "When the spirits call us home, there is nothing we can do."

"I can't accept that," Reed began.

"Reed, you've paid." She ran the pads of her fingers over his eyes. She still held his feather between two fingers.

Resting his forehead against hers, Reed shook his head. "No. Not yet. Maybe not ever. My children will never know the love of their mother. Lizzie was just a baby. Like Caitie was. Neither one will remember their mothers."

"Not true, Reed. Caitie will know of our mother through my memories. And Renny's and Matt's. We keep our parents alive in our hearts. And we share our love with Caitie. All of us."

"It's not the same."

Mattie traced Reed's frown, sighing. "No. But it's something. And it's all she'll have."

"Because I was foolish."

Sitting up, Mattie absently skimmed her fingers over Reed's face, reading his emotions at the same time as trying to heal his broken soul. "Should I blame myself for not being able to stop their murders?"

Reed closed his eyes and copied her movements. "Do you?"

"I did. Do, yes. But in my heart I now know there was nothing I could have done." She smiled sadly as she remembered the torture the gift had brought to her own mother, who'd hated the helpless feeling that was often a part of it. A gift and a curse. And who was Mattie to decide what should have been or should be?

For the first time since losing her parents and her sight, Mattie understood what she'd not known before. Her responsibilities lay only within her abilities.

By accepting the visions, the messages from the spirits, she'd proved she was willing to use her gift for good whenever possible. But when she expected to control the outcome of those visions, she was expecting too much. She could only do what she could do. She could only provide the information with which she'd been entrusted.

Mattie slid her hand down Reed's arm until she found his hand. "Keep this. It is your talisman. Owl is one of your spirit guides, as he is for me. He guides us in the dreamworld. He conveys its messages to us."

Reed took the feather. "And . . . what is he saying?"

Standing, Mattie drew him up. She reached out and took Reed's hand in hers. She placed his palm against her face, placed hers against his. "We must deal with our pasts before we can live in the future."

Reed led Mattie down the steps to the waiting horses. The mare stepped forward and nuzzled her mistress. Mattie stroked the horse's gleaming coat.

"What if we are too late?" She finally allowed herself to ask.

Checking her saddle one last time, Reed walked around the front of the horse and tipped Mattie's chin up. "We won't be."

Mattie turned and stared blindly around. Doubts crashed through her. "Wait. I can't do this." Fear of failing, of losing all that she held dear made the churning in her stomach worse. She'd just been talking bravely, but could she believe in herself like she'd been encouraging Reed?

Strong fingers closed over her shoulders and gently massaged the tension from them. "You can. *We* can." Reed slid one arm down over her shoulder to embrace her, and pulled her against him.

"You have to be my eyes," she said, reaching up to grip his forearm. His hand tightened over her shoulder. His other hand crossed over her. She was cocooned in his warmth, safe with the protection of his hard, strong body against her.

She drew courage from him. He *was* strength, inside and out. Many a man would have crumbled under the load Reed carried. She sighed and let her head drop to his shoulder. Even he thought himself lost, damned forever. But Mattie knew better.

No, she saw the steely core of the man deep inside. He'd not lost himself to the horror of the past, nor was he only a man driven by the demands of the present. Inside, hope for a future still flickered. His soul was not lost to the darkness, he had only to open his eyes to see what she saw: the promise of tomorrow.

Each day was a promise of a new day—and a new night. The sky went from black to blue. Some days were gray, but beauty always shone through in even the darkest of storms. Even at the darkest of the night, there was beauty and promise in the stars.

Mattie drew upon that knowledge, and she dug deep inside her for the woman she knew herself to be. Finding that core of courage, she called it forth, pulled what she needed from Reed, combined their strengths and the driving need they each hoarded—redemption from Reed, independence from herself. Squeezing his arms, she gave the same back to him.

"You have to see what I cannot."

"That doesn't sound so hard," Reed murmured.

Smiling, Mattie laughed. "That sounds a bit arrogant," she murmured.

"Nope. Truthful." He slid his hands down her sides to her waist, and lifted her into her saddle.

Mattie heard the jingle of reins and the creak of leather as he mounted his own horse. Instead of allowing him to lead her, Mattie directed his attention to her broken window. "What do you see?"

Reed sighed. "Broken glass would be too obvious, I suppose."

"I see broken dreams. Yours and mine. I see danger in the sharp shards if they slice through flesh." She held up her hand when he snorted.

"I also see the beauty that comes from having a clean shiny window, gleaming as the sun bounces off it. The protection the glass offers in keeping the cold and wet away. Look up, now."

"Mattie, don't you think we should get going?"

"Some lessons are important. If you cannot see, you are of no use to me. What is up there?"

Reed's horse shifted restlessly. "There's a bird nest just under the roof," he said. He moved closer. "With babies in it. Two—no, four," he added as he watched one of the parent birds land on the edge. Immediately four wide beaks shot up to grab the proffered worm.

"Sparrows," Mattie said. "I hear their song in the morning, the call of the babies. The circle of life. A sparrow shows us how to survive. It will nest anywhere—even in a busy city like Saint Louis; it will find a place to continue the circle of life. It teaches us self-worth, to keep going and triumph in spite of all that is wrong in our lives. It offers dignity.

"What now do you see?"

Reed contemplated the birds and window. Her assessments using something as inert as a window or as small as a sparrow spooked him a bit. Yet it made so much sense. Instead of seeing the obvious, he now experienced something deeper. Staring into the window he supposed that the broken glass could also signify an invitation to enter, and in the birds, he suddenly saw a complete family.

Stunned, shaken, Reed wasn't sure he liked this new sight. What good did it do to see things that were out of his reach? For both things were. Sharing an intimate life with Mattie or creating a family with her was not what he was here for. He nudged his horse into a canter. "I see time being wasted. Let's go."

Renny rode beside Matthew along the James River. "We're going to have to stop soon," she said. Behind her, Caitie was growing tired and cranky. She wiped her face with the sleeve of her shirt. She'd opted to wear trousers for the journey, finding them much more practical when riding.

Matthew glanced behind them. "Kealan too," he muttered.

Renny, upon noticing how far behind Kealan was, whirled her horse around and rode back to him. He was off his mount, kneeling down beside the water. "Kea, what are you doing? I know you're tired. We'll rest when we get to that grove of trees up ahead."

Kealan looked insulted. "I'm not tired. I'm just learning the way so I can go see Uncle Wolf and Aunt Jessie all by myself someday." He pointed to a

193

bent tree across the river. "See, that tree looks like an old man."

"Kealan, we don't have time for you to dawdle." She tried to keep frustration from her tone. She'd actually hoped to have left the James River several hours ago. From there, they'd follow a smaller branch of the James that led to the West, across the plains to another river that snaked east from the Missouri.

Once they reached the Missouri, it was just a matter of crossing the river to reach her aunt and uncle. She glanced at the western horizon. It was clear as far as the eye could see, which was good. The last thing they needed was a swollen river to cross.

She returned her attention to Kea, who was still staring out across the James, and sighed.

"But Renny, Matthew says we should always know where we are and how to read the land. I'm just reading the land."

"Matthew is right. But now we are in a hurry, remember? This time you don't need to pay attention. Now, we're going to take a short rest in that grove up ahead. Then we have to ride pretty hard, and you have to keep up."

"Fine." Sulking, Kealan picked up a rock, examined it, then stuck it into his pocket.

Renny shook her head. "No more rocks. You've collected enough."

Kealan turned away from the bank, his toe kicking another stone. "Hey, look at this. It's got colors in it!" He bent down to pick up the small rock. "I gotta wash it. Then I'll come catch up." He grinned. "Promise. Please? I can take my rest here."

Renny turned away, shaking her head. It wasn't far to the trees. He couldn't get lost between here and there. But she knew she'd probably have to ride back to hurry him along.

"When I whistle for you, you get moving. Don't keep us waiting."

"Oh, boy," Kealan said. "I won't." He turned away, his attention already focused on the rocks near the bank."

"And don't fall in," Renny added. She smiled at his absent agreement and rode to catch up with the rest of her family.

She found Matthew near the stream beneath the grove of cottonwoods. Long flowing flowers drifted down.

"Renny!" Caitie ran up to her and gave her a bruised petal. "For you," she said, grinning.

"Thanks, sweetheart." Renny watched with love in her eyes as her sister pulled up her skirt to collect the fallen petals. Kealan and his rocks, Caitie and her flowers. She glanced at Daire, who was unsaddling the horses to give them a rest. Caitie chatted nonstop and shrieked with joy when the breeze loosened more flowers and caused them to rain down over her head.

Renny joined Matthew, who was staring across the river.

"Mattie's okay, Matt." Though Renny wasn't sure she trusted Reed, she did trust Tyler to keep an eye on their sister.

Thinking of Tyler tended to darken her mood, but this time she was grateful for his overprotectiveness. He wouldn't let anything happen to Mattie.

Matthew turned troubled eyes to her. "I don't like this."

Renny frowned. "I don't either, but it's the only way to protect Kealan and Caitie."

"No. The quiet. It's too quiet here." He was staring around.

Renny laughed. "Well, Caitie is a bit noisy." The young girl was singing and whirling and dancing among the trees. "Maybe she'll tire and fall asleep when we get going again. We'll be able to move a bit faster."

Matthew didn't return her grin. Renny turned and looked—really looked. The grove was shaded with beams of sunlight spearing between thick branches of leaves and flowers. Other than the four of them, there was nothing else. No birds. No squirrels. Nothing.

Watching Caitie dance out of sight, Renny started forward, but Daire, also watching his sister, went after her. "I'm going to get Kealan," she said. She grabbed the reins of her horse and mounted.

Matthew nodded. "I'll get Daire and Caitie. I think we need to get going."

Renny rode fast toward the edge of the stand of

trees, but before she made it, the blast of a gunshot rang out. She jerked on the reins, felt her horse shudder, heard a shrill shriek of pain. Then she was falling with her horse.

She kicked her feet free of the stirrups as she fell, tumbling into the brush. Dazed, she got to her hands and knees, desperate to find the others and make sure they were all right. Then something struck the back of her head and everything went dark.

Chapter Twelve

Reed rode along the James River with Mattie beside him. "How far do you suppose they are?" he asked. He glanced over to be sure she was keeping up. Looking at her he'd never have known she was blind. She rode as though she could see and guide her mount.

"They have a day on us. Renny and Matt will keep moving, but Caitie is young. She'll slow them. I expect they will leave the James before the sun is high." Worry lined her features. "We won't make it that far. Not today."

"You sure they won't take a different route?" Reed's gaze followed the snaking river as far as his eyes could see. He didn't see any other rivers branching off. So far, there were just small streams.

"They won't. Renny promised Sheriff Tyler she'd stick to the route in case . . ."

Reed glanced sharply at Mattie, knowing she'd been about to say in case anything happened to her while they were gone. Tyler had insisted they stick to one route in case.

Silence fell between them for a while. The sun continued to rise and heat the air. Life abounded around them. Not once during the last year had he taken the time to notice the world. He'd learned to do whatever it took to survive, and to do what needed doing. Nothing else had mattered. Until now.

Until Mattie. What would each day be like if he could spend it with her, like this, just riding peacefully across land that belonged to them? Tightening his grip on his reins, he realized it was a dream that had begun to take hold—something deep inside he longed to make real.

But he couldn't. It would remain a dream. He had no place here. There were too many reminders of his past. Too much blood had been spilled, much by his own hand. Even if he should find Malcolm, he still had much of the stolen money to repay. He had nothing to offer any woman. Or even his own children.

"What do you see, Reed?"

Startled, Reed glanced at Mattie. Where his thoughts were turbulent, hers seemed peaceful. "Not another lesson, Mattie." He was not in the mood for any more symbolism. Like the fact that she was the light to his dark, the color that chased away the bleakness. Mattie was everything Reed wanted. And everything he needed.

Mattie sent him a sad smile. "No. I just want to know what the day looks like." She lifted her face to the sun. "I feel the warmth, the absence of the wind. I hear the flow of the river and the call of the birds. I can smell the scent of spring. But I cannot see it."

Reed's gut twisted. He remembered the incredible feeling of sharing sight with her when they'd kissed. They'd used other senses to "see" one another, like touch and taste.

Even the sound of her breathing had triggered in him the need to hold her and never let her go. He wanted so much from her. If a kiss could affect him so deeply, what would making love do to him?

He feared he knew the answer. It lay deep in his heart, waiting for him to acknowledge it and bring it out into the light. Closing his eyes, he forced himself to remember that day at the bank, the fear of those around him when the Granger gang burst through the doors.

He remembered his own shock upon seeing Leo Granger, realizing that he'd been used—and had been stupid enough not to know it until too late. It had cost so many so much.

So he'd searched out each of the Granger brothers by learning all he could about them, going from town to town, talking to folk. And one by one he'd found them, and when it came time, he hadn't hesitated to kill.

"I can't do it," he whispered, fighting a power he feared he was helpless to fight in the end. What if he let her down, or through him, something happened to her? Fear kept him from giving in to what he longed to have. Knowing a family had once been his deepest desire. He no longer deserved one.

"Can't or won't?" Mattie asked.

"Both." Staring at the vast beauty around him, he couldn't speak. Knowing the reason for being there made it impossible for him to describe it. His vision was clouded with pain and death. How could he see beauty or share it when there was none inside him?

Now, had she asked about life on the streets, he could have given her more detail than she'd ever want. But no one wanted to know about the children who lived in the streets. To acknowledge them meant either having to try and do something or to ignore them.

Most chose to ignore.

Yet one man hadn't, Reed thought. His adoptive father had taken him from the streets, given Reed a chance no one else would have.

"What are you thinking?" Mattie reached out for him.

"Nothing pleasant." In order to keep her from asking about things he wasn't ready to share, he deliberately edged his horse away, out of her reach. He hated seeing the light fade from her face, but he couldn't do what she wanted, or be what she wanted.

"We'll stop here. The horses need to rest."

They didn't. Not yet. Dismounting, he reached up

and swung Mattie down, then led the horses to the edge of the bank. Mattie followed, her hand resting lightly on her mare.

After watering the horses, he hitched them loosely to a tree branch. Glancing over at Mattie, he sighed. He just didn't have it in him to hurt her. He'd rather slice his own wrists or stop his own heart than see the hurt in her eyes. She might not be able to see from them, but he saw more than he cared to when he stared into her eyes.

"I'm sorry, Mattie." He had no right to hurt her. It wasn't her fault he was a sorry sonofabitch. He'd taken the image others had of him and made it real. He'd grown up with folk thinking of him as an ill-bred savage, so he'd learned to be cold, hard and unfeeling.

Only those he loved knew that his facade hid a heart easily broken. Only Anne had remained at his side no matter what, loving him, all of him.

He stood behind Mattie, watching her drink and splash water on her face. He remained, ready to help her up and lead her to a spot of shade beneath one of the tall cottonwoods. The silence between them grew. Reed knew she was disappointed.

"It's red," she whispered.

"What's red?"

Mattie held out her hands. Water dripped from her fingertips. "There's blood."

Bending down, he picked up a hand, sure that she'd sliced herself on a rock. He saw nothing; just her smooth, slender fingers. He clasped her hand in his. "There's no blood, Mattie. You're okay."

"You don't see it." It was a statement, not a question.

Reed heard the hollowness of her voice, noted the stiffness of her posture. "Mattie?" He turned her toward him, then sucked in his breath.

She was ghostly white, her eyes nearly black. Her lower lip bled where she'd bit herself. "It's happened. We're too late." Then her eyes rolled back in her head.

A mix of visions held Mattie tight. The river of red split. As though flying above it, she followed, searched for her family. She couldn't find them. Too much was red. It blinded her. Then she felt heat searing her flesh. The river rose up, surrounded her, became a burning inferno, trapping her. The shadow of death pressed in on her, suffocating her. She couldn't breathe.

"Mattie, for God's sake, come back to me!"

Sputtering and choking, Mattie flailed. Water ran into her mouth, her nose. It weighed her down. She was drowning.

"You're okay, I've got you. It's just water from the flask. You didn't snap out of it. I didn't know what else to do." Reed's voice shook.

Mattie's heart raced. She clung to Reed. The air hit her, chilling.

"We have to go. They need us." *Please don't let us be too late.* In her heart she feared they would be. The place where the river split was still a day's ride. Reed picked her up and put her on his horse.

"Raven—"

"She'll follow," Reed assured her. Mattie felt his arms go around her. "Don't worry. Remember, until last night I had only dreamed of those who've already died at my hands. You and your siblings were there." He felt her shudder. "Yes, dead or dying. But it hasn't happened yet. I *know* it hasn't. You have to believe. For me. We're not too late."

His lips nuzzled her hair, and he went on, "I need that hope kept alive, Mattie. I don't think I'll survive if anyone else dies."

"Then let us go. And cling to our hope."

Mattie leaned against him, let his wide shoulders, hard chest and strong arms cradle her close. His scent washed over her and calmed her. She had to believe that there was hope, and it was Reed who gave it to her.

As they rode, Reed told her of the landmarks they passed. Though she saw none of then, she saw the one thing that mattered: their future. The link between her dreams and his, the presence of the owl as a talisman not just to her, but to him as well, and the ease in which he used his eyes to see for them both—even if he didn't know or understand anything yet.

Kealan was just adding another rock to a leather bag filled with rocks when he heard the shot. A terrified scream followed. Wide-eyed, he fell to his belly. What was that? He lifted his head and peered between the bright green leaves of the shrubs growing along the river. He'd slowly been making his way toward the stand of trees where he'd promised to meet his sister.

He glanced over his shoulder. His horse had been munching on the new grass growing along the bank. She now stared white- and wild-eyed toward the trees, nostrils flaring. She looked ready to bolt.

He remembered one time when one of their horses had broken a leg and Matthew shot it. This had been the same scream. All the horses had been spooked, for days. Matt had said they sensed the death of one of their own.

Jumping up, Kealan ran to his horse. He grabbed the reins and spoke softly to the mare, using a mix of English and Lakota. He didn't know as much Lakota as the others, but he knew some.

A second shot rang out. This time, he had to fight his horse. When the animal reared, he clung to the reins and felt his feet dangling in midair. He was afraid, but he refused to let go. Instead, he wrapped his feet around her neck. When her front hooves thudded back onto the ground, he jumped down but didn't release the frightened animal.

Instead, he drew her closer to the water's edge. A burr oak with spreading boughs and thick leaves provided deep shade and concealment. Quickly, he wrapped the ends of the reins around the lower branch. Then he shinnied up the tree. He nearly fell when a third and fourth shot sounded.

Kealan shook. Maybe Daire was just practicing his shooting. Yeah, that had to be what it was. He told himself to hurry and he might get to do some too. But he didn't budge.

Instead, he waited anxiously, listening for Renny's whistle. She'd said when it was time to go she'd call him. And that meant whistling loudly. Both his brother and sister had loud whistles.

When he was home if he heard two short whistles, that meant it was time to come home. One long whistle meant it was time to come home, now. Hurry!

"Whistle, Renny," he said, breathing hard, his heart pounding against his chest. She knew how much he liked to shoot. He was even pretty good, she'd said; so if Daire was getting to shoot, she'd whistle and call him, letting him know he was missing out. He waited.

The whistle didn't come. But he did hear something. He frowned. It sounded like crying. Deciding to go see what was going on, he started to climb down. Riders burst from the trees.

Relieved, he dropped to the ground and ran around the concealing bushes. Maybe Renny had whistled but he hadn't heard. She'd be plenty mad at having to come fetch him. But that was alright.

He skidded to a stop and dropped once more when he realized those horses didn't belong to his family. Matt and Daire's horses were brown and white, like his. Renny's was yellow. The two horses riding across the open land were brown. Red-brown.

And the riders were strangers wearing all black, with black hats. They rode past—far enough away that they didn't spot him or his horse but close enough for Kealan to see the red heads of Caitie and Daire.

He jumped to his feet once more. The riders were heading west, not south. Kealan waited, his heart loud in his ears. As soon as they were out of sight, he took off running. He left his horse behind and kept to the edge of the river.

He found Renny first. Blood covered her head, she didn't move and her horse lay next to her, shot dead.

"Renny, wake up," he cried. No matter how much he shook her she didn't move.

"Matt! Come quick!" Kealan shouted, running toward the small clearing where Daire and Matthew's saddles sat with the supplies. No one was there.

"Matthew?" Fear choked his throat and kept him from screaming when he saw his brothers' horses lying dead in the water.

He ran through the trees. A low moan made his knees shake. He almost fell. "Matt?" He peered around a tree trunk and saw his brother slumped against a tree.

"Matt! Wake up!"

Matthew opened his eyes. "Kea . . ." His voice trailed off.

Kealan shook his brother. When Matthew lifted his hand, Kea shrieked at the blood.

He found the stain of blood spreading on Matt's trousers. He shook his brother. "Don't die, Matt. Please don't die." Tears streamed down his face. He didn't know what to do.

He glanced wildly around and spotted a pair of legs sticking out from some bushes. Cautiously, he approached and saw a stranger. He covered his mouth with his hands. The stranger was looking right at him, but his eyes were dead. Matthew's knife stuck out of his chest.

Kea ran back to Matt. This time, his brother opened his eyes. "Renny," he whispered.

"Matt, you gotta come. She's hurt. Bad. Like you."

Kealan tried hard to lift his brother, but he couldn't budge him.

Matt hissed with pain as he struggled to sit. "Get me a rag, Kea. Gotta stop this bleeding."

Taking off at a run, Kealan skidded to a stop in front of where the family had stopped. He dropped to his knees, thrust his hand into a bag and came out with one of Caitie's calico dresses. One of her favorites. He started to put it back, then decided he didn't have time to be going through more clothes.

He ran back to his brother. Matt took the dress and yanked at the ruffled hem. "She's going to be mad at you." Matt's attempt at humor made Kealan cry.

"You gotta get up, Matt. We gotta go after them. I saw 'em. They took Caitie and Daire and shot the horses." He tried tugging on Matt again. This time his brother stopped him. "No. You . . . have to go . . . for help."

Kealan's eyes grew big. "I can't go by myself," he whispered.

"Got to, Kea. Need to get out of here in case they come back."

"I'll get my horse. You can ride with me." Crying, Kealan stood. Never had he felt so little in his life. Or so scared.

"No. Too slow. You . . . go."

Kealan ran back to the supplies and grabbed the rifle and the sack of ammunition. He gave the weapon to his brother, then approached the dead man. Reaching out, he yanked the knife out of the man's chest with both hands.

He stumbled back and fell on his butt, then wiped the blade clean on some leaves, careful not to touch the blade and cut himself—just as he'd seen Matt do after using it to butcher an animal.

He handed it to Matt, who said, "Now go, little brother."

Crying, Kealan crouched beside him and pulled at his arm. "You gotta come with me, Matt. I'm just a boy."

As much as he wanted to be like his older brothers, Kealan was very afraid he was still too little to do anything as important and dangerous as going for help.

"Yes, you are *hokshila*. A boy," Matt murmured.

210

"But you are brave. And smart and cunning. You are *Matohoksila*, Bear Boy, when you live with the Sioux." Matthew pulled a small leather pouch over his head and handed it to Kealan. "Take this. Go. Quickly."

Kealan took his brother's medicine bag and pulled it on. He tucked the pouch against his heart—for courage—then took off running. His legs might be short, taking a long time to cover the ground back to where he'd left his horse, but with his brother's faith and magic, he felt tall and fast.

Chapter Thirteen

Mac pulled out a pocketwatch to check the time. His fingers clutched the timepiece as memories of the first time he'd seen it gripped him. He'd gone to see that banker for a loan. His Laura was sick, and the local doctor hadn't held out any hope. He'd suggested Mac take her back east.

Yes, he'd dressed in his Sunday-go-to-meeting best, had even brought Laura in so the bank man could see that there were no lies in him; that he desperately needed the funds. But the man sitting behind his fancy wood desk had remained cold and impassive.

Mac had barely finished presenting his case when Harold E. Robertson had pulled that watch out of his suit pocket, making a silent point that Mac was taking up his precious time.

Desperate, Mac had ignored the dismissal and

brought Laura forward, begging the man for help. But as Mac had no collateral, the bank had no money to lend him. It didn't matter that Mac was hardworking. He'd even offered to work in the bank each night, sweeping floors—anything in order to save his daughter's life.

Closing his eyes, Mac pinched the bridge of his nose with two fingers as waves of anger rolled through him. Robertson, the cold bastard, had just leaned back in his leather chair as though conducting a social visit, not discussing whether an innocent little girl would live or die.

"Please," he'd begged. He'd had no pride, didn't care that the tears rolled down his clean-shaven face.

Robertson had stood and paced behind the desk, glancing out the window. "My grandfather was in the banking business. Boston. He didn't make his money by giving it away. Understand, Mr. Clemmings, this is business through and through." And then he'd held up the watch.

"See this watch? It's old. Doesn't keep exact time, but I keep it anyway. Know why?" Robertson hadn't waited for Mac to reply.

"I keep it because it was my grandfather's and he set great store in keeping personal affairs and business separate. Said there was time in a man's life for both. The key is in remembering which is which. It's a daily reminder.

"What you are asking of me is to make a decision based on personal feelings." He turned to face Mac.

While I feel for you, I don't loan out the bank's money based on personal desires. I'm sorry. The answer remains no."

"Please sir, you are my daughter's only hope. You *will* get your money back. Every cent plus. I swear this to you."

"Can't take the risk, Mr. Clemmings." With a snap, he'd closed the watch and dropped it back in his pocket. Then he'd stood and ordered Mac to leave on his own two feet or be tossed out.

Mac shook off the memory that had condemned Laura to her long, slow death. He snapped the watch closed and stared at it. During the robbery, he had taken the watch with the idea of destroying it. He'd hated the watch and all it stood for.

But he had eventually decided to keep it instead, taking great pleasure each time he looked at it, held it, in knowing that for every day of his life, Robertson would suffer as he, Mac, suffered still.

When Mac's young wife had died, he'd grieved. But there'd been nothing anyone could do. She'd died in childbirth, leaving him Laura as a reminder of their love. But Laura's death had been needless. Lack of money and compassion had been what killed her.

Robertson was a hard, cold, unfeeling bastard. He'd killed Laura as surely as if he'd put a gun to her head and pulled the trigger. So Mac had taken his lesson from the banker. He'd taken what the man valued most with the same cold detachment.

Returning his attention now to the ransom note, he tried to write it with the same cold detachment, but his hand shook. A splatter of ink ruined his effort. He crumpled the paper and tossed it aside. Agitated, he dropped the quill and paced.

The past, never far away, seemed hell-bent on making him suffer. He didn't want to remember, but those events had led him to where he was today, and what he was doing.

Damn, it had all been so unnecessary. He'd have repaid all the money, he'd have worked hard and long for the chance to save Laura. He kicked a rock and watched it roll down the bluff.

It dislodged other stones and pebbles. A small cloud of dust rose as the rubble slid to the bottom. It didn't matter that he'd rebuilt his life, for he'd only built a clever facade to hide behind until he found the money he'd been forced to bury.

Grim resolve hardened his features. He didn't want to take more lives, had no quarrel with these kids. Hell, in his own way was even fond of them, but if it was a choice of them or taking what he was owed, then that was the way of it.

Turning, he went back to his task of writing the ransom note, writing it quickly then folding it and stuffing it in his shirt pocket. He didn't anticipate getting any money—in fact, his plan was to make sure the kids found their way home before the demand was met. All he wanted was for the O'Brien siblings to vacate the land. And after nearly losing two of their own, surely they would decide to move into town where it was safer. Standing, he resumed his pacing along the top of the bluff. Staring down at the house in the distance, he frowned. Having the 'breed staying with Mathilda made things a bit more risky. He hadn't anticipated seeing the man again. He grinned. He'd nearly choked on his supper when he'd caught sight of Reed helping himself to a plate of food at the celebration of Mattie and Gil.

Mac had thought himself a dead man when the 'breed stared right at him—but then he didn't show even a flicker of recognition. His new identity was foolproof.

In the distance, Mac saw riders approaching. No one else followed. From the high ridge of land, Mac had a clear view of the rolling hills spread out before him. His plan was working. Soon, he'd have all the freedom he wanted to search for his money.

Grabbing his rifle, he climbed down to a grouping of boulders at the base. It wasn't as secure as a cave, but it would do. He didn't figure on holding the kids for long.

"Eh, mister, we got them brats," a voice called out.

Mac adjusted his false beard and wig and an old, dusty, squashed hat. He stepped forward and scanned the two men and two kids. Frowning, he indicated the two kids.

"Where's the other boy? And your other partner? You said there were three of you." Three men hired to kidnap three kids.

Jasper slid down with Caitie struggling in his arms. She was bound and gagged. "Weren't no others. Took care of the two older ones and killed the horses like you said. Easy. They won't be gettin' nowhere for a while. Mebbe ever." He smirked.

"Dead?" Mac's blood went cold. That hadn't been part of his plan. He'd just wanted them knocked out to slow their return.

"Not when we left 'em. But the injun fought, killed my brother." Jasper was looking uncomfortable. He looked to the man on his right.

"My cousin here is tellin' the truth. These was the only younguns."

Then Mac's eyes went wide as the man pulled off a bandana and leveled a revolver at him.

"Leo!" Mac swallowed nervously.

"In the flesh, ya double-crosser. Thought mebbe you'd got yerself killed 'til I heard you was here." He swaggered forward, handing the reins of his horse to Jasper. "Where's the money, Mac?" His voice was low, as if he didn't want Jasper to hear.

Sweating beneath his wig, Mac swallowed but kept his voice gruff. Controlled. "Don't have it. Had no choice but to ditch the loot and leave the area. When I came back, I tried to find it but couldn't. Still can't."

At Leo's look of disbelief, he hurried on. "It's here. Buried somewhere. Fire took out my landmarks, but I at least know the area. Unfortunately, the land is owned by these kids and their siblings. Too risky to be caught digging. Will raise questions in town."

Mac nodded at Jasper. "That's why I hired your cousins. I needed to drive them away." He kept his voice low so the kids wouldn't hear. He didn't want to have to kill them.

Not trusting his old cohort, Mac kept his rifle trained on Leo, who was doing the same to him with his pistol. "Shoot me and you get nothing. Work with me, help me find it, and half is yours as we agreed."

Jasper approached. He'd tied the horses to a shrub. He glanced from one gun-wielding man to another. "Wha's he talkin' 'bout, Leo? Wha' money? You didn't say nothin' 'bout hidden money. Thought we was gonna rob a bank." Jasper looked excited. "We's gonna be rich! Wait till the boys back home get a load of me in some of 'em fancy shirts and trousers."

A shot rang out, startling Mac. He watched Jasper fall with horrified disbelief. Leo shrugged.

"Expendable. You was a fool to trust them. Stupid idiots, the pair. Now it's back to bein' jest me and you—so start talkin'."

Mac stared at the two wide-eyed kids. He had no wish to kill innocents. But his Laura had been innocent, and no one had cared that she'd died. When the parents of the O'Briens had come across him burying the money, he hadn't hesitated to kill them. It had been a choice of forfeiting the money or making sure they were no threat to him. So he'd taken enough money to see him through, buried the rest and left the area.

Sighing, he stared at the children. The sight of the little girl frozen in terror, chest heaving with silent sobs, got to him. He didn't want to care, caring was dangerous, but inside he knew he could never hurt the little one.

He addressed Daire, keeping his voice low and gruff so the boy wouldn't recognize him.

"If you can keep your sister quiet, I'll take her gag off. And free her hands. She screams, and I tie her back up."

Fury burned in the boy's darkened eyes, but he nodded. Mac motioned to Leo. "Get them inside, then we talk."

"And have you shoot me in the back?"

"Got no choice but to deal with you. Someone needs to stay and guard them while I deliver the ransom note."

He kept his gaze away from the kids. Too much was at stake to go soft now. He also had to be careful. If they recognized him, he'd have no choice but to kill them.

Leo walked sideways to Daire and bent down to slice the rope binding his ankles. Then he yanked the boy's gag off. "Run and I'll shoot ya. Then yer sis here won't have no one. Understand?"

Nodding, Daire went to Caitie and picked her up by sliding his bound hands over her head, bending, then gathering her to him with his arms. "Release her hands," he ordered.

Leo chuckled. "Full of yerself, ain't ya, to be orderin' me 'round."

"Do it," Mac said. He stared down at Daire. "In there. And keep her quiet." With Caitie's arms wrapped tightly around his neck, Daire took her into the shelter.

Mac set his rifle down. "Now we talk. Kill me and no one gets the money."

Leo lowered his revolver.

"Talk."

Sitting a short distance from the fire, Mattie hugged her knees to her chest. The soft pops and sharp snaps of flame didn't comfort her, but neither did they make her break out into a cold sweat. It had taken her a long time to be able to sit close enough to a fire without flashing back to the barn. She could think about it, now, even remember. Only in her dreams did it take on a lifelike reality.

The sound of wood being tossed onto the fire startled her, as did the burst of embers flaring to life. The flames roared, heat reached out. She scooted back.

"Warn me before you do that," she said softly.

"Didn't mean to startle you," Reed said.

"It didn't. Well, it did—but not for the reason you think." She hesitated. It was going to be a long night; she was afraid to sleep lest the dreams return. Or the visions. Talking would help pass the time.

"I tend to be a bit afraid of fires," she explained, not knowing what he knew of her.

"You lost your husband in a fire. I'd forgotten," Reed said. "Day of your wedding."

Mattie wasn't surprised that he knew. Most did. "Collin died trying to save my life. I escaped the barn. He didn't." She heard Reed's sharp intake of breath.

"I didn't know you'd been in the fire." He hesitated. "You weren't hurt?"

"Oh, I was hurt." She ran her fingers down a burn mark on the outside of her thigh. "I have some burns, but that wasn't as bad as having part of the roof collaps on top of me. Lost my sight because of the injury to my head."

Mattie heard Reed shift. His voice was soft when he spoke. "Mattie, I didn't know. Thought maybe you'd been born blind. You seem so comfortable with it." He snapped a twig in half.

"Didn't have much choice," Mattie said, wrapping her arms back around her knees. "Had a family to think of. Couldn't be a burden." She turned her head toward him.

"Do you know that when you lose one sense, you gain others?"

Reed ran a finger down her nose. "You've made it quite clear to me that you see better than I do." He didn't sound resentful.

"I should get your bedding," he said. You must be exhausted. We only have a few hours until it'll be light enough to continue."

Whether it was day or night made little difference to her, and had it been Matthew, they'd have continued on without stopping except to rest the horses. He knew the way so well, traveling in the dark would have posed no problem. Tonight they'd traveled until Reed called a halt.

"I won't need it."

"Mattie, you need to sleep."

"No. I can't." She wouldn't.

"More visions?"

"Dreams. Nightmares. They will come." She heard Reed stand, felt him brush against her as he walked past. Then he was back, dropping a bundle next to her.

"You still need to keep warm." Instead of sitting beside her, he sat behind her, pulling her against him. His warmth once more surrounded her, gave her the comfort she needed but would not have asked for.

"Reed?"

"Hush. It's going to be a long night. Don't think I'll be sleeping either. At least this way, we'll stay warm."

A blanket around her shoulders didn't compare to the warmth of his body, so Mattie silently gave in and relaxed against him. "Thank you."

She sighed. He still didn't believe that they were meant to be together, but with every passing moment the ties between them grew stronger. It worried her that if he broke them, left her to return to his life, that it might destroy her.

She'd grieved over the death of her husband but hadn't known him all that long. He'd been kind, and she suspected that she'd loved the idea of getting married. And of securing her family as a married woman, with no one ever trying to take Caitie and Kealan and Daire from her.

The thought that she might not have loved Collin as much as Reed obviously loved his wife saddened her. Over time, she might have developed that deep love and bond, but fate had taken the chance from her.

"Tell me about your life," she asked.

"Not much to tell," Reed said. Mattie felt him stiffen.

"It bothers you to talk about it?"

Reed remained silent for so long that Mattie gave up. Then at last he spoke. "I was born to a woman who lived off the needs of men."

"Did she love you?" Mattie rested her arms along the tops of his.

"No. I was in the way. I was 'boy.' She couldn't even bother with a name." He paused. "She left one night. I was six. Never saw her again." Reed's voice held no emotion.

Leaning her head back, Mattie wished she could see into his eyes. "What did you do? Who raised you?"

Reed turned his hands palms up so he could thread his fingers through Mattie's. "The streets."

Mattie closed her eyes and reached for the man

behind her. She felt it: the hurt, the despair, the raw need to survive. "How did you do it? Survive?"

"Had no choice. Hell, it was all I knew." Though he tried to hold the emotion from his voice, the bit that escaped told her everything. She'd seen and heard the stories of street children in Saint Louis, had been shocked that there were children with no one to care for them.

"Our people do not abandon children. If a child loses a parent, there are others who will take that child and make him theirs. Children are revered. Not thrown away," she said.

"You are fortunate." His chest rose and fell as he sighed heavily. "Do not pity me, Mattie. I survived. Even found a family when I was ten." He chuckled. "Was caught stealing by a man who took me in. Used to see him going to the bank every day. Had a pretty little girl. Always looked so nice. So I followed him home one day."

His voice grew soft as he admitted, "Snuck around back and saw a pie sitting in the window. Apple." Another chuckle. "I stole it."

Mattie smiled. "Was it good?"

"Heaven," Reed said, stroking her hands.

"You went back again," Mattie guessed.

"Yep. Many times. Made friends with the girl. Anne."

Hearing the love in his voice made Mattie's heart ache. She wanted love that ran so deep. Renny was right: marrying Gil just to please his father was wrong. For her, for him . . . In fact, looking back, she wasn't even sure Collin had loved her—certainly not with the same devotion she heard in Reed's voice.

They'd been in love. But maybe they'd been more in love with the idea of becoming independent; her for her family, him because that was what was expected of him by his father. But not his mother. His mother had fought the union and lost.

"Tell me more." The warmth she felt came from the man holding her. In front of her the fire was dying.

"Anne used to sneak me food. She'd come out and talk to me. She was younger by a couple of years. At first, she just amused me. She was so innocent. I used to tell her she wouldn't last a day living on the streets." Mattie felt his smile against the back of her head. "She'd get so mad and stomp her tiny little foot at me. Then she'd stop bringing me food until I apologized. Used to be worth it, though, to see her so mad. As long as she didn't cry. Couldn't handle that. Not as a boy—"

"Or as a man," Mattie finished.

"No. She had me there. She was my best friend. My only friend." Reed told Mattie how her father had found out what she was doing, how Anne had begged him to give her a brother. A brother named Reed.

"When he asked me to move in with them, told me he needed a son to leave his business to one day, it was the best day of my life. I wasn't just Reed with no last name. I could be Reed Robertson."

"When we first met, you didn't give us your full name. You said it was just Reed. Why?"

Reed was silent so long, Mattie feared he wouldn't answer. Then he said, "I don't deserve the name."

His tone told Mattie that it hurt to talk about it. "Who gave you the name Reed? You said your mother didn't name you."

She felt him shrug. "People used to call me ''breed.' So I took the name Reed."

Mattie found that part of his story the saddest. "I like the name—Reed," she said. "It's a strong name. Like the reeds in a pond. Straight, tall. With many uses. A hollow reed offers a swimmer air to breathe while beneath the surface."

"There you go, seeing things that aren't there." Reed hugged her tight and buried his face in the crook of her neck.

Reaching up, Mattie ran her fingers through his hair. It was soft, silky. She rubbed a strand between her thumb and forefinger. "I see what I see," she murmured. "And in you I see strength and courage. A man who survived where most would not have. You could have turned out so different."

"Anne saved me," he murmured.

"No, Reed. Even as a boy you had the strength to save yourself."

"Who will save the man, Mattie?"

"The boy deep inside you, Reed." At her words she felt him jerk, heard him moan. She turned in his arms, gently ran her fingers over his face and felt the wetness of tears.

Chapter Fourteen

"Mattie."

"Shush. I need to touch you, Reed."

Reed closed his eyes and let her fingers feather over his face. He lifted his hands and, like before, used just his senses to touch her. He needed her in a way he'd never needed anyone else.

Her fingers wiped the tears from his face. At first he'd been horrified to find himself crying. But not now. What she'd said had been incredible, made him feel things about himself he'd never before felt.

Drawing her around, one of his hands slid from her face to cup her head. When her fingers slid into his hair, he lowered his head and touched his lips to her brow. Her head shifted, fell back as she offered up her mouth.

With a groan, he gave her a kiss that lacked the

gentleness of their first. This time he needed passion, and she gave it to him, meeting his demands with those of her own.

Their mouths parted then came together, opening, inviting each other in. Each gave. Took. Drank and sighed. Reed's hands roamed over Mattie's back, down her sides. Her hands ran down his chest, splaying across that hard wall of muscle, trailing up to grip his shoulders and sliding back down the bulge of his arms.

She turned, twisting to her side. He pulled her close until they were chest to breast, her arms wrapped tight around his neck, him stroking her back, one hand trailing down over the curve of her buttocks, along the line of her thigh until cloth gave way to flesh.

Slowly, his fingers retraced their path, sliding along flesh. He felt the patches of her scarred flesh, felt her tremble when he ran the pads of his fingers gently over those places of injury, all the while keeping to his upward journey.

She sighed. He swallowed that sweet sound, then claimed her mouth. "Mattie. I *want* you," he said.

"You have me, Reed," she breathed back at him.

He left her mouth. His rougher cheek slid against her soft flesh as he used his mouth to follow the line of her jaw. Her head fell back, leaving her open and exposed. He couldn't resist tasting her, nuzzling her.

His tongue found her pulse. He licked. She shuddered as his mouth trailed down to the neckline of her dress.

She was soft. Smooth. Sweet. His hand found the curve of her bottom, then the slope of her spine, before the confines of her clothing stopped him. Reed groaned. He wanted no barriers. He needed all of her, as much as she'd give. "I want to see you, Mattie. *All* of you."

Mattie sat, swiveling around so she faced him, then rose to her knees. She untied the sash of her simple cotton dress and drew it over head.

Reed sucked in his breath. Firelight washed over her, giving her skin a rich warm glow. She showed no shyness as she bared herself to him. He reached out but didn't touch her. He was afraid to touch her, for fear that he'd never be able to live without her.

"Beautiful," he murmured, staring at the proud tilt to her breasts, the dark nipples that begged to be kissed and suckled.

Mattie reached out, found his hands and took them into her own. "Now see me again." She turned his hands and placed them on her waist.

Reed closed his eyes and closed his hands over her tiny waist. Then he let himself go. Slowly his hands traveled up. "Soft, like the feather of the owl." The tips of his fingers trailed over her navel. "Incredible," he said, feeling her breathing turn rapid. "Heaven." He felt each rib, each breath of air, each

231

shudder. "A true gift," he said, cupping her breasts, using his hands and fingers only to "see" her.

She moaned with each gentle tug, each tender squeeze, then protested when his hands went around to her back. Keeping his eyes closed, he whispered, "Feel what I can give you." He closed his mouth over one pert nipple.

Mattie cried out, her hands gripping his shoulders. "Let go, Mattie. Let go."

Trusting him, she let his shoulders go, let herself go limp. He opened his eyes, needing to see her with all that he was. She lay curved over his arm, her breasts begging for him to touch and taste, her head back, hair trailing on the ground.

His mouth went dry as it followed the firm line of her belly down over the dark patch of her womanhood. "Mattie!" he cried. Then once more his mouth closed over her—tasting, suckling, exploring. His fingers skimmed over her flesh, down the hard wall of her abdomen and into those tempting curls.

"Reed. . . ." Her voice trembled as he laved her moist center.

Gently, he laid her down. Sliding his hands over hers, he gripped her fingers between his and slid up over her. "Mattie, I have no right."

She opened her eyes and stared at him with complete trust. "You are the only one. What's mine is yours. I give myself to you."

Reed had never felt so humbled. Or so loved.

He sat up and took off his shirt. "Then take me as well. I am yours, Mattie. God knows I don't deserve you, but I'm too weak to say no." He took her hands and placed them on his chest, his own breath hitching as she ran her fingers over his male nipples and rubbed.

"Reed. It is the strength in you that allows you to say yes." Her fingers slid below his waist, over the material and down until she found the aching bulge that cried out for her touch.

"Then touch me, Mattie. All of me," he begged as he released his sex.

Mattie gasped slightly when she felt him spring out and into her hands. With both hands, she cupped him, felt his soft sac and hard length. Slowly she traced her fingers up to his tip.

"Soft," she said, rubbing her thumb over him. "Moist." One hand closed around him.

Reed jerked and fell on top of her. He found her mouth with his, and she opened her legs to him, cradling him against her moist heat. He moved against her. She ground her hips upward.

"Feels so good," she breathed into his mouth. Her hands strummed the nerves down his back, making him shiver with incredible need. He reached down between them, shifting so he could feel her. His fingers pressed lightly over her mound.

She lifted her hips, pressing herself against him. His finger slid down her moist folds and found her entrance; hot, wet and wanting. "Damn good," he agreed, lifting himself onto his elbows.

"Take me inside you, Mattie. Join with me. Share what I feel, need what I need."

Mattie stroked the lines around his mouth. "Come to me, Reed. Join with me, let me feel you, all of you. Share with me all I have to give." She let her legs fall open.

Reed positioned himself at her entrance. "Don't close your eyes, Mattie. I know you cannot see me, but I see so much in you."

She trembled beneath him. Her fingers fluttered over his mouth. "What do you see, Reed?"

Reed took her lips in a gentle kiss. "I see into your heart. I see my own heart reflected back. You are the light shining on my path, Mattie." Staring into her tearful gaze, he pushed slowly into her. He waited for the pain of breaking through her maidenhead to cloud her eyes but he saw only love—hers, which reflected his.

His heart swelled, his eyes misting. He felt her love as she gave herself to him, as she accepted him deeply inside her. His own love for her throbbed deep inside him. Merged with her, Reed rested his forehead on hers.

"Mattie, I think I love you. I know it's not the time for it or even this—"

Mattie lifted her legs and wrapped them instinctively around Reed's hips, causing him to groan as she pulled him even deeper. Her heat sheathed him, pulsed in time to his own throbs. He shifted, trying not to start a rhythm that once begun would shatter what control he retained.

She smiled. "I know you love me, as I love you. There is always time for love, for it is part of the circle of life. As is *this*."

She pulled away then eased back until he moved with her, slowly at first, each of them holding their breath as though afraid of shattering the other. His mouth mated with hers, his strokes grew longer, came faster and harder. Her breath became shallow gasps; his, hoarse groans. Her hands touched him, caressed him, learned the feel and shape of his tightly corded arms, the dance of muscles along his back, and even the tautness of his buttocks. Her fingers lingered there, squeezing the rounded flesh. Each time he thrust into her, she felt him tighten beneath her fingers.

She moaned when his hand slid back down between them, finding her center. He touched her, over and over, circling, his fingers matching the rhythm of his organ sliding in and out of her throbbing sheath.

Her hands fell to her side, her fingers digging into the grass as he drove her up toward some distant peak she had never known existed. Mattie watched the light grow brighter, felt her heart pounding, the ache in her swelling, building.

She called out, arched her body upward as

tremors began rocketing through her body. They started deep inside her and pushed relentlessly outward, zeroing in on the spot where she and Reed were joined, where his fingers stroked her.

Sure that she'd burst if he didn't stop, die if he did, her body suddenly convulsed.

"Yes, Mattie! Now. Let go. Let go, now," Reed begged, his voice low, hoarse.

Mattie did; and she found herself flying through heavens the color of Reed's eyes.

Later, Mattie lay curled next to Reed. They faced the fire. She felt the ebbing warmth but with him lying at her back, she was warm. She smiled. Her journey into womanhood had been all she'd believed, all she had hoped it would be.

Even the breaking of her maidenhead hadn't been as bad as she'd feared. The love in his touch, his voice, had numbed any pain with pleasure greater than anything she'd experienced.

Mating, she thought, was indeed as wondrous as her mother promised. Cocooned in warmth, she smiled with contentment. The time would come soon enough to pick up the threads of worry and fear. This time right now, she took and made hers. And Reed's. The past didn't belong here.

Nor did the future, for she couldn't bear to think of what tomorrow might bring. She hugged herself tightly. She'd either have her family or not, and she found that she just couldn't think what that might mean to her. At that moment, Mattie only knew she had Reed to help her through the darkness.

"What are you thinking?"

She started. "I thought you were asleep." She rolled over, forcing him back. In a smooth movement, Reed adjusted the blanket over them, drawing her head down onto his chest as though he couldn't bear to let her go.

"Was. For a brief while. Then I had this incredible dream and had to wake up to be sure it was real."

Smiling, Mattie stroked her fingers over his chest. "Was it? Real?"

She felt Reed's answering grin as he ran his hand down the back of her head. "Oh, yeah. Very real. Incredibly real." His voice dropped. "Still don't believe that you're here, in my arms."

"I too feel this way." She sighed. She wanted it to last, forever. She wanted what they shared, what they had between them to hold and keep all the bad at bay. But she knew that as soon as the night passed into day, this would fade, become a shared dream. Reed wouldn't stay. Somehow, she knew in her heart he couldn't.

"I wish . . ." She broke off.

"Wish what, Mattie?" Reed's voice sounded as wistful as the cry in her heart for him to never leave.

"You know what I wish. Our hearts are joined. You see into mine."

This time he sighed, long and heavy. "I can't stay. I have to return."

"She's gone," Mattie whispered. Though she had no wish to hold him to her with guilt.

"She lives in my son and daughter. For them I have to go back."

"You have children?" Mattie sat up. Reed reached over and fingered a long strand of her hair.

"Two. A boy and girl. Daniel is nearly four. He's about the same age as Caitie. He has Anne's blond hair and her blue eyes." His voice drifted off. "And her laughter."

"And the other?" Reed had gone silent.

"Elizabeth. My Lizzie girl. She was only a year when her mother died. She won't know who I am anymore."

Mattie had a vision of dark curls and bright blue eyes. A solemn child. Stretching back out beside Reed, needing to touch him, to be with him, she drew the blanket back over them. "She takes after her father."

Reed tugged her back against him. "Yeah. She does." Pride rang in his voice before it turned sad. "She won't remember me."

Mattie splayed her hand over his heart. "She'll know you *here*."

"God, Mattie, I can't live without them."

"You won't. You'll go back to them."

"But how can I leave you?"

Tears fell from Mattie's eyes. She understood now. "You'll leave because you must."

"Mattie, I don't know if I can return. I can't leave my children without a father, but neither can I take them away from their grandparents. Danny and Lizzie are all that is left of Anne. I don't have the right to take them."

Mattie didn't know what the future held. For now, they had each other. "Then hold me for as long as you can and think of tonight."

The moon was high, the stars bright when Kealan woke with a start. He jumped to his feet. He hadn't meant to fall asleep, just to rest. His horse, he reminded himself; it was the horse that needed to rest. He could have ridden all night. Never mind the fact that he'd fallen asleep on Rider's back more than twice.

Sitting back down on the grassy bank, he stared out at the shimmering water. He wanted the sun to hurry and return so he could get home. To Mattie. His sister would know what to do. She and that man, Mister Reed, they'd find Matt and Renny. Then Daire and Caitie.

Kealan tried not to remember all the blood, but he knew Matt was hurt bad. And Renny too. He stood again. Maybe Rider was rested. Maybe they could go. But it was so dark. A distance chorus of wolf howls also reminded him that there were animals out there.

"I have my rifle," he said, reaching over to be sure it was still nearby. He might be small, but he could shoot. Even if it wasn't as big a shotgun as what Daire had. Or Matt.

Grabbing his blanket, he wrapped it around himself, wishing there was something he could do. On and off, he dozed, determined to remain awake and on guard, but the needs of a young boy won out.

The next time he woke, it was still night but not so dark. The stars were fading from the sky as a grayness chased away the black. A dark shadow flew over him.

Kealan pushed himself up and stood. It was just an owl. The bird flew over his head, circling. Excitement sang through him. His brother and sister were always telling tales of how animals and birds knew things and tried to tell the humans, but most people didn't understand.

Matthew and Mattie did. Owl was his sister's helpmate. She wore his feathers and a claw in her medicine pouch. Putting his hands on his hips, he called out, "Owl!"

To his surprise, the bird swished lower. Kealan tipped his head back, felt the push of air from the wings. Something soft drifted down.

"A feather!" He ran to catch it. Staring at it, he saw the bird flying away.

"Thank you, Owl," he cried out.

He ran a finger over the long feather. Now what should he do? What would Matt or Mattie do? He'd thanked the bird. He frowned, then grinned.

They'd try to find out what message there was for him.

He turned in a circle and stared at the feather. It was a long feather. The feather Mattie carried in her medicine pouch was small. He'd seen her pick one up and tuck it inside. He also knew she had the talon of an owl.

Kealan grinned. The owl was his sister's totem, and the owl had come to him. "Mattie is coming!" His voice shouted the words. His sister knew things. Saw things no one else could see. He forgot what they all called it. He just remembered how neat it sounded to be able to see things that no one else could—except when she really did know when he'd broken the rules, without Caitie or Daire tattling even.

Matt and Renny and even Daire were always telling him to be good when they went out because Mattie would know.

He grinned. Sometimes, she didn't know. Sometimes, he just couldn't help doing something he oughtn't. Like teasing Caitie. Or like sneaking off to practice shooting his bow and arrow.

He touched his owl feather carefully. Maybe it was Owl who saw things and told Mattie. Maybe Owl had told her about Matthew and Renny. And him. He glanced up into the sky.

He hoped Owl had told her how brave he'd been. He hadn't cried at all! His lips turned downward. Well, maybe just once. Or twice.

But he didn't care, as long as she was coming.

He grabbed the sack of food, the blanket and the water skin that he'd managed to unload from Rider, and stuffed it all back in his saddle bag. Then he mounted, using a fallen stump to regain the back of the animal.

"Come on, Rider. Let's go. We gotta go find Mattie!" He clutched his feather in his hand as he directed the horse to head toward home.

Chapter Fifteen

Riding along the James once more with Mattie at his side, Reed took the time to notice his surroundings. The land was all shades of green—pale bushes, bright, rich grass and deeper hues among the trees. Earlier, he'd made a stab at describing what he saw to Mattie.

She'd opened his eyes to so much, he wanted to do the same for her. Of course, it helped that she asked very specific questions instead of leaving him floundering for the words.

Still, he thought, he could grow used to this. All of it: her, the untamed land, her family and the wondrous feeling of renewal taking place deep inside him.

He glanced at Mattie. Last night had been incredible. She'd given him so much. Hope, love and joy now filled him so deeply, so fully, that he thought for sure he'd burst. It was almost more than a man could bear.

She'd given herself to him last night with no hesitation, no doubts. She'd accepted all that he was, and made him see that without being the boy he'd been, the young man he'd been a year ago, he would not be the man he was today.

Thinking back on his childhood, his youth and even only a few years past, he saw what Mattie saw: his will to survive. But, would he survive the day he had to leave her? Could he live without Mattie?

That worried him. He didn't think he could. She was the air he breathed, the music in his ears and the most beautiful sight he'd beheld. He watched her as she rode. Sometimes he felt guilty for staring at her so much, but he couldn't help it.

The proud tilt of her chin, the gentle slope of her nose, the soft fullness of her mouth made him feel like a smitten boy in love for the first time. But when he looked in her eyes, he saw so much more.

He saw wisdom that made him want to beg her to teach him all she knew. He saw kindness, tenderness and the love that had freed his heart and put light back into his soul. There was also sadness, fear and worry. Those he would take from her if he could, and replace them with the light of laughter.

How could he walk away from all that this woman was? Yet when the time came, he would return to his children. He *had* to.

"Come with me," he said suddenly.

244

Mattie turned her head. "Where?"

He hesitated. "Never mind." He couldn't tell her where he meant. He could name a town, a city, a bunch of places; but he had no idea where he'd end up. All he knew was that he had to return home to his children. Then what?

He had no job. No money. No place of his own to call home. In short, there was nothing he could offer.

Except his love.

He firmed his lips. Love wouldn't feed her, clothe her or provide her with a place to call home.

"You know I would." Her voice was soft, compelling.

"I know. And that's why I can't ask." But he stared at her hungrily.

She smiled. "You already did. Before you leave, you'll have my answer."

"I can't ask you to leave your family. The youngsters need you as much as I need Danny and Lizzie."

"And as much as they need their father," she added.

"I'd like to believe that to be true." He worried about how they'd react when he went back to see them and claim them. Would they hate him for inadvertently killing their mother? Would their grandfather and grandmother fight him? Reed knew he wouldn't take the children from them if they did, but he would insist on seeing them, and on being a part of their lives.

He glanced at Mattie. She had her eyes closed, a

dreamy expression on her face. He reached over and touched her shoulder lightly. She turned her head and smiled.

"Tomorrow will take care of itself," she said. She didn't know how she fit into the future, but she knew Reed would be with his children. As it should be. She was determined that it would be so. A faint sound came floating on the breeze. The call of a bird. She frowned. *No.*

She whipped her head around. "Kealan," she whispered.

Reed stopped their horses, his hands over hers on her reins. "Where?"

"I hear him," she said.

"There. I see him. He'd riding toward us." Reed took off. Raven followed.

Mattie gripped her horse's dark mane. Her heart pounded. "The others. Where are they?"

"Don't know," Reed shouted back.

Minutes later, Reed brought them to a halt. Mattie slid down, then used her horse to steady herself. "Kealan! Reed, is he alright?" Where was he? "Kealan!"

She stepped away from Raven, placed each foot hesitantly, held her arms out before her like a toddler just learning to walk. Like she'd done when first blinded.

"Got him, Mattie."

Reed was beside her, his arm around her as her brother rushed into her outstretched arms.

"Kealan!" she cried, running her hands over his face, down his shoulders. Relief poured through her. He was here. Safe. Unharmed. She cried and hugged him tight. Even when he pulled back, she couldn't let go. He was here. With her. She ran a hand back over his face.

"I'm fine, Mattie," he said, breathless. He took her hand with his. "I knew you were coming. Owl told me so. Feel this."

For the second time in as many days, she felt a feather thrust into her hand. "Owl came to me. Like he comes to you. He gave me a feather."

Mattie couldn't help but smile at the pride in the boy's voice. "That's wonderful, Kea." She released him from her arms but kept hold of his hand. "The others, where are they?"

Kealan tightened his hold on her hand and started walking. "Have to come fast, Mattie. Matt and Renny are hurt. Bad."

Mattie's heart stopped. "How bad, Kealan?" *Please, don't let us be too late*, she begged the spirits. In her heart and mind, she both thanked the spirits for Kealan's safe return and asked them to look after the rest of her family.

"They were both bleeding. Matt woke up. He talked to me. Made me leave to get help. Said I was big enough to do it."

Her heart pounded. "And so you were," Mattie said, stroking her hand through his hair, striving to remain calm for all of them.

"What about Renny?"

"She . . . she wouldn't wake up." Kealan's voice broke.

"They are where the river splits?" Mattie had to fight to keep the terror from her voice.

"Yep." He threw himself back into her arms. "I knew you'd know. Did you know I was coming like I knew you were coming?"

Mattie saw he needed comfort and took a moment to give it to him. She was tempted to lie to him but didn't. "No, I only knew that something bad had happened. I'm glad Matt and Renny had you, Kealan."

She was afraid to ask about the rest, but did so. "What about Daire and Caitie?"

She felt his forehead furrow. "Some bad men took them."

Mattie felt sick. Her legs gave out and she sat heavily, pulling Kealan into her arms. She needed him as much as he needed her.

Reed hunched down beside her. "Easy, Mattie. We'll find them. Remember my dream. Kealan was very brave. You have to stay strong as well." He slid his hand across her back as he addressed Kealan. "Did you pay attention to where they went?"

At the firm, no-nonsense, authoritative tone, Kealan stood. "Yeah. Back there." He pointed the way toward home. "I waited until they got past where I was hiding, then I left Rider tied and hidden in the bushes. I ran really fast to find Matt and Renny, but I made sure no one saw me."

"Very clever," Reed said. "Now, we need you to lead us back to Renny and Matthew. Can you do that?"

"Of course I can," Kealan said. "I might be a *hokshila*, but I am a brave *hokshila*. That means 'boy' in our tongue," he told Reed. "I was smart and cunning. Just like Matthew said I was. Today I am *Matohoksila*. Bear Boy."

Mattie was grateful for Reed. She was so overwhelmed by emotion, she felt sick and dizzy. The calmness in his voice and the strength in his touch kept her from breaking down.

She mounted her horse. When she asked Kealan if he wanted to ride with her, he agreed. Both brother and sister needed the comfort of the other.

"Why are you stopping?" Breathing heavily, Matthew leaned heavily on the branch Renny had managed to find for him to use as a crutch.

The last thing Renny wanted to do was stop. She was too worried about Daire and Caitie. Where were they? Were they alive? Her mind was tortured both by fear and pain. She rubbed her head. But, "You need to rest," she said, dropping the supplies and rifle she carried.

Matthew glared at her.

"All right, we both need to rest."

She dropped down and put her head in her hands. Her head felt like it was going to explode. She carefully touched the back of her skull. It was still bleeding, but not as badly. Whoever had bashed her had done a good job. She tried to swallow her moan of pain. A hiss escaped.

She supposed she was lucky. Matthew had found her in the bushes where she'd fallen off her horse. Her head had hurt so bad, it had been all she could do to tend Matt's wound.

Her brother put his arm around her. "At the rate we're going, it's going to take us weeks to go home."

Renny didn't care at the moment. Her head ached fiercely, her vision blurred and she still felt sick to her stomach. Traveling yesterday or the day of the ambush had been impossible. Today she was determined to start on their trip back. Maybe.

The grass felt cool against her neck, the breeze soothing and the sun warm and comforting. Maybe they'd just stay right where they were. The deep sighs coming from Matthew told her he was in as bad a shape as she.

His wound was nasty, but the bullet had passed through the flesh, leaving a torn and gaping hole that she'd mustered up the courage and stamina to stitch and pack with herbs.

"You better not pull any of my stitches out," she

grumbled. "You know how much I hate to sew. I'm gonna be pissed if I have to do it again."

"I'm going to have a scar the size of a dinner plate," Matthew replied.

Renny grinned. She couldn't stand to sew clothing and such, but when it came to stitching up her brothers, she wielded a needle like a pro. "Better be nice to me. I might not be so gentle next time."

"Gentle, hah! I felt like you were using your knife to sew me. You probably made it worse."

They both laughed. Renny moaned as the movement sent pain radiating through her head. "Come on. Let's get going."

She rolled over and got slowly to her feet, trying to minimize her dizziness and nausea, then helped Matt get steady on his feet and pulled his arm over her shoulder. "Come on. If they find us only this far, we'll never live it down."

Renny kept a sharp lookout for Kealan as they went. She'd been horrified to find that Matt had sent him off on his own. But he'd had a point when he'd said he hadn't known if Renny was dead or alive, or whether the men who'd attacked would be back. He'd wanted his small brother out of danger.

"Kea's fine. He'll make it."

It didn't surprise Renny that Matt knew what she was looking for. He read them all well. "I hope so, Matt."

"And Mattie will know what to do. She'll likely see him coming."

Nodding, Renny agreed. Mattie's visions were powerful, and they had returned. She'd know something was wrong and come after them. Unless the Troll stopped her. She grimaced. He always thought he knew best for them. She kicked a rock. He made her so mad sometimes, but never as furious as when he'd tried to take their three young siblings away.

Yet look where fighting to keep together had gotten them. The O'Briens were scattered. She and Matt were hurt, both lucky to be alive. Kea, she could only hope was okay. Caitie and Daire were gone.

Renny had to believe they were alive. She couldn't bear anything else. Which left Mattie. Who also had to be all right. And on her way, for Renny didn't think she could make it much farther.

In fact, she didn't think she'd make it another step. But she had to. Matthew wasn't complaining, though she'd noticed him slowing. His breathing was harsher.

They were in truly bad shape. Renny stared out into the distance. The river and grass and sky seemed to stretch forever. One more step. Two. Make it to that tree. Those rocks. Renny pushed herself by giving herself small goals.

Her head pounding, her vision blurring, she tried to pick out the next easy goal. Her eyes widened. She rubbed them, then her head, and blinked. "Matt?"

They both stopped. "I see them," he said, his voice weak with exhaustion.

"They really are coming for us! I could jump for joy."

"Yeah, okay. Do it," he teased.

She grinned. "Later." Much later. Maybe in a week. She winced. Or two. She gave in to her need and sat.

"Renny, what are you doing?" Matthew had started forward, one painful step at a time.

She laughed softly. It turned to a groan. "I'm waiting. Right here. I'm going to let them come to me. You want to be brave, go for it."

"I'll save the brave for another time. I'm with you on this one." He lowered himself to the ground. Both brother and sister kept their gazes on the riders coming toward them, as if afraid their rescuers would veer off the trail and leave them behind.

Reed watched from his saddle as the O'Brien sisters and brothers hugged each other. He slowly dismounted and stood off to the side. He didn't want to intrude, but inside, he was as excited and relieved as they.

He shared a connection with them through not just Mattie, but his own feelings of coming home. The O'Briens had started out being strangers, then a job. Now they were much more.

He glanced at Mattie. Especially Mattie. *He loved her.* Awe filled him. Even saying the words in his head gave him a thrill. Reed hadn't planned on falling in love again. Truth was, he hadn't thought it possible. Anne had been his life.

One I threw away.

For whatever reason, he had a second chance. Not just with love, but with everything. His gaze settled on Kealan. Already he felt like he belonged to this close, loving family.

Worry churned deep inside him as he thought of Caitie and Daire. He vowed to find the other two.

Mattie turned her head. He knew she was searching for him with her mind. He smiled and walked toward her. When she held out her hand to him, his breath caught in his lungs. He reached out, placed his hand in hers and allowed her to pull him deeper into the circle of love.

Where were they?

Sheriff Tyler paced, wondering. He'd come as promised the day before, but neither Mattie nor Reed had been there. He'd waited until nearly nightfall before returning to town. He'd returned early this morning, going immediately into the barn. Raven was still missing. She wasn't in the corral or the pasture.

Though he knew no one would be home, he went to the door of the cabin. He entered. Maybe he'd missed something.

A note.

On the table.

He frowned as he removed his hat. Now how had

he missed that yesterday? Picking up the note, he unfolded it.

Got the brats. If you want to see them
alive again, it will cost you two thousand
dollars. Each.

Tyler sat heavily as he read the note. *Dear Lord,* he thought, staring at the heavy, scrawled print. What was going on? None of this made sense. The O'Brien kids had no enemies; they were well liked by all. Even the fights and pranks the boys pulled were tolerated, for all children were prone to such. Even Renny's bad temper—

Tyler jumped up.

Renny!

If the youngsters had been kidnapped, then something must have happened to her and Matthew! His heart pounded. Chills ran down his spine at the thought of anything happening to Renny. The woman was a damn stubborn mule, a sharp thorn in his side, but hell, their butting of heads livened up the dull days and eased the loneliness of having lost his brother.

Hearing the sound of a horse outside, Tyler shoved the door open. Instead of Mattie and Reed, he spotted Paddy dismounting.

"Sheriff." Patrick mounted the steps.

"Hello, Paddy." Tyler moved aside to allow the older man to enter.

Paddy removed his hat and glanced around. "How's Mattie? Came to check on her, see how she's holding up."

"Mattie's not here. Neither is Reed." He returned to the table. And the note.

Paddy sent Tyler a sharp look. "What's going on? You said we could trust the stranger to look after her."

At Paddy's accusing tone, Tyler sent the man a sharp glare. "Wouldn't have agreed to it if I'd believed otherwise." Though he believed what he said, his confidence in Reed didn't tell him where the man was or where he'd taken Mattie.

He handed Paddy the note. "Found this. Wasn't there yesterday. Bet my life on it."

Paddy read the note and whistled. "Two thousand each! Them kids don't got that kind of money. Hell, I bet Henley's the only one with four thousand to his name. He's the richest man around. Why not kidnap *his* children?"

"Don't know, Paddy." Tyler was worried. "I think we should ride out and find them. If they ran into trouble, they can't be more than two days' ride."

"I'll get Gil." Paddy turned to leave.

Tyler reached out and gripped the older man's shoulder. "No. Leave the boy here. I don't want your wife or daughter left alone. Not until we find out what's going on. We'll ride over and let them know where we're going." With that, Tyler strode out the door and down the steps.

In less than an hour, he and Paddy were riding away from the two homesteads. Worry for the O'Brien family slammed against his ribs with each breath he took. Especially for one hot-headed, hot-tempered, sharp-tongued woman who had somehow latched onto his heart like a tick to a bull.

Chapter Sixteen

Tyler and Patrick came upon Reed and Mattie and Kealan less than a day from the two homesteads. Mattie still felt the quiver of relief at their arrival, for it meant that they'd been able to get both Renny and Matthew home faster, and start the search for Caitie and Daire that much sooner.

Restless and sick with worry, Mattie paced. Paddy had gone into town to gather men to help search for Caitie and Daire, and Reed had ridden out to look around on his own. Tyler had elected to remain at the homestead, determined not to leave any of them unprotected. Mattie appreciated his concern and help. She made her way silently to the alcove where Renny and Matthew were sleeping.

Sitting beside Renny on the bed, she wished she could see them and know for sure they were all right. Reaching out, she found a tin cup sitting on the table by the bed.

"Have more tea, Renny," she begged.

"No more, Mattie. I just want to sleep."

"Just another sip. A small one."

Pleased when she heard her sister obey, she left the bed, felt her way around and sat carefully next to her brother. "Matt? Are you awake?" She rested a hand on his chest. His breathing felt slow and even. She breathed a sigh of relief.

The last two days, ever since finding them, she'd cursed her blindness more than once. She hadn't been able to see for herself the extent of their wounds, or to tend them. She had to accept what others told her.

She hated it. She'd come so close to losing Matthew and Renny, and she wouldn't rest easy until they were both up and doing as normal. The fact that they were both in bed worried her. A lot.

All she could do for the moment was take care of them as best as she could. Whether they liked it or not. She smoothed the covers over her brother's sleeping form.

"He's awake. He's faking," Renny grumbled.

"Matt?" She shook him. "You better not be!"

Matthew groaned, proving he was. "Mattie, we're fine. Go away!"

Mattie sat up, uncertain. He sounded so unlike himself. Matthew never snapped. She started to leave.

He snagged her hand. "Stay. We're worried. And we're mad that we're stuck here when we should be out looking for Caitie and Daire with everyone else."

Mattie settled on the bed. "You feel as helpless as I do," she said softly.

"Yeah."

Renny struggled to sit; Mattie felt the mattress shifting. "Renny, you are *not* getting up."

"I can't just lie here all day," she groaned.

"You can and you will." The deep voice had all three O'Briens glancing toward Tyler. "You so much as step one toe out of that bed and I'll truss you up like a pig."

"You can't tell me what to do, Troll," Renny bit out.

"I can and did." His heavy boots stalked away from them.

"I think he means it, Renny," Mattie said.

"Let him try," Renny muttered. But she lay back down. "As soon as he's gone, I'm up and out of here."

Mattie smiled. Truth was, Renny would fall flat on her face if she tried to get up, and she knew it.

A soft snore made her smile. It didn't come from either Renny or Matt. Kealan was asleep in the middle of the bed, sandwiched between his older siblings. Their reunion had been full of tears and praise, but even a boy who felt like a man had to give in to his young body's demands. Kealan had fallen asleep almost immediately.

"How's your leg?" Mattie asked Matt.

"Fine."

She lifted a brow.

"Warriors don't admit to hurting. But if it makes you happier, it hurts like hell, okay."

"You were lucky. The bullet passed through." And the herbs Renny had put on the wound would take care of the rest. Luckily, there was no sign of infection.

"What are we going to do if they can't find Daire and Caitie?" Renny asked softly.

"They'll find them. They have to." Mattie couldn't believe otherwise. She *wouldn't*. After all, she'd feared once that they'd all been lost to her, and that had done no one any good. She stood and went to the window. Paddy had removed the canvas. The breeze coming into the room felt good. Fresh. Healing.

"We have to get the money, Mattie. That will take time."

Mattie nodded. "We have some here, but not nearly enough." Her father had been a wealthy man. Few knew that he had enough to buy a house wherever he wanted, but the family had chosen to live simply. She smiled sadly.

Grady O'Brien had planned to build them a grand house after a few years, but she and the others had loved this small home that had been, and still was, a place filled with love.

She thought of Reed and imagined them together. Here, or in their own house. They'd have his children, her brothers and sisters, and maybe babies of their own. *Babies with dark hair and blue eyes,* she thought as she lay down at the foot of the bed.

Drowsy, she allowed herself to dream.

It was a clear day. A good day to get married. There wasn't a cloud in the sky. She glanced up at her groom— Reed. He was there, smiling down at her. The minister stood in front of them. They were in the church, surrounded by their family.

Without warning, the door crashed open. "Stop this wedding. Stop it, I say!"

Mattie turned to see Katherine O'Leary stalking up the aisle. "You won't marry my son. I will not have it!"

Confused, Mattie turned to Reed. Then she screamed. It was Gil staring down at her. She turned back to her mother-in-law, but couldn't see her. Smoke filled the church.

A wall of flame rose in front of her. She heard the crackle of fire. It sounded as though it were laughing at her.

"Gil," *she cried, grabbing his arm. He didn't move. She glanced up. This time, it was Collin she saw. He fell back, into the flames. His mother shrieked and ran toward them.*

"It's your fault. All your fault. He shouldn't have died!"

The words faded as a wall of flame lifted Mattie high into the air. No, it was wings—soft wings, carrying her away from the heat and hate.

She clung to the giant bird as they soared. The owl

turned his head. Mattie saw blue eyes. Brilliant blue eyes.
Reed had saved her, and he was taking her away.

They soared across the land, dipped down into valleys
and rose high over the bluffs. The feeling was incredible.
She felt free.

"Mattie."

"I love you," she whispered.

"I love you too," a voice whispered in her ear. "But
perhaps this isn't the time to be telling everyone
that." Reed's hands were gentle on her shoulders as
he helped her sit up. "Come on. Renny and Matt are
sleeping."

Mattie realized then she'd fallen asleep. She heard
the low murmur of whispers and realized everyone
was back from searching.

She let Reed scoop her up off the bed. He set her
down in a chair. "Did you find them?"

"No." He sounded weary.

Mattie, knowing they weren't alone, resisted the
temptation to reach out and touch him. "What
now?"

"We wait until day and start searching again,"
Tyler said. "Paddy and Gil went home. They'll be
back at first light."

"Tyler, we have the money. We'll pay." To her
mind, four thousand dollars was a small price to pay
for the safe return of her brother and sister.

A scrape of feet on the floor had her turning.
"Why didn't they just ask for money before? Why all

the pranks? That shot taken at Mattie . . . ? And why
didn't they grab the kids at the picnic? Anytime.
Why wait?"

"Renny, what are you doing up?"

· "I've slept enough."

"You sound terrible," Mattie said.

"Looks it, too," Tyler added.

"Thanks, Troll."

"One day, Renny. One day . . ."

"Promises, promises."

Mattie smiled. Renny was obviously fine. She was
going to be okay. Her first fear had been that the
blow to her sister's head would leave her blind. It
looked like that worry was unfounded.

"If you're going to talk all night, then at least put
some coffee on." Matt's voice was coming from
closer. Mattie heard his crutch hit the floor as he
slowly made his way to the table.

"Matthew, you shouldn't be walking on that leg."
She felt him lower himself into the chair beside her.

"Don't fuss." He tempered the words with a fond
ruffling of her hair, then he pulled her to him and
hugged her close. "This involves us all."

Mattie was too happy to have him and Renny alive
to argue. She smiled. "Come on in, Kea. You might
as well join us."

Kea ran over. "How did you know I was awake,
Mattie? Did you see me?"

She laughed and pulled him onto her lap. "No. I

265

just happen to know my brothers and sisters very well." She felt the brush of his owl feather. He hadn't let go of it since they'd found him.

Listening to the others talk and argue, Mattie closed her eyes and sought Reed.

He was there. Across from her. As before, the blue of his eyes chased away the darkness, and his warmth beckoned. She felt herself drifting toward him. The closer she got, the clearer he became.

He had a face, a shape. Before, she'd had only the impression of the man behind the blinding blue blaze. She hadn't minded not seeing him because she found such comfort and beauty in the blue that she now knew was part of Reed. His eyes were the shade she saw, but the blue meant so much more.

The home of many spirits was in the heavens. Just as Reed's heart and soul were home to her. Her people passed on to the spirit world through the sky. She would move from her world of darkness into his world of light. He was her heaven. She smiled against Kealan's head.

The fact that she could now see the man behind the blueness also meant he was seeing—*truly* seeing. And now, in turn, she could see him.

Oh, it was her own conjured image based on what she thought he looked like, but didn't we all see what we wanted to see, not what was there? She saw Reed not with her eyes but with her hands and heart. She knew the feel of him, every line, every scar, each feature intimately. His scent was locked into her mind as well. The sweat of him, the freshness after he'd bathed, and even the heat that engulfed her when they'd made love.

Thinking of that wonderful night, Mattie sighed. Yes, she knew Reed. The man in her vision was the man who'd claimed her heart and shared her soul.

Chapter Seventeen

The new day dawned gray and overcast. Reed cast an anxious eye to the sky. Rain, he thought, grabbing his coat. He strode out of the barn, leading his horse to the yard. Noise filled the morning as men and horses arrived. Some talked. Some stood, their features tight and grim.

The town had come to Mattie's aid with a vengeance. Even the women were here, cooking, serving coffee and helping her through the wait and worry.

Renny walked out of the house. Reed saw the sheriff cut her off. "You're not going, Renny."

"You can't stop me, Sheriff."

"Someone needs to stay here, in case your brother and sister are found."

Renny waved at the people. "I think there's plenty of people here, Sheriff." She winced. "Besides, I don't think I can take any more of Mattie's fussing. I'm fine, and it's my family we're searching for."

Reed stepped in. "You can ride with us. You know your land better than anyone, and that's what we're searching. Paddy will lead a second group over his land. The rest of the searchers will spread out."

The town had already been searched, but there were a lot of places to conceal two children, dead or alive. Reed's plan was to start here and work north, the idea being that whoever took the kids had arrived back here to leave a ransom note. Unless there was more than one kidnapper.

Even then, they would have to be close enough to communicate. He went group to group with Tyler, making suggestions, noting the areas covered and those not.

Tyler whistled and drew everyone's attention. "We meet back here at dark. If they are found, send the signal: two shots followed by three." The groups of men, boys and even some women mounted up.

It was the largest search party Reed had ever seen. He figured most of the town turned out.

Mounted, Reed looked toward the house where Mattie stood on the porch. He didn't ride over to her and pull her into his arms as he longed. Until she broke off the wedding to Gil, they would keep their feelings to themselves.

He frowned. At least, he assumed she was going to break it off. After all, they'd talked about her coming with him or him staying. He wouldn't worry about that for the moment.

As though she saw him, she started down the steps. At the bottom, he saw her put her fingers to her mouth. He groaned as the shrill sound stopped every man in his tracks and startled a good number of animals. He glanced toward the corral.

Raven was taking a flying leap. People and horses parted. Beside him, Tyler stared in disbelief. "She's not!"

Reed grinned. "She is." He rode toward her.

Mattie felt him. Among all the people, she felt Reed. When his strong hands closed over hers, she turned her face toward him. "I'm going," she said softly.

"You need a saddle. Wait here," he said.

Mattie smiled as he led Raven from her without arguing. Behind her, women entered and exited her small house. Food cooked, women chattered and children played quietly.

When Reed returned, she let him lift her onto Raven. "Come on, before they leave without us," he said.

Pleased, Mattie held the reins loosely. After the last couple of days' riding, Raven would automatically follow Reed's horse. Surrounded by the people she loved and knew well, they rode from the yard.

Mattie felt better at taking part in the search. The last thing she'd wanted to do was be stuck in her own home where she couldn't move. Nor did she want the looks she knew would be thrown her way or the soft whispers as everyone talked about the kidnapping.

No, this was her place, where she belonged. Sighted or not.

"Hey, wait for us," Kealan called out.

Mattie grinned when she heard him ride up beside her. The length of leg that brushed against her told her Matthew was there, too. She called out, "Got your feather, Kea?"

She wasn't the least bit surprised that both brothers were here. After all, they were family, and they were all in this together.

"Yep. In my medicine bag. Matthew gave me his, too, so I have lots of good medicine now."

"Bye, Mattie." They rode off to join a different search party.

Reed dropped back to ride at her side. "Some family you've got, Mrs. O'Leary."

"Yes. It's a wonderful family." She turned her gaze to him. "Some family *we* are going to have someday, Reed." She added *Robertson* silently. He'd told her that until he cleared his father's name, and his own, he would not use the name he'd once cherished. He refused to bring further dishonor to the name of a man he loved, but had been too stubborn to say the words that might have prevented a lot of heartache.

Reed listened as Renny made suggestions as to

where their group should search. They split into twos and threes, then arranged a time and place to meet when they were all done.

Staring around him, Reed knew it would be a daunting task.

Riding away from the O'Briens' cabin, Mac was worried. Things were not going as planned. He glanced at the men around him, at the men spreading out over the land like ants leaving their nest.

Damn. What was he going to do? He didn't dare ride over to where the kids were hidden. It was too risky. Yet if he left the kids where they were stashed, he'd lose all his chance of getting the O'Briens off the land. He frowned. Right now, he needed his young hostages alive. If anything happened to them, the rest wouldn't have any reason to vacate the land. But if the kids were returned as he intended, the O'Briens would leave; they'd move to town where it safer.

No, he didn't need or want the ransom money. There was far more than that hidden. He just needed time to find it. Time, and no one around to catch him searching.

He'd been assigned to check the eastern border for the kids, where a long narrow ridge rose high above the prairie. It would take a bit of time to reach it, search the base, then climb up. Even going around it would take a bit of time, but when they did, his party would find Leo, Daire and Caitie.

Glancing north, he saw other riders approaching the same ridge. It looked like the sheriff and Reed were concentrating there.

He tightened his lips. After all this hubbub over the kidnapping was over, he was going to have to lay low for a while. The money would have to wait.

Which left Leo to deal with. He whistled to the men around him, indicating that he planned to hit the area at the south end of the bluff where the property narrowed. Two young men rode over to him. "Going to go around from here," he told them.

"We'll go with you."

"No. Start here, work your way south. Search every bush and outcropping of rock. When you reach the end of the ridge, head for the river, follow it to the mill, then search the other side back up to here."

The boys nodded and hurried off, keeping them away and giving him time to do what he needed to do. A plan was forming in his mind. There might be a way to come out of this with none the wiser.

Riding hard, Mac followed the bluff, keeping an eye out to be sure no one was around. He reached the other side then stopped. From one of his saddle bags, he pulled out his wig and beard and old hat and scarf and put them on.

He smiled as he stared at the saddlebags. They were old, as he'd borrowed one of the O'Brien horses. There was nothing on this horse that would tie it to him.

Keeping his pace even, he approached the boulders where the kids were hidden. He spotted Leo sitting on a fallen tree, out in the open. As soon as the bank robber spotted him, he jumped to his feet. Once more, they were each pointing a gun at the other.

"Got the money?" Leo asked, spreading his feet wide.

"It's not going to work," Mac said. "They're searching right now. On the other side of the bluff. They'll find us."

"Then we take the brats elsewhere," Leo said.

"Can't. They got most of the town out searching. We're going to have to back off and wait. They'll give up the land now. If they get them kids back safe."

Leo spat on the ground. "I ain't gonna wait. I want my money now."

"Listen, you fool, we can't get it until the kids are gone! If we try to dig and find the money before, it'll raise questions. If someone sees us, or finds the spots we've dug . . . I already tried. The kids buried their parents in that area. Renny goes there almost every day."

"Then I say we kill them. *All* of them." He moved toward the rocky prison where Daire stood holding Caitie.

"If what he says is true, if they are searching, they'll hear your shots," the O'Brien boy said. He set Caitie down and shoved her behind him. The girl clutched his leg.

Mac met the boy's eyes. They were wide, scared, but he put on a brave front. Like Laura. She'd had blue eyes too, and soft brown hair. She'd been afraid. So afraid and in pain. But she'd never cried. Never whined. She'd been brave all right during her illness, during his own moments of despair and even in death; she'd met the end without a tear or complaint. She'd simply said she loved him and asked him not to forget her.

Mac's eyes blurred. He'd never forgotten her. Or the fact that her death could have been avoided if only he'd had money to take her to the best doctors, the best hospitals for treatment.

Instead, she'd died in the flea-bitten tenement building where they'd lived.

Leo's bark of laughter broke the spell of the boy's eyes.

"Then let 'em come. We'll be long gone by then," he sneered. He pulled out a small revolver, cocked it and pointed it at Daire.

Reed rode toward the bluffs with the rest of Mattie's family. The other searchers were already spreading out along the base. He led the group to the north end.

Kealan spoke up. "Reed, I know the way up," he said. "I go up there all the time. It's my thinkin' place. I could go up there to look around."

Matthew smacked him in the head. "You aren't allowed up there without us, brat."

Reed grinned. He liked the boy's spunk.

"Can I go?" the kid repeated.

"No!" The answer came from all the adults.

Kealan sulked.

Reed felt a growing love for the boy, and he hoped that his own son would be so quick to love and accept him back into his life. "We all stay together," he said, to soften the blow to the boy's pride.

"Yeah." Kea glanced around, as though making sure no one had sneaked off without him.

The boy chattered away while they searched. Reed suspected that Kealan truly could not understand the dire circumstances his siblings were in; he had childish faith in those he loved. He could accept no other outcome than their finding Daire and Caitie, and that everything would be right with his world again.

Reed wasn't so sure. From the grim set on the faces around him, he knew the others also feared the worst.

"What are we going to do if we don't find them?" Mattie asked. She was riding beside Reed.

"We pay what they want," Renny said fiercely. "I'd pay double to get them back."

Reed shot a look at Kealan, who was out of earshot. "It's a wonder they didn't get him. Probably meant to take all three of the kids. Would have made it six thousand."

"I'm glad Kealan was being Kealan that day," Renny said. "Otherwise, they would have."

"Just better hope they weren't angry that they only got two instead of three," Tyler said. He stopped, a frown darkening his face. "Wait a minute. Just wait a minute."

Reed clucked and made his horse back up. "What's wrong?"

Sheriff Tyler looked at each of them. "They only got two."

Renny rolled her eyes. "That was just established. A bit slow today, aren't you?"

For once, Tyler didn't fight back. "When I read the note, I assumed all three had been kidnapped. No one knew that Kealan was safe."

"Your point? We're wasting time—"

Reed held up his hand. He recognized the fury building in Tyler's gray eyes. In the space of a second they'd gone stormy. "What do you have, Sheriff?"

"I think I know who is behind this. But it can't be."

Mattie shifted. "Tyler, tell us. Please."

"Patrick O'Leary came over the day I found the note. He read it. Said he didn't know where you kids would get four thousand dollars."

"It can't be Paddy," Mattie said. "He's been like a father to us. Why would he take the children?"

"Don't know, Mattie, but he knows something."

"He's also our neighbor, and he knows us well. Even the children. Who else had the access to poison the cattle?" Renny shifted restlessly in her saddle.

"Could have been anyone," Mattie argued, but she sounded doubtful.

Renny glanced at both Reed and Tyler. "Yeah, but Paddy especially would know how Mattie would react to a blackbird tossed through the window."

Reed went to Mattie and took her hand. It was cold. Ice cold. "How long has Patrick lived here?"

Mattie bit her lower lip. "He moved here a couple of months after our parents were killed." Shocked silence fell over the group.

"He's the one, isn't he?" She gripped Reed's hand tightly. "He's the one who killed Anne. And our parents. Our mother and father died for the money he stole, didn't they?"

Reed was sure that he'd found Malcolm Clemmings, but he said, "I hope not, Mattie." For her, he hoped it wasn't. The man was her father-in-law, and a man she admired greatly.

"But makes sense now," Mattie went on. "He pushed me and Collin together. Like me and Gil. It didn't matter to him that Katherine hated us."

Reed nodded. "Sounds like. But why not just come back and get the money at night? You'd never know." Reed and Mattie had told everyone everything their first night back. Why had Paddy felt he had to drive the O'Briens off their land?

Renny looked at Reed. "If he is the one who killed our parents, that means they probably found him burying the money in the first place. Right?"

"Makes sense," Reed said.

"Well, we buried our parents in a place I go almost every day." She sounded excited. "Then we had that fire. It wiped out everything. Even the cross we put up." She looked at Reed and Tyler. "We buried them like we normally do. The Indians wouldn't do that. So Mattie and Matthew never went there." She glanced around. "We never put a new cross up. But I know where it is."

Reed whirled around. "Patrick was taking the other side of the bluff. If the kids are there, he'll get to them first."

Renny whipped her horse around as well. "Not if I can help it."

But just as she took off, a shot rang out in the distance. A second shot followed.

For a moment, no one moved. They were waiting for the next series of three shots that might mean Caitie and Daire had been found. But there weren't any more shots, so Reed reached out and pulled Mattie onto his horse in front of him.

"Hold on," he ordered, and he kicked the horse into a gallop.

Chapter Eighteen

Mattie's heart was in her throat. Something had happened. Something terrible. She closed her eyes.

Come, she invited. *Tell me. Show me.* She waited for a vision to come to her. She didn't see anything.

"Hang on, Mattie. We'll find them," Reed whispered.

Tears squeezed past her eyelids and ran down the side of her face. Giving up on trying to call forth a vision, she opened her eyes. Reed was pushing them fast, rounding the bluff. The thunder of hooves told her everyone was riding together.

A slight squeeze around her middle from Reed's arm gave some comfort. He was here, with her. No matter what they found, she had Reed.

Above her head, she heard a distant rumble. The air had grown cold, and the wind was whipping around them. She smelled rain. As they rode, the rumble of thunder grew louder. Soon, a storm would be above them.

When the rain started, Mattie felt all hope die. As far as omens went, it was not good. She so desperately needed to believe that her siblings were alive and unhurt. But . . .

"Don't give up, love," Reed said. "I have a feeling that they are fine."

"Seems impossible," she said, holding on to his arm tightly. "It's so dark and stormy."

"But I see something you don't. I see sun."

Mattie turned her head slightly. "Where?"

"Ahead. A small patch breaking through the clouds. The light is shining down there. That is our hope, Mattie."

"It might not mean anything," Mattie argued. What if he believed it was a sign and was wrong? Would he choose not to believe again? Would he go back to believing only what he saw? What would that mean for them?

No, he couldn't. Which meant she had to believe as well.

"Let us hope, Reed," she said. "Ride toward the light."

The closer they got, the harder her heart pounded. Her mouth was dry, her lips cracking. Even her eyes were stinging from the force of the wind and the salt of her tears.

Without her eyesight, the passing of time could be marked only by her thoughts. To her, the ride went on forever. She wished she could see the land go past, see where they were headed, see the gap closing.

The worry and fear and suspense were too much. Without warning, the air was filled with shots. Two. Then three. Over and over. The wind carried with it wild screams.

Mattie sat as high as she could. "What's happening, Reed? Who's screaming?"

Reed let out his own whoop. "Everybody, Mattie. From the top of the bluff. They are there. Coming toward us!"

"What? How?"

Reed kissed her on the cheek with his lips, making a loud smacking sound. "I was right! The light was the way! That's where Daire and Caitie were. They're riding toward us!"

Mattie cried, "I need to see them."

"Hang on, we're almost there."

Around her, she heard her sister yelling, her brother whooping, Kea's higher-pitched imitation, and even Tyler was shouting.

Then they were stopping so fast, Mattie would have gone flying had Reed not had his arm around her. He slid off with her in his arms.

"Put me down."

"Hang on. The ground's rocky here. It's faster this way."

Then Reed was setting her down, and someone handed her Caitie. Mattie hugged her sister. When a second pair of arms went around her, she knew it was Daire. Suddenly she was in the midst of a joyous reunion. She didn't know which arms belonged to whom as everyone was hugging, laughing and crying. All she knew as she felt one body, then another, heard the voices of her siblings, and even smelled the overwhelming smell of body and sweat, was that it was the most wonderful sight of all.

Mattie spent the afternoon with Caitie clinging to her. The little girl, aside from not allowing Mattie out of her reach, seemed no worse for the ordeal; Daire had apparently taken good care of her.

Sitting on a blanket spread out on the ground, Mattie heard a large group of boys walk past. Since arriving back at their home, both Daire and Kealan—to Kea's surprise and pleasure—had been the center of attention. Even most of the girls demanded firsthand accounts of their adventures.

The O'Brien house was still filled with people. Searchers were still arriving back, hungry and tired, but as soon as they learned the children had been found, celebrations started all over again.

Mattie sighed. There was one family not here to celebrate. The bodies of both Leo and Patrick had been found. Daire had also told them about another man that Leo had shot. The rest of the mystery had quickly unraveled. Katherine O'Leary had been taken home. She was inconsolable, accusing everyone of lying. Gil and Brenna had gone with her.

Mattie sighed. Four more deaths. Hearing the firm

footfall of someone's approach, she turned her head. As much as she appreciated all the love and support shown to her and her siblings, she really longed for time with only her family around. So much had happened; they needed time to rebuild a cocoon of security. Especially her young sister. She stroked a finger over Caitie's brow.

"Hey. We're back."

Mattie smiled up at Reed's voice. "You sound tired." She patted the spot on the blanket beside her. It didn't matter that they were in view of most of the town. She and Reed belonged together now.

He sat. "Hell of a day." Gently, he tucked a strand of hair back behind her ear. "For you as well."

"It's over, Reed. For all of us." She still had a hard time believing that Patrick could have wished them harm. Her heart went out to Gil and his family. They had known Patrick for three years. He'd married Katherine and adopted her children. All as part of his plan, it seemed. He'd betrayed all of their love for a plan of revenge.

He'd had not one child who loved him, but three. And he'd never seen that. Gil and Brenna would hurt for a long time. Mattie was more determined than ever to make sure Reed got his children back.

"Almost. Not over yet."

Startled from her thoughts, Mattie sighed. "The money."

"Yeah."

"And your parents and children."

"Them too."

Reaching out, she found his face. Using the fingers of her free hand, she traced the deep grooves etched around his mouth. "We'll find that money, Reed. Then you'll return it and be free to make amends with your family. You'll hold your children again."

Reed took her hand in his and kissed her palm. "Thanks to you, Mattie. I'd given up hope of ever getting my family back."

Mattie allowed him to pull her close. "I wish we were alone."

He smiled against the side of her face. "We will be."

"Promise?" She tipped her head back, her forehead sliding across his cheek. She felt the dimple in his cheek when he smiled.

"Promise." He got to his feet but leaned down. "Tonight."

As he walked away, Mattie felt the glow of his promise in her heart. She was so happy. Everything was right with her world again. And tonight, with Reed, she'd get another taste of heaven.

The soft scent of nightfall soon swept over the land, helping to erase the horrors of the day. Darkness fell, cloaking all, hiding the blood that had soaked into the earth. Above, the stars seemed brighter, the moon larger—a reminder of the wonders of the world; that with death, came life.

And life would always go on. A circle, Mattie said.

Reed drew in a deep breath, filling his lungs. His eyes took in the twinkling of the heavens while the glow of the moon's light washed over him.

Yes, he could see that now. And he'd come full circle.

"Are you happy?"

Reed glanced down at the woman walking beside him. "Very." He pulled her close. He'd promised her a walk in the moonlight. He grinned. He'd sneaked her out of her open window clad only in her nightshirt.

"Where are we going?" But Mattie didn't care. As long as they were together, she was content.

"To a special place," Reed said. He nuzzled the side of her neck. Mattie turned and wrapped her hands around his neck. She kissed him. Slow, then deep.

Reed groaned. "Not yet. A bit farther."

Mattie swallowed his protest. "I think here is just fine." She opened to receive the thrust of his tongue, then closed her lips around him. The heat in her center started a slow burn.

Reed pulled away. "Come on." He scooped her up into his arms.

"This is becoming a habit, Reed."

He chuckled and gave her a quick, hard kiss. "Get used to it. I like the feel of you in my arms."

"I think I like being in your arms," she whispered.

She opened two buttons on his shirt and slid her fingers inside. His skin was smooth. Warm. Leaning her head against his shoulder, she nuzzled this throat and drew in his scent. Heaven. His was a mixture of promise and man.

In her heart, they were married. She'd told Gil she couldn't marry him earlier. She'd thought she'd seen relief in his face, but he hadn't been able to talk.

Mattie couldn't blame him. His world was in shambles even as hers was righted once more.

She looked forward to sharing this night with Reed. Their future was still uncertain. Tonight was not. Tonight was theirs, shared only with the stars and moon beaming down upon them. She breathed in clean, fresh air. Soon, the sounds of their love and passion would travel up to the heavens, carried by the gentle breath of the wind.

Impatience made Mattie lick the warm flesh of Reed's throat. She stroked him with the tip of her tongue and smiled when she felt his pulse jump and his jaw tighten. She chuckled.

"Witch. You best watch yourself. I'm hanging on by a thread."

"I don't want you controlled." She nipped him none too gently. "I want you *now.*"

Stopping, Reed groaned. He took her mouth, plundered his way inside and drank. And tasted. He took her tongue and lips hostage. His control had snapped. He could wait no longer to have her.

He let her slide slowly down the length of him. With her feet almost to the ground, he wrapped his arms around her lower back and held her there, tight against his throbbing need.

Mattie clung to him with hands and lips. When she felt his hand slip beneath her nightshirt and draw the fabric up, she moaned. The feel of his hand sliding over her bare buttocks made her jerk herself hard against him.

She felt the bulge in his pants, needed it against her. Restless, she tried to shift, to lift herself a bit higher. Mattie lifted one leg, gripped his shoulders with her hands, and wrapped her legs around his waist so she could straddle that which she so desperately had to have.

"I want this to be perfect," Reed moaned in her ear. Each hand cupped a rounded cheek.

Mattie drew her head back. "This couldn't be more perfect, Reed. This is what I want. You. Now." She slid her hands down his chest, tearing at his shirt, uncaring that the buttons were being torn from the material. She spread his shirt wide, ran her hands down the hard, warm, smooth flesh.

Reed sucked in a breath when her fingers made quick work of the buttons on his breeches. His hard, throbbing member sprang loose, jumping into her hand.

"Mattie," he breathed as she took him in her hand, enclosing him with her warmth and love.

"Reed. Come to me. Like before."

Without waiting, Reed lifted her slightly, let her guide him to her, then into her. Slowly he slid her down over him. "Home," he breathed. He'd found a home at last.

Chapter Nineteen

It should have been a gloomy day, a day full of cold, wind and rain. A day when most wouldn't set foot outside the house. As fate would decide, the skies were clear, the sun bright and the wind a gentle breath of sweet spring air.

It was not a day for a funeral, but that was where a goodly number of Pheasant Gully citizens were. It wasn't the dead that had them paying their respects; it was curiosity, pure and simple.

Patrick O'Leary had been a citizen for a short time, but most were new to this area and homesteading. He'd been well liked and well loved for his booming, good-hearted voice, his cheery attitude and his willingness to work hard. If a man needed help, he had only to ask Paddy.

The man's wife was another matter. It was clear from the beginning she had no wish to be there, and she'd made no effort to hide that fact. Some congregating in the tiny, sun-filled meadow felt sorry for Katherine.

Others were there to collect gossip the way many gathered their eggs each morning—one at a time. A tidbit here, whisper there. The ambush of Matthew and Renny, the kidnapping of Caitie and Daire, and the killing of four men, including one most had called a friend, would feed the gossip mills for years to come.

Also, those who looked closely saw love simmering in the air between Reed and Mattie. Reed didn't stray too far from her. And, as though it were the most natural thing in the world, he'd touch her on the arm, smooth a strand of hair from her face or offer his arm.

Mostly, his feelings were seen on his face. He couldn't take his eyes from Mattie, and those blue eyes were always filled with love. Mattie did her own share of touching, or leaning close to talk to him. And with uncanny accuracy, her gaze followed him. It unnerved many.

Reed provided his own fuel for talk. Men admired the man for taking control of the three dead criminals. The bounty due him for Leo Granger had been donated to the town. A committee was being formed to decide how to best put the money to use.

The women admired Reed for an entirely different reason. He was a hero. In him, they saw the tall, dark, handsome prince riding to the rescue. More than one envious eye followed the couple.

To Mattie, the day seemed surreal. For once she was glad she could be "oblivious" to what was going on around her. She easily pretended not to hear the rampant gossip and the personal questions she didn't want to answer. Most meant well, but normally there was no such excitement as this in Pheasant Gully.

Listening to yet more talk about Patrick and his betrayal of the town, Mattie turned away. What bothered people the most was the deception. Had Patrick been mean, kept to himself or otherwise fit the image of a criminal on the run, it wouldn't have hurt so much. But the man had deceived them all. Patrick O'Leary was really Malcolm Clemmings. O'Leary had been his mother's maiden name; Patrick, his father's given name.

Mattie was torn by her feelings. The man had done some horrible, unforgivable things. But he'd also helped prevent Tyler and others from splitting up the O'Brien children.

He'd been there whenever they needed advice or help, and he'd made them all part of his family. Had the whole thing been a lie? A way to try to get access to the money?

Mattie didn't know. She wished she could talk to him one last time, but he'd been dead when found.

She sighed. How could she still think of the good in Paddy—no, she could never think of him by that name again—the good in Patrick O'Leary?

Sadness gripped her. She had no desire to be angry or resentful. She wanted to understand, to forgive and to put all to rest. No one around seemed of the same mind. Did no one understand that grief did things to people? That it changed them?

Why did no one talk about how Patrick had chosen death in order to keep Leo from killing Daire and Caitie? They only talked about his being behind the kidnapping.

But from Daire, they knew at least some of the truth. Before Leo could shoot Daire, Patrick had shot Leo. But when Leo had pulled his revolver to kill Daire, he'd kept a rifle trained on Patrick. As a result, Patrick took a bullet to the chest and died. Mattie would forever be grateful to the man for doing the right thing in the end.

Strong hands closed over her shoulders. She inhaled Reed's warm scent.

"It's so sad," she murmured. "I want to be angry but I can't."

"Life is twisted sometimes. I think he was basically a good man driven mad by his loss." Reed sighed.

"It's not your father's fault either, Reed."

"I know." He threaded his hand through her hair. For him, she'd left it loose.

"Will you be all right if I head down to see Tyler?" he asked. "We have some business to finish." Reed slid a finger down the side of her face.

"I'll be fine." Mattie knew he was wrapping up the last details of organizing an operation to find the money. Before they started digging in the area Renny suggested, Reed and Tyler wanted backup. They wanted marshals there to guard the site once the search for the money began, then to take charge of the money once found.

She heard him groan. Then he said, "Your mother-in-law—Katherine—is coming toward us. Want me to stay?"

Mattie shook her head. "No, you don't have to."

Behind her, Reed gently squeezed her shoulder. "I'll stay." He remained right where he was. Mattie was glad. She wasn't sure what to expect of her mother-in-law. Yesterday, Mattie had found Gil and told him that she couldn't marry him. She'd made sure Gil understood that it had nothing to do with what his father had done.

Of course, her mother-in-law was sure to be pleased that the wedding was off.

"Mattie, dear child. Could I have a word with you?"

The happiness in Katherine's voice confirmed Mattie's thoughts. Life was strange, she thought.

Mattie nodded. She'd never figured on hearing her mother-in-law addressing her in so friendly a manner. "What is it, Mother O'Leary?"

"Come. We can talk in the church. There's no one there."

"All right." She turned back to Reed. "I'll be fine." She walked away from him, allowing Katherine to lead her away.

Brenna stopped them. "Mattie!"

"Hi, Brenna." Of everyone in Patrick's family, Mattie worried about Brenna the most. The scandal was sure to affect the girl.

Katherine stopped. "Brenna, I'm going to talk to Mattie. Run along."

"Mother—"

"Not now, Brenna! Come along, Mattie."

Following her mother-in-law, Mattie felt sorry for her. Mattie couldn't fathom what it felt like to have lived with a man and never really known him.

She sighed. It was over. Life would go on, and for that she was grateful. What life had to offer, she wasn't sure. But she knew it would soon be time to give Reed her answer. She smiled. He wouldn't be leaving alone.

She'd held a family meeting early that morning. Daire, Kealan and Caitie were coming with her. Together, with Reed, they planned to help him regain custody of his children. No matter how long it took.

Mattie figured if his parents saw that he had her, and that there were other children, they might not fight to keep Danny and Lizzie from Reed. Mattie didn't know what Reed had as far as money, but she had enough to buy them a house near Reed's children. From there, they'd have to wait and see. She knew only that they'd be together.

"Here, my dear. Up the steps."

Mattie heard the squeak of the door. The sickly-sweet scent of flowers overwhelmed her. The church was filled with them.

"Wait here a moment." Katherine O'Leary hummed as she walked away. Mattie heard her up at the front of the church.

Strange, Mattie thought, for a woman grieving to be in such good spirits. She reached out, felt the pew to her left. "Mother O'Leary, are you all right?" Feeling the bench so she'd know for sure which direction she was facing, she walked toward the front of the church.

"Oh, just fine, my dear." The woman laughed as she walked back toward Mattie. "Just fine," she whispered close to Mattie's ear.

Mattie froze. She'd heard that eerie laugh once before. In the barn. Over the roar of flames. She turned slightly, needing some distance and a moment to think through her revelation.

Something struck the side of her head. As she fell, she remembered that on the day of her marriage to Collin, Katherine O'Leary had asked Mattie to help her with a surprise for Collin in the barn. Mattie had gone with her, just as she'd come in to the church today.

Too late, she'd forgotten that last vision of the fire in the church.

Outside the church, Brenna didn't know what to do. She'd tried everything to protect Mattie from her mother, but the glow of madness in her mother's eyes said that it was useless.

Brenna whirled around. Spotting Reed walking away, she ran after him. "Mattie needs you."

Reed glanced down at her. "She's with your mother."

Brenna bit her lower lip and ran her sweat-slicked hands down over her dress. She could no longer protect her mother either. "Mattie's in danger. You must hurry." Each breath came faster. She glanced back at the church. The door was closed. Mattie was alone with her mother.

"It's okay, Brenna. The danger is over." Reed's gaze strayed to the church and to the surrounding groups of people. Nothing looked out of place.

Brenna grabbed his arm. Her voice rose. "You don't understand. She'll kill her this time!" As she spoke aloud the words she'd hoarded deep inside her for so long, she felt some of the tightness in her chest ease.

Reed's eyes sharpened on her. She didn't give him a chance to talk. "My mother hates Mattie, always has. But now . . . she's crazy. She blames Mattie for everything." Tears spilled down the girl's cheeks. "Please, just go to her. Get her away from my mother."

To her relief, Reed took off at a run toward the church. Brenna's shoulders sagged. Her world was in shambles. What was she going to do? If her mother hurt Mattie, she'd go to jail. If anyone ever found out that it had been her mother who'd set fire to the barn, killing Collin, injuring Mattie so severely that she'd lost her sight, she'd be hanged.

Brenna closed her eyes, reliving the horror of last summer when her mother had tried to kill Mattie by setting the barn on fire.

Strong hands gripped her shoulders. Fear held her still. "Explain," came the soft voice. "Why is your mother trying to hurt Mattie?"

Brenna shook with fear at the sound of Matthew's voice. He'd appeared from nowhere, and he was the one person she feared most. "You know she hates Mattie."

"Tell me, Bren, did she ask you to shoot Mattie?" His voice was soft. Dangerously soft.

Brenna whirled around, her eyes wild. "No." Her heart stuttered as she stared up into the harsh planes of his face. He knew. She saw it in the darkness of his eyes, the set of his jaw, and felt it in the hard grip of his hands.

"I had to do that. I had to protect Mattie." Tears coursed down her cheeks. "And my mother."

She told him the truth that she'd kept for the last year. "I saw her and Mattie go into the barn. I followed, and sneaked around to the back. There was a crack. I figured Ma was going to talk to Mattie about the marriage bed." She bit her lower lip. "I wanted to know. Ma refused to tell me anything, said it was something I'd have to wait for until my own wedding day. Then she . . ." She couldn't say it.

"She what? No games, Bree."

Brenna stared down at her hands. "Ma hit Mattie on the head. I saw her," she whispered, clutching her stomach, gasping at the burning pain as she remembered how horrified she'd been, so shocked she couldn't move.

By the time she'd run around to the other side of the barn, it had been engulfed in flame and her mother was nowhere in sight.

"Your mother started the fire." Matthew's voice was harsh, cold.

Brenna nodded. "I didn't see her do it. I ran to find Pa. Then everyone started screaming that there was a fire in the barn. Ma had to be the one who set it.

"Collin went in looking for Mattie and never came out. He died. She—my mother—went crazy, Matthew. I was afraid for her. She acted as though nothing had happened—that she hadn't done anything. Only when she learned that Collin had gone in and died, she did go crazy."

"Yet you told no one!"

Crying, using her skirt to wipe her eyes, Brenna shook her head. "I wanted someone else to find out. She was saying things, horrible things. I knew what they meant. I prayed that someone would ask questions."

She paused. "She is my mother," she whispered. "I couldn't say anything. Mattie didn't die. If she had, I'd have told someone. Only Collin died. He was her favorite of us all, and I figured that was her punishment. Telling anyone wouldn't bring him back or make Mattie see again."

She looked at Matthew, then away. "When Mattie and Gil decided to marry, Mama started acting funny again. I thought if I got you guys to leave, or got Mattie to change her mind about marrying Gil, then Mama would leave Mattie alone."

Matthew glanced at the church. "Wait here, Brenna, while I go get Tyler. You leave, I'll find you," Matthew snarled. He took off at a run.

A wall of people stood between Reed and the church. He shoved his way through, ignoring startled gasps and angry shouts. The closed doors seemed so far, his steps slow, as though he moved through molasses.

If anything happened to Mattie, he would blame himself, for he should have questioned what he'd seen with his own eyes: Katherine O'Leary being friendly, too friendly.

Yesterday, after returning Mattie and her siblings to the cabin, he'd ridden back out to where searchers were gathering around the area where the dead men lay. He hadn't been surprised to see Leo's body.

When he'd first seen Patrick O'Leary, dead from a gunshot, he'd first assumed Leo had killed Mattie's father-in-law when he'd tried to rescue the kids. But one of the searchers who'd arrived first on the scene had held out the old wig and beard, saying he'd taken it off Paddy.

Reed recognized that disguise from the bank robbery. As he'd glanced down at Patrick O'Leary, he realized he'd truly found the man who'd killed Anne.
His search for Malcolm was ended.

But when he and the rest of the search teams had
returned with the news, Katherine had gone crazy.
She'd screamed, accused him and everyone else of
killing her husband.

Mattie had gone to try to comfort her, but the
woman had turned on her, blaming everything on
Mattie—the death of her son, and now her husband.
Reed had taken Mattie away while others had
helped the hysterical woman home.

Today, he'd been relieved to find Katherine quiet,
a normal grieving woman. After yesterday and all
that Mattie had told him about her relationship with
her mother-in-law, Reed should have suspected all
was not right.

Breaking through the crowd, he took the steps
leading to the double-wide church doors in one long
bound, crashing through the door. He hadn't taken
the time to see if it was locked or not. He was moving purely on the fear pumping through him.

Flying through the broken door, Reed landed
hard, skidding across the polished floor into the
back row of pews. Standing, his chest heaved. He inhaled the strong aroma of oil.

"Stay away," a shrill voice screamed.

Reed's heart stopped. At the front of the church,
Katherine stood with a lantern in her hand. Oil

dripped from its base. In her other hand, she held a match.

"Wait," he said, his gaze finding Mattie on the floor. The altar where Katherine stood with the lantern was behind her.

His heart flipped when he saw Mattie open her eyes. She looked right at him.

Alive. She was still alive!

"Mattie, come to me. The way is clear. Run straight to me."

Katherine screamed when Mattie scrambled to her feet. She shrieked, "No! No! You killed them. You'll die. You'll all die!" The woman struck the match.

Reed rushed forward. Mattie slipped on the oil-slicked wooden floor that Katherine had doused. She grabbed the corner of the altar to gain her footing. With a burst of speed, she ran down the aisle toward Reed, her eyes never leaving his.

Reed grabbed her as she fell into his arms. He pulled her behind him, shielding her in case Katherine had a gun. To his horror, he saw Katherine hold the flaming match over the altar where the lamp sat.

"No," he shouted. "Don't do it! It's not worth dying over."

Katherine stared at him. She was calm as she dropped the burning match. "Die, savages. Indian pigs! Burn in hell!"

The flames shot to life, feeding eagerly on the oil spreading out over the floor, then licking at the dry hewn-timber pews. Katherine's mad laughter rang out. She grabbed the lantern and heaved it over her head. Taking a step toward them, preparing to toss it, she yelled: "No escape. You'll both die!"

"Come on, let's get out of here," Reed said, scooping Mattie into his arms.

Rushing forward to toss her weapon, Katherine gave a horrified shriek as her foot slid across a patch of flaming oil. In horrifing slow motion, Reed watched her feet go out from under her. She fell, landing on her back beneath the burning altar. The lantern crashed down on the floor at her head and exploded.

Reed set Mattie down and took one step toward the woman, now on fire and shrieking in pain and terror, but it was too late. The entire front of the church roared into a thick wall of flame. Intense heat kept him from trying to get closer to the crazywoman. Smoke billowed out, making his eyes water.

A hand on his shoulder, a cough, and the tremble of fear coming from Mattie spurred Reed back to action. He grabbed Mattie and ran out of the burning building as people ran to see what was going on.

"It's too late for her," he choked as Tyler and Matthew pushed themselves forward through the crowd. "She tried to kill Mattie. I couldn't reach her in time."

The low buzz of talk started, grew. Men found pails and formed a line from the river behind to try to save the burning church.

It was too late. The building was engulfed. Reed

carried Mattie far from the commotion. He sat beneath a tree, with her still in his arms. "I will never let you go, Mattie." He bent down and kissed her, uncaring who might be around to see.

"You won't have to," she said, her hands all over his head and face. She traced his eyes, his mouth, each line the fright had put there on his face. "When you leave, I'm going with you."

Reed hugged her tightly. "Thank God," he murmured. "I don't have the right to ask you to leave your family, but I can't live without you."

Mattie pulled away, her hands framing his face. She smiled up at him. "As the man I love, the man who holds my heart in his hands, you have every right."

"Well, I love you, Mattie." And Reed did. All of her. He no longer saw her as blind, but as a strong woman with incredible gifts and the intellect and ability to use all of them with a wisdom that made her the most incredible person he'd ever known.

And she was his.

"You hold my heart and my soul, Mattie. I couldn't live without you in my life. But what about your family?" He was surprised that Caitie and Kealan were not there. The two had barely left her side since their ordeals. He framed her face with his hands.

Mattie smiled. "They will come with us." She reached out and put a finger to his lips. "You worry about supporting us, about finding us a place to live. Do not. What is mine now becomes yours. We will find a place to live while we sort out what is best for Danny and Lizzie. If it takes years, so be it. If we can return here, then return we will."

"You are beautiful, Mattie. Here." He kissed her mouth lightly, then placed his palm over her beating heart. "And here."

"No more so than you are to me, Reed," she whispered back.

Reed stared at the wild scene around them. People were crying as their church burned. He saw the minister and sheriff standing off to one side.

"Guess we won't be getting married for a while," Mattie said. She sighed.

Reed scooped her up. "The hell we won't," he said. He wasn't waiting. Not a single day. Not an hour. He was making her his. Right now.

Matthew stalked back over to where Brenna sat facing the stream that ran behind the church. Her shoulders stiffened at his silent approach.

He should have been surprised that she knew he was there, but he wasn't. The moment the O'Learys had become their neighbors, all the children had grown to be friends, and Brenna and her brothers had loved learning the stuff he took for granted.

Matthew had always walked like the Sioux, being able to approach anyone on silent feet. Usually, he startled most people who didn't hear him. Especially Brenna, whom he'd loved to make shriek when he scared her. Brenna, finally having enough of him, had demanded he teach them all the ways of his people.

Matthew had agreed, believing it to be good for them to know how to survive in the wilderness. Now, what he'd taught had been used against him and his family. He was beyond furious. Inside, he was cold. And deadly intent upon exacting punishment.

Matthew didn't touch her. "Your mother. She's dead. By her own hand. I won't lie to you, I am not sorry."

Brenna's shoulders shook with silent sobs.

Part of Matthew wanted to join her, to sit beside her and offer a friend comfort over the loss of not one, but two parents. He did neither. "Had you said something when all this started, we could have helped you."

"I'd have lost her anyway," Brenna whispered. "This way, there was hope."

"No. Your way put others in danger. Again. Your silence could have claimed more lives."

Brenna ducked her head. "I was afraid. I didn't know what to do."

"Are you afraid right now?" Matthew's hands were fisted. He deliberately relaxed them.

Brenna didn't answer. Matthew reached down and yanked her to her feet. When she still refused to answer or look at him, he forced her chin up. "Answer me!" He closed off his heart to the fragility that seemed so much a part of his young friend.

Brenna looked at him then. Her eyes, a mix of green, yellow and brown, like fall leaves, grew wide. The green from inside turned bright.

"Yes," she whispered.

Matthew stared into her eyes. He saw the fear. The regret. He saw pain, and grief. He also saw confusion and a small spark of defiance.

"Good," he said. "Be afraid."

He stalked away.

Mattie was back home, sitting in her bed. She was fine, without even much of a headache. She'd been a bit dazed after Katherine had hit her in the head, but her slight movement before being hit had kept her from being knocked out.

She'd pretended to be unconscious, staying down to wait for her chance to escape. The first splash of oil had nearly frozen her with fear. Just the thought of facing another fire had almost made her jump up right then and there.

But she'd been afraid that if Katherine was given a second chance to hit her, she might succumb. So Mattie had used all her will, forcing herself to be calm. She'd silently called Reed to her.

He'd arrived just as Katherine was pouring oil from the lamp over the altar and floor. As soon as Mattie heard his voice, she'd waited for his command. And he'd saved her!

She smiled when she felt someone plumping the pillows at her back. Reed not only refused to let her out of bed, he refused to leave her alone. It didn't matter that her entire family was here, in her bedroom. Reed was not leaving. The thought warmed her from the inside out, chasing away the chill of the ordeal. Instead of allowing her thoughts to linger on what was over and done with, she thought of her family.

Renny sat on the edge of the bed, and Caitie and Kea were on either side of Mattie. Daire sat at her feet, while Matthew paced back and forth across the small alcove.

"I'm fine," she repeated. Inside she was still reeling. Not just from Katherine's attempt today, but from learning that the woman had hated her so much that Mrs. O'Leary had tried to kill her last summer.

She stared at Matthew. What still shocked her was Brenna's involvement in all of this.

"How did you know Brenna was involved, Matt?"

Matthew's voice when he spoke came from the window. "Whoever was sneaking onto our land was too good. No footprints. No sound. The night the rock with the bird was thrown through Mattie's window, I knew it was her. I couldn't prove it, so I said nothing."

He laughed, a low, harsh sound. "Whoever was behind it all had the skill of a Sioux warrior. It only made sense that it would be Brenna or Gil, as they'd each learned those skills from us."

He sounded disgusted with himself. "The night

you were shot at, she seemed paler than normal. And when she came back down from her room and suggested you leave as well, I suspected her most."

Mattie smiled sadly. "She did like learning about our way of life." They'd had many contests between them, including ones where one person ran to hide. The others had to find him or her by using their tracking skills.

"I thought Padd—Patrick was responsible for all of it." Mattie leaned her head back against her pillows.

"I'm sure he was responsible for the poison. We won't ever really know. But Brenna was the one pulling all the pranks. She wanted us to leave, but for a different reason: she knew if Mattie married Gil, her mother would make another attempt to kill Mattie." Matthew sounded furious.

"Matt, she was trying to protect me." Mattie felt sorry for her. And afraid. She'd never heard Matthew so angry and barely in control. Her brother prized control most of all.

"She *shot* at you. What if she'd not missed?"

"No. She's too good. She missed, and missed on purpose. You know that she's good."

"Best of us all," Renny muttered.

"Don't be hard on her. She needs us. Now more than ever." When Matthew remained silent, Mattie leaned forward. "Matt! What are you planning to do? It will serve no purpose to go to the sheriff. It will only hurt her and Gil."

"Her silence almost cost you your life."

"But it didn't."

"She will be punished."

Mattie sighed. "There's been enough pain. No more, Matt. No more."

Matthew went to her. "The punishment will fit the crime, sister."

Mattie felt his features. They were hard, unyielding. "As the one who was affected, I have final say."

"Agreed." He returned to his pacing.

They all waited. When he stopped, Mattie held her breath. She would not allow any harm to come to Brenna.

Matthew decided, "She will come with me to our people. There she will learn to live as one of us, and in doing so, she will learn how to use her skills for the good of all. She needs to learn right from wrong. What she did was wrong."

"From her viewpoint, it was all she could do. She's young yet." Mattie stopped her brother's protest by holding up her palm. "However, I agree. There is nothing but shame for her here." She speared Matthew with a sharp glance. "But she must agree to go with you. And after one year, if she wants to leave, you must bring her back."

Matthew remained silent so long that Mattie was afraid he'd reject her wishes. Then he spoke. "Agreed. We leave when the sun rises." He left the room.

"Wow," Renny said. "I've never seen him like this. Are you sure it's safe for her to go with him?"

Mattie grew quiet for a moment. Then she smiled softly. "It's the safest place for her, Renny. It's the only place for her to go."

"What did you see?" Renny demanded.

Mattie shook her head. "Some things are best revealed in their own time."

"Come on, Mattie." Renny edged closer. "Just a hint."

Mattie grabbed one of her pillows and tossed it at her sister. "Mind your manners, Renny." With a flurry of activity, the bed came alive as everyone grabbed a pillow.

Laughing, Mattie held out her hands, grabbing pillows to toss or attacking sensitive bellies with her fingers.

Watching the playful antics, Reed laughed and imagined being in that bed with Mattie, his new wife, and with her three young siblings mock fighting with his kids. He grinned. And maybe one or two of their own kids. Lost in dreams of what he hoped to be, he didn't see the pillow that smacked him.

"Got you," Daire called out.

With a playful growl, Reed launched himself onto the bed. He pulled Kealan over on top of him and tickled the boy's soft belly. Then the unthinkable happened. Daire was on him, giving back in kind, finding just the tender spot in his side that had him shouting out his own laughter until tears ran down his face.

Mattie smiled through the antics taking place on

the bed. She even heard Caitie's shrill giggles. Then it happened—with a loud groan, then a snap. The bed collapsed.

Stunned silence gave way to shrieks of laughter. Renny had landed on top of Mattie. She pushed herself up.

"Okay, enough. Daire, Kealan, Caitie—let's go!"

Protests came loud and swift.

"Out," Renny repeated. Her voice softened. "I think it's time to let the married couple be alone."

Daire made some smacking sounds. "They're gonna be kissing all night," he teased.

Mattie tossed one of her pillows at the voice. His muffled "hey!" told her she'd gotten him in the kisser.

Kealan scrambled over her. "Are you really gonna be kissing Reed all night?" he asked.

Reed's low growl came, "Yes, she is. And I'm going to be kissing her too! A lot!"

Kealan made a disgusted sound in his throat. "Ick. Not with me here you're not. I'm leaving!"

The adults all chuckled. Renny reached over her sister and grabbed Caitie. "Come on, kid. Let's go up to bed. I'll read you a story."

"Two stories," Caitie said slyly.

"Chocolate, too?" asked Kealan.

"You bet, punkin."

Mattie heard the quilt that separated her sleeping quarters from the main room fall into place, and she knew she and Reed were finally alone. She shifted on the broken bed. Reed crawled up beside her and drew her close.

"Some family you've got, Mrs. Robertson."

Mattie snuggled close. "No. Some family *we've* got, Mr. Robertson." She reached up and pulled his head down to hers. "Some family we are going to have, my love."

"A man couldn't ask for much more than that," Reed said, claiming her mouth with his.

Epilogue

"Caitie! Lizzie! Girls, hurry. We're waiting for you." Mattie stood at the ladder leading up to the loft.

"Coming, Mattie."

"Coming, Mama." Then came the flurry of starched skirts and stiff petticoats as the two girls climbed down.

"Are you wearing your new dresses?" Mattie reached out and felt the stiff fabric, yards of lace and ribbon and ruffles.

Reed's mother kept the girls dressed so well that there was no point in saving their best for Sundays or other special events. Only for the dirtiest of chores did the kids put on their plain, everyday clothing.

"My dress is green," Caitie said.

Mattie smiled at her. "Perfect with those red curls," she said, running her hand over Caitie's head to be sure she hadn't messed up her hair. She straightened the big bow she'd tied.

"Mine's blue," Lizzie piped up. "And Caitie found me a blue ribbon." She held it up and placed it in Mattie's hand.

Mattie tied the ribbon around the young child's braid. It was hard to imagine that nearly three years had passed.

Caitie was now seven, and Lizzie nearly five. "There. Your father is going to be so pleased with his beautiful daughters. Go get in the wagon. We're late, and that will not make him happy!"

The girls squealed with laughter. "Thanks, Mama!" Lizzie ran out.

Mattie listened. She'd heard only one set of running feet. "Caitie? Is anything wrong?"

Caitie leaned against Mattie. "She gets to call you Mama."

Kneeling, Mattie hugged her young sister. "I am her mama, now. Just like her father is now your father. You call Reed Father, just like she does. We are a family."

"Yeah. I like that. But—"

"But what, sweets?"

"When baby Annie gets bigger, she'll get to call you Mama and you'll be her real mama." She paused. "I won't ever have anyone to call Mama."

Mattie's heart bled a little. It was true. She'd always be Caitie's sister. But where it counted, she was the girl's mother. "In my heart, Caitie, you are my daughter."

Reaching out, she drew her sister to her and ran her fingers over her face. "Would you like to call me Mama?"

Caitie hesitated, then let her breath out with a rush of air. "I'd always know you were really my sister."

Smiling, Mattie nodded. "Yes, you would. I think what you call me doesn't matter as long as you love me and I you."

Caitie wrapped her arms around Mattie. "I love you, Mattie." She pulled back, happiness shining in her blue eyes. "Mama."

"Love you too, sweets." She stood and listened to Caitie run out the door.

"If she gets to call you Mama, then me too!" Kealan had been in the doorway and had apparently heard. He came to stand beside Mattie. "Unless I'm too big now."

Mattie laughed. "You'll never be too big to call me Mama if that's what you wish."

"Oh, boy!" Kealan shouted. "Oh, Daire said he has the horses ready and for everyone to hurry up."

Grinning, Mattie gave him a push. "Then tell him I'm ready."

"I'm here," Daire announced, his voice deep. "Now get out and into the wagon, Kea." His voice cracked, ruining the deep, authoritative command.

Kealan imitated his brother's unpredictable voice

as he ran out. Daire groaned. "You too, Danny! This time, stay in the wagon. Don't got time to be chasing the two of you all over."

Mattie grinned as Danny ran out, doing the same thing as Kea. Daire took a stomping step after them, which just sent the boys running wildly. She went to the doorway.

"No one had better get dirty!"

Daire walked back up the steps. He put his hand on her shoulder. "You won't be offended if I don't . . . um, you know, call you Mother?"

"Of course not, Daire." She hugged him. She didn't expect him to think of her as his mother. He'd been plenty old enough to remember their mother.

"That's good. I sure love you—"

"I know what you mean. Now, let's get going."

"Right. I'll get the baby."

Mattie heard Annie's soft little squeak as her morning nap was interrupted by Daire's lifting her out of her cradle. Mattie held out her arms for her daughter. She cuddled Annie close and let Daire take her arm, then she walked outside, down the steps.

Her brother was fast becoming a man at nearly eleven. His experience with Leo and Patrick had matured him, and he took his role as the eldest son of the household seriously. Whenever Reed was gone, he took command of the family.

They reached the wagon. "Hey, settle down, you

guys. Your mom's here." He took the baby, waited till Mattie was settled, then hopped up and gave her Annie once more.

Taking up the reins, he snapped them.

During the drive to town, Mattie listened to the good-natured arguing behind her, along with Daire's threats when things got too loud. Smiling, Mattie couldn't have been happier.

"Hey, here comes Pa," Daire called out.

Mattie's smile grew wide. Having Reed home safe always made her happy. She worried over him each day he left to go to work.

Reed drew up beside the wagon. "Afternoon, Mrs. Robertson. Can I offer you a lift?"

Mattie didn't have time to answer. Reed simply dismounted, scooped her and his daughter into his arms and set them on the back of his horse. He climbed up behind her.

Mattie rode with her legs to one side, her back flat against his chest, his arms securely around her. A tiny dig in her back made her sigh. Who'd have thought that Reed would take on the task of deputy of Pheasant Gully? But after all that had happened, and after finally finding the stolen money, it just had seemed natural for him to take his place at Tyler's side.

A short ride later, they arrived at the home of Reed's parents. "Here, love. Let me take her," her husband said.

Reed took his tiny infant daughter, cradled her

close to his heart. Then he wrapped his other arm around Mattie's waist.

Around them, the children were running for the open door with shouts of "Grandma! Grandpa!"

"I'm so glad they returned to Pheasant Gully with us," Mattie said. She reached up and touched the brooch that had been found among the bags of money.

Reed had cried when he'd seen it. Anne's mother had cried when he'd given it back to her, and Mattie had cried when she'd insisted Mattie take it. It was the greatest compliment her new mother-in-law could give her. It was love and acceptance as her daughter.

Reed had also returned the pocketwatch to his father. To their surprise, he'd tossed it in the fire. They weren't sure why, and Harold Robertson wouldn't tell them. He'd simply said there were other things more important than hanging on to the past.

Reed's homecoming had been all she could have wished for. His parents, especially his father, had actually been relieved to see their son. Mattie smiled softly. Both Reed and his father had burst immediately into apologies, both trying at once to beg forgiveness.

Reed's young son had been overjoyed to see his father. Lizzie had been shy at first, but with Caitie, Kealan and Daire, it hadn't lasted long. Neither had Reed's parents' wariness of Mattie.

They'd accepted her after just a few days, knowing how happy their son was, how right she seemed for him, and the love of all the children.

It had been Mattie's idea for them all to move to Pheasant Gully, especially as Reed's father had sold the bank and retired. He'd built a home in town and was considering opening a business.

Reed hugged her tightly "We have it all, Mattie," he whispered. "We have it all."

"Yes, Reed. We have it all."

A vision came, soft and sweet like a spring morning. Mattie smiled. When the time was right, Reed would have a son with blond hair and with eyes the same shade of blue as his own.

And as all the children arrived and rushed into the house, Mattie's vision faded and the plainly furnished room she was in became alive with the sounds love and laughter.

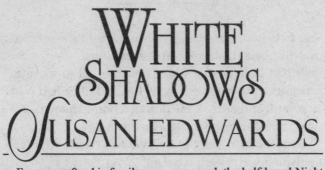

WHITE SHADOWS
SUSAN EDWARDS

For years after his family was massacred, the half-breed Night Shadow harbored black dreams of vengeance—and the hope of someday finding his kidnapped younger sister. Now is the chance. His enemy shows himself and is to be wed. It should be a simple maneuver to steal the man's bride-to-be, to ride off with the beautiful Winona and reveal the monster she is supposed to marry.

But it is *not* simple. Winona is not convinced. Even the burgeoning desire Night Shadow sees in her eyes has not convinced the Sioux beauty of her betrothed's evil. Can love be born of revenge? There seems but one way to find out: Take Winona into the darkness and pray that, somehow, he and she can find their way to the light.

WHITE DUSK
Susan Edwards

A winter of discontent sent Swift Foot on a vision quest, and he returned ready to be chief. Where his father brought shame upon their family by choosing love over duty, Swift Foot will act more wisely. He will lead his people through the troubles ahead—and, to do so, he will marry for *all* the right reasons.

Small Bird is the perfect choice. But for their people to survive the coming darkness, the two will have to win each other's hearts. On the sleeping mat or wrapped in furs, on riverbank or dusty plain, passion must blaze to life between the half-breed chieftain and his new wife . . . and they have to start the fire soon, for dusk has already fallen.

WHITE DREAMS
SUSAN EDWARDS

Why has the Great Spirit given Star Dreamer the sight, an ability to see things that can't be changed? She has no answer. Then one night she is filled with visions of a different sort: pale hands caressing her flesh, soft lips touching her soul. She sees the flash of a uniform, and the handsome soldier who wears it. The man makes her ache in a way that she has forgotten, in a way that she has repressed. And when Colonel Grady O'Brien at last rides into her camp, she learns that the virile officer is everything she's dreamed of and more. Suddenly, Star Dreamer sees the reason for her gift. In her visions lie the key to this man's happiness—and in this man's arms lie the key to her own.

Also includes the twelfth installment of Lair of the Wolf, a serialized romance set in medieval Wales. Be sure to look for other chapters of this exciting story featured in Leisure books and written by the industry's top authors.

White Dove

Susan Edwards

White Dove was raised to know that she must marry a powerful warrior. The daughter of the great Golden Eagle is required to wed one of her own kind, a man who will bring honor to her people and strength to her tribe. But the young Irishman who returns to seek her hand makes her question herself, and makes her question what makes a man.

Jeremy Jones returns to be trained as a warrior, to take the tests of manhood and prove himself in battle. Watching him, White Dove sees a bravery she's never known, and suddenly she realizes her young suitor is not just a man, he is the only one she'll ever love.

___4890-6 $5.99 US/$6.99 CAN